STREETS OF HONOR

A Novel by
Erling H. Kolke

Erling H. Kolke
cover artist - DeVaughn Kolke

Jerry & Mary Beth -
Its a pleasure to
autograph a book for someone
interested in these events and
times.   October 13, 2005

First Printing, June, 2004
Second Printing, December, 2004

ISBN 0-9755035-0-2

Printed in the United States of America by: Bang Printing
Brainerd, MN 56401

Cover Artist: DeVaughn A. Kolke

**Distributed by
Appleseed Art Works
12276 Tanglewood Road
Audubon, Minnesota 56511**

Author's Notes

This novel is dedicated to all the courageous soldiers of the 34th Infantry Red Bull Division with special honor to all who gave their lives fighting for their country.

The novel is based on historical events but the story and the characters are a work of fiction.

Audubon, Minnesota
April, 2004

E.H.K.

Acknowledgements

The author gratefully acknowledges the following who, with their help, advice, knowledge, and lives made the novel possible.

Manuscript editor, Alys Culhane, Palmer, Alaska; Janet Pratt, copy editor, Detroit Lakes, MN; and my wife, DeVaughn Kolke, editor, cover artist and for her encouragement; and to the other members of my family for their help and support.

Appleton, Minnesota National Guard members, Philip Anderson, 1941; Bob Hayes, Pre WWII; Harry Nordby, 1941; Dennis Kohlman, Present M/Sgt.

Ernest Hanson, Detroit Lakes, MN, wounded Fondouk, Africa; Melvin Holden, Appleton, MN, Artillery, WWII.

Prisoners of War, Bill Eckholm, Willmar, MN; Ray Swann, Audubon, Mn; Wilfred Carmo Lundberg, Ulen, MN (Wife - Maxine).

References - Daryl Podoll, Valley City, ND. - State College Librarian; Merle Sagen, Lake Park, MN. American Legion-Burial Service; Rudy Ronning-Appleton Dental Clinic.

The Appleton Press, Appleton, MN. for their excellent coverage of servicemen killed in action in WWII and the events surrounding the lasting Memorial and to the Appleton National Guard for the use of their excellent archives.

To the members of the Fergus Falls, Minnesota Writer's Group for their suggestions and encouragement.

To the organizations and individuals whose names may have been left out but their contributions were greatly appreciated. Thank you.

STREETS OF HONOR

Chapter 1

Friday afternoon, March 24, 1939, a week after his 22nd birthday, Dean was playing in an impromptu basketball game in the gym of Valley River State College. Roger, Dean's roommate, rushed into the gymnasium and hollered at Dean, "Hey, Dean, you're supposed to get over to the Placement Office right away."

"What's up, Rog?" Dean yells, shooting another basket.

"Skogan sent a note to the dorm that there's a superintendent from Minnesota that wants to talk to you about a teaching and coaching vacancy."

"I told him that I don't want to teach in Minnesota," Dean said, continuing to jostle players around under the basket. At 6'1' and 180 lbs., his presence dominated the play.

The game stopped. Jim Foley, Dean's friend said, "Here's your chance to learn about Minnesota, Dean."

Jim from Breckenridge, Minnesota was also planning on teaching. They were co-captains of the 1938 college football team and had often debated the merits of where to teach after graduation.

Walking off the floor, wiping his face, neck and blond hair with a towel, Dean asked, "Why should I drive way over there when I can teach right here in North Dakota?"

"I already told you that with income tax relief you'll pay less in Minnesota," Jim said.

"Jim, I don't give a hoot about income tax because I just want to teach in North Dakota."

Roger had been standing silently listening to these two friends. "Whatever," he said when he could get a word in edgewise, "I just wanted you to know that Professor Skogan said you should come for the interview. He expects you," Roger said, walking toward the door.

"Dean, remember what Pinky told us in the Placement Office meeting for seniors?" Jim asked. The students had given Professor Skogan the nickname 'Pinky' because of his pink complexion that extended from his chin to the back of his bald head. "He said that we shouldn't be so particular our first year out."

"But what if a superintendent from North Dakota wanted to see you, Jim? Would you go?"

Jim paused and decided there was no use arguing with a stubborn Norwegian. "Well, it wouldn't hurt you to go just for the interview...good practice, you know."

"I guess you're right, Jim. It would be good experience." Dean turned to leave shouting over his shoulder to the others who were still shooting baskets; "I've got to go, guys." In the locker room, he decided not to shower. Maybe if I smell sweaty the superintendent won't waste too much of his time on me, he thought, as he strolled leisurely to the Placement Office.

Professor Skogan met Dean and led him to one of the interview rooms. "Supt. Grafstrom, this is Dean Brandum. Dean, Supt. Grafstrom from Applegrove, Minnesota. He's had a chance to look over your folder, so I'll leave you two alone."

The superintendent gave Dean a firm handshake. He

was a stocky, energetic man with a full head of gray hair. Dean liked his air of confidence and the toothpick that appeared occasionally from one side of his mouth gave him a down-to-earth quality.

"Sit down, Dean. I see you're from Auburn, North Dakota, and have applied for several positions here in North Dakota."

Dean said, "I know it's early yet, so I haven't heard too much about openings." He had planned to adopt a disinterested attitude; but remembering that Ma had often said he should always be polite, he sat up straight and listened intently.

"I hope I can interest you in teaching in Applegrove. Our town is in western Minnesota, not too far from the Dakota border. The town itself has a population of about 1200 and it's an agricultural community."

Dean just nodded. Supt. Grafstom leaned back in his chair, put his fingertips together and looked up at the ceiling. "Our present coach has accepted a position in a larger school near Minneapolis and we have a vacancy for someone that can teach math, physical education and take on coaching responsibilities. You appear to be well qualified for all these areas." His gaze met Dean's now. "Are you at all interested, Dean?"

"Well, it's what I want to do, but...." his voice trailed off. Dean didn't want to mislead the superintendent into thinking he was seriously interested in the position.

"The classes would be seventh, eighth, and ninth grade math, chemistry one year and alternating with physics the next year. The physical education classes would be combined seventh and eighth and combined ninth and tenth. Six classes and no study halls. You'd be the coach for football in the fall, basketball in the winter and baseball in the spring. Someday we would like to add track."

Dean's interest grew. It was the kind of challenging assignment he'd anticipated. But he was still having conflicting thoughts about leaving North Dakota. Dean shifted slightly and said, "Mr. Grafstom, what you told me is exactly what I want to do and I like the fact that it's a farming community. It's what I'm used to."

Now Grafstom leaned forward. "Well, Dean, I spoke to our school board members before I left on this recruiting trip. This is what we can do. I can't include anything for the coaching duties but we can pay more on the salary. Next year our coach who left would have gotten $1400.00 for the year. I am prepared to offer that amount to you."

Dean caught his breath. That was more than he had hoped for. None of the other seniors had been offered anything like that. And he knew the teaching profession in North Dakota was in jeopardy.

"School starts this fall on the day after Labor Day, September 5, with the usual Thanksgiving, Christmas and Easter breaks. School ends on May 24. How does the job sound now, Dean?"

"I'll admit I'm impressed!" Dean said. "I've told all my friends that I'd never teach in Minnesota. But I can see that I might have to change my mind."

"What I would like to do, Dean, is to use a typewriter here in Professor Skogan's office and make out a contract for you."

"Okay with me. And I'll talk to my family and friends and decide very soon."

Dean hung around the Placement Office reading the vacancy notices. The missionary church in Tanganyika needed an English teacher and the Episcopal School in Hawaii wanted a mathematics teacher. Dean thought, I'm not so sure yet about teaching in Minnesota, but it's not as far away as Tanganyika or Hawaii.

Grafstom came out of one of the offices and handed Dean a large manila envelope. "I might have made a few mistakes...my typing skills are a bit rusty." He chuckled,

"You'd never know I taught business and typing many years ago. And Dean, if you could let me know your decision by April 7th, I'd appreciate it. By the way, if you'd like to come to Applegrove to visit, just let me know. I'll show you around."

Dean dashed into the dorm, up the steps and into his room, waving the large manila envelope at Roger. "Hey, Rog, I'm in a dilemma. I know I've been saying that I want to teach in North Dakota, but I've got a great contract here ...for Applegrove, Minnesota! What do you think?"

"Do you know how lucky you are to get a contract you like right off the bat? But you'll have to decide."

Dean ran into Jim Foley and rather sheepishly told him the same thing. Then he spent some restless nights comparing the good points and the bad. Dean had put a note on the bulletin board in the cafeteria that he wanted a ride to the Auburn area this weekend. A girl from a nearby town responded; and by Saturday, he was in Auburn where Dean's Uncle Eric met him.

Arriving at the farm, Dean had to explain the whole thing to his mother who was delighted by his unexpected trip home. "Ma, I treasure your advice. What do you think?"

Pauline sat in her usual place at the kitchen table, her sturdy arms on the table, her work-worn hands around her favorite mug of coffee. Dean knew about the many things that she had faced in her life, the loss of two children as babies, and her husband dying of pneumonia had taken its toll. But she still had the twinkling blue eyes and the smile that brightened her face.

"It's what you've always wanted to do, Dean. When you were little you started kicking a ball around. And after Eric put up that basketball hoop down by the barn, I thought you'd never get the chores done. I always knew where to find you."

Dean felt his mother had really heard him, and knew him well enough to give him good advice. "That's true, Ma, but if I teach in Minnesota, I'll need a car."

Ma took another swallow of coffee and set her cup

6

down. "Well, Minnesota isn't as far away as Alaska or California. We'll see you several times during the year, won't we?"

A broad smile crossed Dean's face. "I'm going to sign it and send it back tomorrow," Dean said, banging the table in his excitement, so Ma's coffee cup bounced. Uncle Eric had come in from doing chores and was washing up at the sink. "Uncle Eric, could I use the Chevrolet to mail a letter in town tomorrow morning?"

Uncle Eric was Pauline's older brother, and had been like a father to Dean ever since Dean's dad died in 1929. "Sure, Dean," Eric said, "and did I hear you say something about needing to buy a car?"

"If I'm teaching in Minnesota, I can't keep using your car. I've got to have my own."

"Well, I happen to know of a car that might work for you. Peter Andrud had a slight stroke. Peter told me his doctor said he shouldn't drive. His muscles on his left side are so weak that he can barely walk."

"But won't they still need a car?" Dean asked.

"No," Ma said, "his wife's like me...she doesn't drive."

"They're planning an auction sale, Dean, and will move to Valley River," Uncle Eric said. "I know his car will be sold."

"I'm sorry about Peter," Dean said. "Didn't he drive that '33 Studebaker with the spare tire on the side?"

"Yah, that's right. And it doesn't have many miles on it."

"Eric, that would be great! And I won't need a car 'til this summer. Will you help me bid on it?"

"Sure, if it doesn't go too high, I might even be your banker." He paused, "Of course, after you get this high paying teaching job, I may have to charge you interest," Eric said with a smile. "I'll let you know when the auction is."

"How about one of you used car dealers setting the table?" Ma asked, getting up to check the beef roast.

Dean caught a ride back to college and was busy unpacking. Ma had sent some food back with Dean. Life seemed good. To Dean and many of the graduating seniors the situations developing in Europe seemed so remote from their daily lives...except for Ben Weinstein.

When Ben heard Dean was back with food he hurried into Dean's room. "Oh, oh," Dean thought as he remembered what had happened to the goodies Ma had sent with him at Christmas.

Ben was a good friend of Dean's from out east and the only Jewish student on campus. Ma had sent some julekake and lefse back with Dean after Christmas, so he invited Ben to stop by his room for some "good Norwegian food."

Ben laughed, "Sure, Dean. Mother sent me some food too, since we just finished Hanukkah and I didn't get home this year. I'll bring some "good Jewish food."

The two friends ate and talked about the food they were eating, the traditions connected to it.

Ben explained that the 'challa', soft and delicate, was made of small pieces of bread dough, baked and glazed with egg whites. Part of their ceremony was tossing the rabbi's share into the fire, a sacrificial token.

Dean said that the Norwegians wouldn't do anything like that; they would consider it a waste of good julekaka. It was an evening of sharing and learning about each other's customs and gaining a new appreciation for their own.

When Ben left, Dean surveyed his empty baking tins and thought, next time I'll hide some.

Now Ben, entering the room, greeted Dean and Roger. "What did you bring from home this time, Dean?" As he was eating one of Ma's sandwiches, he suddenly became serious and said, "Things are really bad in Germany for the Jews."

8

"What happened, Ben?" asked Dean.

"My mother got a letter from her cousin who has a clothing shop in Munich. About five months ago the Germans had 'Kristallnacht- the night of broken glass'. His store windows were smashed and his goods thrown in the street."

Dean was quiet, shaking his head. "My uncle said he heard Hitler on the radio and he sounds like a fanatic."

"My mother hasn't heard from her cousin and his wife since, Dean. She's afraid they were sent to a concentration camp." Ben's eyes dropped to the floor. He laid his half-eaten sandwich on the table. Everyone was quiet. Ben got up and left without saying a word.

Dean and Roger stared at each other after Ben's quiet and abrupt exit.

"He's really upset," Dean said.

Roger reached for another sandwich, "Seems kind of remote for us to get involved, doesn't it?"

"I don't know, Rog. I don't know."

The big news on campus was the upcoming graduation and everyone's future plans. Dean was relieved he didn't have to worry about finding a job but found it difficult to focus on his classes.

Winnie, a physical education major and in many of Dean's classes, squeezed by him in the lecture room. She playfully stepped on his foot. She didn't know it, but she had helped Dean get over his shyness around girls. "Hear you changed your mind about teaching in North Dakota, huh?" she said.

"Yes, I got a good job," Dean answered.

"Well, I'm going to Montana. That ski trip with the Delphi Society clinched it for me. I was hoping you'd be in Williston or Bismarck so you could come to Montana once in awhile."

Not sure how to express his sadness about the distance that would separate him from this good friend, Dean said, "I'll write to you, Winnie." He didn't want to lose her friendship.

The days rolled on; spring emerged greening up the lawns, shrubs, and early flowers. The students handed in last minute papers and returned their equipment. Dean got a letter from Uncle Eric that the auction sale would be the second Saturday in May and the Studebaker was listed on the auction bill. Despite having two finals the following week, Dean decided to go home for the sale. With Eric's coaching and his loan, he returned to campus with the Studebaker.

Graduation was bittersweet, knowing he would miss Jim, Roger, Winnie, Ben and other classmates. He had an uneasy feeling he might never see some of them again. But these thoughts were outweighed by his excitement about the next phase of his life - Applegrove and the new friends that awaited him there.

STREETS OF HONOR

Chapter 2

Carrie didn't feel the pain. Only after she watched in shock as the pitchfork toppled from her knee onto the manger floor and the dark red stain spread over her overalls did she realize what had happened. It was then she felt the stabbing pain.

"Joe, help me! The pitchfork stuck me in the knee!"

Joe scrambled down the ladder. "Carrie! What were you doing in the manger?"

"I was going to chase that heifer out of Bess' stall," she said. "Joe, please! Help me up to the house so Mom can look at it."

"Okay, I'll be right there, Carrie," Joe said, and hurried to shut the stanchion on Bess, their oldest and orneriest cow.

Carrie leaned against the barn wall, her teeth clenched stoically against the pain that was starting to throb in her leg. Her eyes squeezed tight together, Carrie wanted to be sure her big brother wouldn't see her cry. She didn't want Joe to know her mind hadn't been on what she was doing, but on what he had teased her about earlier.

"You're getting fat, Carrie. The players and coaches don't want a fat cheerleader." A hundred and fifteen pounds distributed over five-feet-four inches, Carrie Swenson was not getting any taller, but she could tell now, most of her clothes were too tight across her hips and breasts.

She'd continued to fret. Since she'd been a cheerleader since tenth grade and now a senior, she'd been chosen captain of the squad. I surely don't want to get fat. She had been stewing about this when she went to chase the heifer.

Carrie hobbled alongside Joe. "Just let me hang onto

your shoulder." They struggled toward the small, white house just far enough from the barn to leave a respectable amount of grass.

Carrie's straw hat slipped to the back of her head; it was Joe's hat, too big for her, tied down with a piece of blue chambray torn from her dad's old shirt. It kept the sun away from her fair skin and sun-bleached blond hair.

The early August evening and the pain in her knee made small beads of sweat appear on her upper lip. Limping along with Joe, she thought, brothers can be pests but sometimes they come in handy.

"Mom!" Joe yelled and pushed open the door from the entry into the kitchen. "Carrie got stuck in her knee by the pitchfork!"

Sophie Swenson rushed to the door, "How in the world did that happen?"

"Aw, Mom, I dropped the pitchfork down from the hayloft. Pa said he wanted some hay for the horses when he comes home from threshing. I didn't know Carrie was there."

Mom looked hard at Joe and took over the burden of Carrie. "You better go start milking," Mom ordered. Joe hurried out the door, only too glad to escape to the barn.

"Let's see how bad it is. Slip off your overalls, Carrie." She looked at the wound, a small puncture just above the knee, and said, "Dr. Raleigh will have to see this. We'll disinfect it first," Sophie said bringing a cotton swab filled with iodine to soak the wound. Carrie bit her lip as the iodine worked its way into her leg.

Sophie got the can of Raleigh salve from the medicine chest and covered Carrie's wound with the pungent ointment. She tore a piece from an old pillowcase and taped it over the puncture. Swenson's kept a can of Raleigh salve in the house and one in the barn where it helped heal the cuts from the barbed wire fence the cows got on their teats and legs.

"There, that should draw out any infection, Carrie.

We'll have to let Pa look at it."

Carrie's pert nose wrinkled, hiding the freckles the sun had sprinkled across her face. Carrie really loved her father, Carl Swenson, and his homey wisdom: "When you do something, do it right" and "think of what could happen" were words of wisdom she'd heard him say over and over many times. She knew both she and Joe would hear them again tonight!

Pa had told the kids several times, "Before you throw the fork down from the hayloft, be sure to yell to see if anyone's there" and she knew Joe's response would be, "Well, I can't think of everything!"

"It looks like you should stay off that leg for awhile," Sophie said with a sigh. "You probably can't even bake bread for awhile." She appreciated Carrie doing that chore. Baking five loaves every other day was a big help. It took a lot of her time.

Carrie braved a wry smile, a dimple appearing in her right cheek. "Mom, can I still go to town tonight and see the show?" Carrie asked wistfully. "It's *Treasure Island* with Wallace Berry and a parrot."

Tonight was Saturday night with the free show on the big wooden screen by the Old Towne Cafe. Like many Minnesota farm families, the Swenson's spent their Saturday nights in town.

"If I can't go, you'll have to tell Louise I won't be coming." Louise was Carrie's cousin and best friend. They would both be in the twelfth grade, rode the same bus, talked about the boys and even exchanged clothes at times.

Mom replied, "Let's wait and see what Pa says."

When Pa came in from taking care of the horses, he washed up while Sophie told him what had happened. He shifted his snuff to his other cheek, inspected the wound and told Carrie, "You have to stay off that leg and keep it propped up. You better not go to town tonight." And that was that.

Her whole family left after supper for Applegrove while Carrie sat on the couch with her leg propped up on the hassock. She had some quiet time to think. Why did this have to happen to me? she wondered. I could've hobbled around town if Pa would've let me go. Well, maybe it's better I stayed home. At least, Tim Thoreson, the new implement dealer's son, won't get to tease me. He's such a pest. Since he moved to Applegrove last year he's always bothering Louise and me. Yet he can be very nice at times. Carrie hadn't made up her mind whether she liked him or not.

Her mind wandered into dreams of the future. I suppose some day I'll marry a farmer and raise a family. It would be nice to live in town in a big house and not have to do chores, but I can't see marrying someone that wears white shirts every day either. What a job to wash, starch and iron those!

Carrie tried to stand up but then dropped back onto the couch when she felt a stab of pain move up into her thigh. She thought back how she wanted to be a cheerleader since she was little. Cheerleading had helped her overcome her fear of being in front of people. She worried, what if my leg doesn't get any better and I can't be a cheerleader? But if I do what Mom says, I'm sure it will be okay. She settled into the couch to wait for her family to return.

Mom's home remedy kept Carrie's leg from becoming infected. She had to stay off her leg for awhile. Carrie was sitting on the couch and folding the clothes her mother brought in from the clothes line.

Sophie came in and sat down next to Carrie and sighed, "Oh, it feels so good to rest! I've been on my feet all day, washing clothes all morning and baking all afternoon for the Church Bake Sale."

"I'm sorry I haven't been much help the last two

weeks," Carrie apologized and slid closer to her mother. "But look, I can bend my knee and I can walk without it hurting. Mom, you're a good doctor. I'll be ready for school to start."

Sophie slipped off her shoes and said, "That's good."

Carrie said, "I was worried for awhile that I wouldn't be able to start school again, like when I was in first grade."

"Oh, you mean when you had rheumatic fever. Yah, that was too bad," Sophie lamented.

"I remember crying because I wanted to start school, but now I'm glad I waited," Carrie remarked. "If I had started earlier, maybe I wouldn't have been a cheerleader."

"It was a good thing we kept you home that whole year. Dr. Midthune recommended it."

"Well, it makes me whole year older than any of the other seniors, but I guess that's okay. Just think, the class of 1940," Carrie said.

"Yah," Sophie reflected, you kids have grown up in a hurry. Where in the world does the time go? First Delores, then Joe, now you, Pete in two years. Before long, Dawn will be graduating."

They were startled out of their reminiscing by howls of anguish.

"Land's sakes, what now?" Sophie said as she slipped on her shoes and hurried out the door. She brought Pete in, blood was dripping down his chin, and his hand was over his mouth. Sophie pulled his hand away and peered into his mouth. "Oh, no. I think you've knocked out a tooth. What happened, Pete?"

Pete, still holding his hand over his mouth mumbled, "When Pa was gone, he wanted me to take the oil pan off the tractor so he could fix the leaky gasket. The wrench slipped."

"For goodness sakes, first Carrie, now you. Carrie, we've got to take Pete to the dentist."

"How are we going to do that?" Carrie asked. "Pa's got the car and Joe took the truck to go fishing down at the creek."

"Oh, that's right!" Sophie said, losing her usual calm. "Can you go and get him?"

"Yes, It looks like I have to," Carrie said and hurried off to the creek in the pasture.

It wasn't long before Carrie and Joe drove into the yard. Carrie climbed out and said, "Mom, I should get my license, then I could drive in emergencies." She rushed on with her argument. "Remember I told you Willie at 'The Corner Cafe' is going to need a waitress on Saturdays this fall and he said it's possible I could have the job."

Mom, anxious to get Pete to the dentist said, "Okay, Carrie, the week before Labor Day, I'll take you to Benton for your license. You three will have to take the truck to the dentist. Carrie, you stay with Pete." Handing Joe a slip of paper, Sophie said, "I want you to buy these groceries for me when you're in town."

Pete, with a towel over his mouth, climbed in the truck and Carrie squeezed in beside him. "You're supposed to see Dr. Bob," Mom yelled over the noise of the old truck. She slammed the truck door and with a worried look, watched the truck leave the farmyard.

Carrie said enviously, "Joe, you get to drive all the time. I need the practice so I can get my license now before school starts."

Joe said, "It's no big deal, Carrie. All you have to do is fill out this form. It just took me a few minutes."

Pete mumbled something through the towel, "I should get mine too."

Joe teased, "I've got an idea, Carrie. Why don't you get Tim Thoreson to drive you around?"

"I don't like him!" Carrie exclaimed, shaking her head to emphasize her feeling. She was quiet for awhile then asked, "Do you know where the dentist's new office is?"

"Yah," Joe said. "When you take Pete to the dentist I'll go to Moe's Store and get Mom's groceries."

Joe parked momentarily in front of the new dental office on main street down from the Applegrove Farmers Bank. Carrie dragged the reluctant Pete along by one arm.

"What's he going to do to me?" Pete protested.

"You'll have to wait and see," Carrie answered. Hanging on to Pete with one hand and opening the door with the other, she almost bumped into Hazel, the receptionist.

"Dr. Monson will be right with you," she said. "Your mother called so Pete won't have to wait. You can put your jackets on the chair."

Dr. Bob appeared in the doorway of his office. "Come right in, Carrie and Pete."

He knew everyone in the area. A big man for a dentist, he was not so tall but wide in the shoulders. In uniform, he could easily be identified as the Captain of the Applegrove Co. M - 135th Regiment, 34th Infantry Red Bull Division of the Minnesota National Guard. However, few could picture him as the same man who bent over his patients each day at the Applegrove Dental Clinic. Bob and his brother Rick had built their new office in 1937. The shiny dental chair, porcelain bowl and sink, the mahogany instrument cabinet with its many drawers and milk glass top, were all new.

"What happened? " asked Dr. Bob.

Carrie answered, "Pete was working under the tractor when the wrench slipped. Mom thinks he knocked out a tooth."

"Oh, I see! Hop up in the chair, Pete, and I'll give you a special ride." With that he pumped up the chair and tipped Pete back.

"I'm going to squirt some water in your mouth and you can rinse and spit in the bowl. It's like a cuspidor only this one has running water," joked Dr. Bob. "When I get a little more light I can see what's what," he said as he pulled on the large reflector then adjusted the light beam. Dr. Bob swung his table of instruments over.

"Open wide, Pete. Mmm. Well, Pete, you did as good

job of pulling that tooth as I could. Carrie, you can tell your folks that it was one of his permanent teeth, but it's off to one side of the mouth so the other teeth will move over and fill the opening. I don't think we'll have to make any impressions or put in any crowns. Let's just keep an eye on it. Pete, your jaw will probably turn black and blue."

Pete hopped quickly out of the chair, his mechanical curiosity aroused and said, "You sure have a lot of stuff, Dr. Bob."

Dr. Bob laughed heartily. While Pete investigated the new dental equipment, Dr. Bob asked Carrie, "Since your brother Joe graduated, has he ever said anything about belonging to the National Guard? We can always use more good men."

Carrie replied, "Yes, he did. He talked to Bill Bradford, the janitor at the school. He told Joe what they did on maneuvers at Camp Ripley. But, Pa's talking about renting the Peterson place, so Joe will be needed on the farm."

Carrie and Pete picked up their jackets, ready to leave. "Mom will be coming in about the bill, Dr. Bob."

"Okay, maybe we can barter with some chickens or steaks," Dr. Bob smiled.

As he closed the door to his office behind Carrie and Pete, his smile disappeared. A letter from the Minnesota National Guard office lay opened on his desk. The General's Office in Fort Snelling had recommended all units be brought up to full strength.

On this August morning in 1939, the radio reported, "Europe is on the brink of war. Diplomacy cannot stop Adolph Hitler. There is no peaceful resolution of the conflict between Germany and Poland. The German Reich and the Nazi ideology, with Hitler as their leader, has become a real threat to many of the free countries of Europe."

Dr. Monson sat for a moment in his office chair, a vacant stare in his eyes as he looked out the window. What would all this mean for the young men under his command and for all those he might recruit? How was this menace going to be stopped?

STREETS OF HONOR

Chapter 3

After finishing the morning chores, Carrie took a sponge bath then brushed her thick blond hair until it shone. When she put on clean slacks, she noticed these too, were getting tight for her. She chose a white blouse with decorative embroidery down the front. She attributed her nervousness to the fact that she was finally going to get her driver's license.

"Mom, it's a good thing you could take me to Benton today," Carrie said excitedly as she rode beside her mother. "This is the last day I can get my license before school starts and tomorrow I start my waitress job at The Corner Cafe."

"I promised I'd take you. It'll be nice that you'll be able to drive yourself." Noticing Carrie's nervousness she added, "It's only 11 o'clock, Carrie. You don't need to fidget around. You only have to fill out an application to get your driver's license." She looked at her pretty, blond daughter, "You look very nice, Carrie," she said.

Dawn piped up from the back seat, "Yes, and she smells nice too. She put perfume behind her ears, and dabbed some on her wrists."

Carrie smiled, "When you get big, Dawn, I'll bet you'll use a whole bottle of perfume at one time."

"I'll drop you off at the courthouse parking lot. Dawn and I will buy groceries and we'll come by in about half an hour or so to pick you up."

"That's fine, Mom. According to what Joe said, it shouldn't take too long to get a license."

"You might have to wait for us," Sophie called out the window and watched as Carrie walked across the parking lot to the courthouse steps. "My, but she's grown up, Dawn, and filled out. It looks like we'll have to shop for new clothes."

Dawn was happy to report; "She told me that the last time she weighed herself at Louise's she weighed 115 pounds."

Sophie failed to notice the well built young man that had parked nearby and now followed Carrie into the courthouse.

Dean had started out at 6 a. m. Friday morning. He knew he had to get an early start if he was going to stop at Benton before going to Applegrove. Superintendent Grafstrom had written that he could apply for his Minnesota driver's license and get license plates for his car at the courthouse in Benton.

Dean drove around Benton, the county seat, and located the courthouse in the north end of the city. Parking the Studebaker, he noticed the pretty, blond girl walking up the courthouse steps and opening the door.

I wonder if she's getting a driver's license. She looks like she knows what she's doing. He had guessed right when he saw her stop by the counter under the License Bureau sign. The clerk was handing her a form.

"You can fill this out over at the next window," the clerk told her.

Dean stepped up to the counter, "I'm from North Dakota and I need both a driver's license and license plates for my car."

"Oh, where will you be living?" the clerk asked.

"I'll be teaching in Applegrove." Dean couldn't help but notice the girl gave a little start and glanced his way.

" Do you have an address?"

" I haven't found a place to live yet."

"You'll have to fill out this form, sign it, then leave it here. I can't give you a license until you establish a residence. When you find a place to stay you can write me or call. The license bureau number is in the telephone book under the courthouse offices. My name's Bertha."

Moving over from the window, Dean noticed the blond girl smiled at him, revealing a dimple in her right cheek.

"I heard you say that you'll be teaching in Applegrove. That's my school," Carrie said proudly. "I'm a senior there this year. What will you be teaching?"

"Math, chemistry and physical education," Dean said, adding, "I'll also be coaching football, basketball and baseball."

"I'm captain of the cheerleading squad." The smile and dimple returned to Carrie's face. She handed her application form to the clerk.

The clerk said, "You could have gotten your license free last year. If your Dad paid the 25-cent fee, each member of the family could be issued a license. The new law passed this year raised the fee to 35 cents for each license."

"I brought a dollar, just in case."

Bertha finished filling out the form, signed it, tore off the license, handed it to Carrie with her change. Before leaving, Carrie said to Dean, "I hope you like teaching in Applegrove."

"I think I will. It sounds like a nice place."

Carrie heard him good-naturedly tell the clerk, "I'm 22, so I suppose it will cost me 35 cents too, unless it's more for North Dakotans."

Carrie skipped down the steps and waited with a smile still on her face by the driveway entrance to the courthouse. Ha, wait 'til I tell Louise I already met the new coach. She always seems to know everything, but this is one time I did something first! I wonder what Pete and the other players will think of him.

Dean told Bertha he would call as soon as he got an address, picked up his license plates and headed for his car.

He noticed the blond student waiting by the entrance to the parking lot and rolled down his window, "Can I drive you someplace?"

"No, my mother is coming by for me in a few minutes. Thanks, anyway."

"By the way, what's your name? I should know someone from Applegrove."

"My name's Carrie, Carrie Swenson. But, I don't live in Applegrove. My folks farm north of town."

"My name's Brandum, Dean Brandum," Dean said with a smile. We'll see you at school, Carrie."

Dean was happy for a couple of reasons. Being at Valley River Teachers College had built his confidence and helped him get over being afraid of girls. And now he knew someone from Applegrove. If, he thought, the other students are as nice as she is, I'll like the school. She had a nice smile and seemed older than a high school senior.

Sophie drove into the courthouse lot to turn around. "You sure look happy, Carrie. They must have let you have your license."

"Yes, and it only cost 35 cents. And... you know what?...I met the new coach."

"Really? What's he like, then?"

"He's from North Dakota, has broad shoulders, is tall, and blond and has a nice smile."

"You sure must have looked him over good."

"Oh, Mom, he's 22...too old for me."

"How do you know he's 22?"

"I overheard him tell the clerk when he was getting his license. I told him we lived on a farm. Living on a farm has its advantages; I think Willie at the Corner Cafe hired me because I'm a farm girl."

"Yah, he knew that you'd be a good worker."

Driving down the highway after noon lunch, Dean reflected, I should have asked Carrie if she knew of any places to rent in Applegrove. I'll have to check those two places the superintendent sent me. I hope I don't have to stay at the hotel.

Dean introduced himself as a new teacher to the owner of the Applegrove Cafe.

"Hi, my name's Bruce Strong," the cafe owner responded. "Are you the new coach?"

"I'll be coaching everything, Mr. Strong."

"You can call me, Bruce. I go to all the sports events. If my customers miss a game, I have to report. We should have an average football season but a pretty good basketball year," observed Bruce.

As a newcomer in town Dean was a little surprised at the interest shown in himself and sports. But he suddenly realized that the high school team was an important part of main street and the subject of community conversation and pride. He would have to live up to some high expectations.

"Do you know of any places where I could rent a room?"

"I know a number of the teachers have rented from Mrs. Bogenreif over the years. They seemed to like staying with her."

"Thanks, Bruce. I'll be eating out quite a bit so you may be seeing more of me."

Looking at the list from the superintendent, Dean saw Mrs. Bogenreif's name. I'll try there first. He decided to drive by the school and was pleased to see a brick, nicely landscaped building. Mrs. Bogenreif's house was only two blocks from the high school.

Dean sat for a moment and gazed at the old, two-story house with four pillars holding up the roof of the large screened-in porch. Two large windows on the second floor peered out like two eyes. Sure is a big house. Should be rooms available he thought.

Walking up the sidewalk, he failed to notice the elderly lady in her rocker on the porch. She rose and greeted him. "Hello, young man, can I help you?"

Surprised, Dean said, "I'm Dean Brandum, ma'am. I'll be teaching here and I was told maybe you could maybe rent me a room."

"Yes, come on in. I do have a room available you can look at. It's the only one on the second floor. I have one of the downstairs apartments and I rent out the other. The stairway to upstairs is at the end of the hallway." She added, "Where are you from?"

"From North Dakota, but from now on, this will be my home." Dean liked the cleanliness and privacy of the second floor room and the fact that the house was close to the high school. "I'll take the room, Mrs. Bogenreif. Can I pay you the rent when I get paid?"

"Oh, yes and you can call me Mrs. B. If you want to bring your things in, I'll make some sandwiches and coffee." Over the years, she had treated her renters like the children she never had.

"Do you know if there's a Studebaker dealer near here?" Dean asked Mrs. B. as he munched on the sandwich she had just made. "I should have my car checked and get whatever filters I need."

"When my husband was alive, we sometimes went to a movie in Willmar. It's about 60-65 miles and there are a lot of car dealers there."

"I need to drive over there later this month or the first part of October," Dean said.   "I'll have to wait until I get paid...and after I pay the rent, of course," Dean smiled.

"If you're short of money, I can wait,"   Mrs. B. encouraged.

"You're a good listener, Mrs. B.. I can see why the teachers like to stay here."

"I've rented to lots of teachers over the years."   She added, "When my husband died, I moved to town and bought this house. If you ever want to talk about anything, I'll be around."

"Tomorrow I'm going to look Applegrove over. I see there's a drive-in eating place at the edge of town. I'll eat there and go to bed early."

"I suppose you're tired from driving?"

"Yes, but we just finished harvesting and I need to get caught up on my sleep. Would you happen to have an alarm clock I could borrow?"

"Yes, I do. Use it as long as you like."

"Thanks, Mrs. B., and thanks for the sandwiches and coffee," Dean said, accepting the alarm clock Mrs. B. offered.

The soft and comfortable bed looked inviting to Dean who lay down with the intention of resting for only a few minutes.

When he awoke the sun was rising in the east. He couldn't believe he had slept through the night. Feeling rested, he finished unpacking and went to get some breakfast.

Dean decided to try Willy's Corner Cafe. Seated around one table were men dressed in bib overalls or in denim pants and flannel shirts covered by an overall jacket. The summer sun had faded their straw hats and striped denim caps. Treating him like all strangers that came into the cafe, the men stopped their conversation when he entered. It started again promptly when one of them said, "Must be a new teacher."

Dean sat on a stool by the counter and immediately felt right at home. Looking over the menu that he found tucked away behind the napkin dispenser, he was surprised when someone said, "Good morning, Mr. Brandum."

Glancing up, Dean noticed Carrie Swenson. She was wearing a small waitress apron.

"You remembered my name. I'm surprised you work here. I thought you lived on a farm."

"I work here from 8:00 a.m. until 2:00 p.m. on Saturdays."

"You're going to be a busy lady this fall."

"Willie needed help. Pa said I could drive in now that I've got my driver's license. At least for a couple of months until the roads get icy. Do you want coffee?"

"Yes, please. I'll have the #3, eggs over easy, whole wheat toast and bacon."

Carrie poured him coffee and then took menus and water glasses over to a couple just sitting down in an adjacent booth.

Dean found the Applegrove paper from last week. All new students were asked to register for school and he found an article on the football schedule. He studied the names of the other schools on the schedule.

Setting Dean's breakfast before him, Carrie asked, "Did you find a place to stay?"

"I have a room at Mrs. Bogenrief's. Do you know her?"

"I know who she is."

As Carrie refilled his coffee cup, he asked her, "I'm going to look over the community today, Carrie. Is there anything special to see?"

"Besides the uptown area, there's the Johansson flour mill with a water wheel and a dam on the west side of town. There's a nice park by the river." She hesitated a moment. "Farther out in the country there's a game refuge with lots of geese and once in awhile you can see deer. It's just a little town, Mr. Brandum."

"Thanks, I'll just drive around." Not used to eating out, Dean hoped he'd left an adequate tip. Dean soon discovered that Applegrove was a lot like Auburn, only larger.

Saturday afternoon, Dean spent drawing up a football handout. It included what he expected of his players, but mostly offense and defense formations he wanted to use. It was his hope that the school would have a way of copying the information for himself and his players.

Sunday morning Dean thought about going to church, as he'd promised Ma. But instead, he slept in. Heading down town to the Applegrove Cafe for breakfast, Dean noticed there were lots of cars and dressed up people either coming or going to the various churches. Mrs. B. had told him, "Applegrove is a churchy community. There are five churches in town, so you can take your pick."

He was finishing up his breakfast when a young man with a big mop of curly black hair and black bushy eyebrows came over and offered his hand. "Hi, I'm Bill Bradford. Bruce said you were the new coach. You'll be seeing a lot of me. I'm the janitor at the high school."

"I'm glad to meet you, Bill. Our coach at college told us the one person we have to be good to was the custodian."

Bill smiled and sat down in the booth opposite Dean. "We just came from church. That's my wife Sally over there. Bridget, our girl, is three and we're going to have another one this month."

"You have a nice looking family."

"Thanks, Dr. Midthune thinks our next will be a boy. He's been right in the past. Are you anxious to get started at school?"

"Yes, I am. Is it possible to get in there today?"

"Don't worry about school. Major has started school two hours late on Tuesday after Labor Day ever since I can remember. There's a teacher's meeting first then classes are only twenty minutes long. Just enough for the first day."

"That's good. I planned to get here earlier but we had so much rain out in North Dakota we couldn't get the harvesting done."

"Same here in Minnesota."

"Who's Major?"

"Oh yeah, I forgot you're new. That's Supt. Grafstrom. He was a major in the Great War--everyone calls him by that nickname when he's not around. He's been in Applegrove so long, some of the parents had him as their teacher. On one day he might be ornery and on another he doesn't mind anything that happens."

"I was wondering about my classes and thinking about football equipment."

"The players have got that all under control too. The ones that are coming back either kept their same equipment or took the equipment of the seniors that graduated. They've marked it so they can be sure to get what they want. It's stored

in the gym storage room. I'll be around after school and help
you get it passed out."

"That's really swell of you. I'm also needing a
chemistry textbook."

"I'd let you in but we're on our way to visit Sally's folks
in Willmar. But like I said, you won't have time for anything
much on Tuesday anyway."

Bruce Strong came by with the coffeepot. "Is the head of
the school telling you what to do?"

"Just because you're my first sergeant, I don't have to
listen to you when I'm out of uniform," joked Bill.

Bruce continued down the booths and Bill explained.
"We're both in the Guard although I'm only a private first class.
He's a good first sergeant - a little blustery at times, but he gets
along with the men. Have you ever thought about joining?"

"I'm going to be busy this first year, but I'll see later on.
Thanks. Say, Bill, maybe you can tell me. Is there a
Studebaker dealer in Willmar?"

"Yes, there is."

"Next month I have to have the oil changed on my car.
If your wife can travel, you and your family sure can ride with
me."

"We'll have to see how Sally feels after the baby is
born. But thanks for the offer."

As Bill got up to leave he said, "See you Tuesday."

Dean was glad to have a friend at school and relieved to
learn that the first day of school was shortened. He decided to
finish his football project and spend time reviewing his
chemistry notes. He felt a little shaky in that area. If, he
thought, he had some good students in chemistry class, they
might learn together.

On Monday after breakfast, as he walked around the
football field, he thought about how nice it was of Bill to offer
to help with the equipment. Dean spent the afternoon driving
around the game refuge and looking over the area lakes and

farms. They raise a lot of corn here, he observed. When he ended up north of town, he drove his Studebaker down gravel roads looking for Swenson's farm, but couldn't find it. I wonder where Carrie lives? he asked himself.

STREETS OF HONOR

Chapter 4

The morning of the first day of school, Tuesday, September 5, 1939, was bright and sunny. The dew, covering the green grass like a hazy carpet, sparkled in the early morning. The sun, filtering through the trees, made a pattern of light and dark green grass as Carrie and Pete finished their morning chores and hurried up to the house. Dawn, done with her breakfast, was already wearing her new school clothes.

Mom reminded them, "You don't have to eat so fast. School doesn't start until 10:30 today. The bus won't be coming until after 9:00." Swenson's were one of the first families on the bus route; they normally had to wait at the driveway by 7:15.

The night before, Carrie had laid out her clothes, a new skirt and blouse. Carrie, Pete and Dawn, bright and shiny in their new clothes, boarded the bus. "My, you look nice today," Fred, the bus driver, greeted them.

Carrie's cousin, Louise, waited by the mailbox at the end of her driveway. As she slipped into the seat beside Carrie, she asked, "How does it feel to be a senior?"

"It's wonderful! I've been thinking about my classes. I'm taking accounting and shorthand in the morning and chemistry and home economics after lunch."

"Chemistry!" Louise exclaimed. "What do you want to take that for?"

"I would like to find a job in a bank when I graduate, but if I take a job in the hospital or doctor's office, then I should know some chemistry." Carrie refrained from telling Louise that Dean Brandum was going to teach chemistry.

Fred stopped at the school and his passengers,

disembarking noisily, entered the Applegrove School.

Dean was up early on the first day of classes. As he put on some of his best college clothes, he frowned. When I get paid, I better go to Willmar and buy some new clothes. After a quick breakfast at the Applegrove Cafe, he hurried to school for the 8:00 a.m. teacher's meeting. The familiar smell of floor sealer and fresh paint greeted him as he opened the high school doors.

Dean stood looking around for the office, when he heard a voice say, "Can we help you?"

"Thanks," Dean said with a grin, "I'm new here and not sure where to go. I'm Dean Brandum."

"I'm Russell Wagner, Dean. I teach social studies. This is Mrs. Collins, the band director." Dean nodded and shook hands with them both. With her black hair cut short, her eyes shaded with dark glasses and wearing a snappy, dark blue suit, Mrs. Collins appeared ready to take the band on parade.

Russell continued, "We've both been here for several years, so don't be afraid to ask for help. Our teacher's meetings are in the study hall upstairs."

Walking up to the second floor study hall for the meeting and hearing the squeak in the wooden steps, Dean commented he felt like he was back in the college Annex dorm. Following the two teachers through a door marked, STUDY HALL, Dean saw Supt. Grafstrom up front helping a slender young man unpack books. Seeing Dean, he brought the young man over.

"Welcome, Dean. Good to see you," he said. "This is Mr. Rogstad, the high school principal. He and I were just unpacking the lesson plans and grade books. Remember, Dean, if anything good happens, come and see me...bad, see Mr. Rogstad," the superintendent joked.

"Hi, Dean, welcome," Rogstad smiled and shook his hand. "Supt. Grafstrom has been telling me about you. We have two new teachers this year - you and Berniece Wright - the business teacher. I'll introduce her to you when she comes."

The superintendent added, "We've got a few minutes before the meeting starts. Why don't you see Maybelle in the office and get your keys? She can tell you what they're for. The office is down the steps to the right."

"Could I talk to her about copying some pages for the football players for me?"

"Yes, I'm sure. There's a duplicating machine in the office. Maybelle's very helpful."

On his way to the office, Dean met Bill Bradford in the hallway. "You have things looking nice, Bill," Dean commented.

"Yes, if it would only stay that way. I'll be around if you need help, but after school for sure, to help with the football equipment."

Maybelle explained which keys were for what and said she'd be happy to make copies after he put them on a duplicating master. I bet she's got a lot to do with running the school, Dean guessed as he returned to the study hall.

The high school staff stood around, waiting for the meeting to begin. Principal Rogstad motioned for Dean to join a small group. "Dean, this is Berniece Wright, the other new teacher."

Berniece smiled and extended her hand. She was small, dark, and appeared to Dean like she could be mistaken for a high school student. Dean shook her hand, smiled, and said, "Hi, glad to meet you. It's nice that someone else here is new to teaching."

Supt. Grafstrom's voice halted the buzzing going on around the room. "Will you please find a place to sit." Dean looked for a large desk where he might fit more comfortably.

The superintendent welcomed everyone, introduced Berniece and Dean and encouraged the staff to make them welcome. "After Mr. Rogstad reviews lesson plans, grading, school discipline and the class schedule, I'll go over the school policies."

Principal Rogstad took only a few minutes, then said, "If you have any questions, I'll be happy to answer them."

One of the older women teachers asked, "What about the big seventh grade class?" Dean learned later it was the junior high English teacher, known for her strict discipline.

"I had to leave the seventh grade in one section, as we don't have enough staff for two sections. Any other questions? Okay, then we'll hear from Supt. Grafstrom."

Some of the staff slid down in their seats as Supt. Grafstrom opened a well-worn school board policy book, one that they'd seen in past years. To Dean it was a little more interesting. When the superintendent's eyes went up to the ceiling, Dean observed that he must have known the policies by heart. Dean's mind wandered when he talked about school board relationships, and he began to wonder how Berniece will handle those big high school boys.

After relating the staff policies for sick leave, snow days, and travel, he took his eyes off the ceiling and began reading policy number nine."

"Instructors attached to the staff of the Applegrove Schools will not date students. Faculty members should not mingle socially with students and every effort must be made to maintain a proper faculty-student relationship. General overall faculty conduct shall be good and misbehavior will not be tolerated."

Dean, cramped in the desk, stretched his legs out in the aisle. The thought came to mind that he didn't anticipate any problem with that policy.

The superintendent concluded, "The students should start coming in about 10:30 a.m. so take the rest of the time until then to prepare. Good luck, and have a good school year."

The morning went by quickly. Dean found a place

across from Berniece for noon lunch in the lunchroom. Dean confided to her, "I got a good class schedule. How's yours?"

"I've got accounting, typing and shorthand in the morning and after lunch, a business class, typing, and then last hour study hall."

"Ouch! How'd you end up with a last hour study hall?"

"No one else wanted it, and I only had five periods assigned. How does this face look?" She made a grouchy face and then smiled.

Dean laughed, "Very good. I like the smiling one better."

"But, Dean, our education teacher told us we shouldn't smile for the first three months."

"My math classes are in the morning with chemistry after lunch and the two phy. ed. classes after that, so I don't have to change again for football. It should work out fine. Good luck with your afternoon classes," Dean said, unwinding himself from the table.

Dean then noticed Bill Bradford leaning on a broom, talking to Russell Wagner. He stopped for a minute before going to his chemistry class. Bill said, "We were just talking about last summer's bivouac at Camp Ripley. Russell is in the Guard too."

"Yes, it's a good experience for me, Dean. It's going to help in my social studies classes. Are you interested at all in joining?"

"Like I told Bill, I'll have to wait and see. Right now, I'd better open up for my chemistry class."

Dean was pleased to see Carrie Swenson in chemistry class. He was nervous about teaching this class, and was encouraged by her smile. "With only twelve in our class we should be able to move right along." He added, "It looks like we don't have too many chemicals, but I'll talk to the superintendent and perhaps we can order some, along with more equipment." A ripple of applause and "yeah, yeah!" told Dean they were happy to hear this.

After his last class, Dean hurried to the storage room where the football equipment was stored. He was anxious to meet the players and was eager to start practice. Bill Bradford was already there and a great help; he knew all the players by name and could determine what they needed.

A sturdy, muscular boy with dark hair and glasses introduced himself, "I'm Ed, Mr. Brandum. I was the quarterback last year and I hope to be again."

Dean shook his hand. "We need someone with experience at quarterback." Dean walked over to a tall, lanky, blond boy, struggling to put on his jersey. "Now, who are you?" Dean asked.

"Hi, I'm Clarence."

"What did you play?"

"I played tackle on both offense and defense last year."

"Good," Dean said. "You'll be doing that again this year."

After the players were dressed, Dean had them huddle up outside on the football field. He cautioned them, "We have only twenty-eight out for football; so you need to stay in shape, take care of yourselves and stay out of trouble."

Carrie's concern whether Pete and the other players would like him was quickly dispelled. The players took to Dean right away after he gave them a short workout and said each one would get a handout on what was expected of them and team formations.

The first three weeks of school went quickly for Dean. Even chemistry, despite being the first class after the noon hour, turned out to be rewarding. Supt. Grafstrom agreed to place a large order of chemistry supplies and equipment. Dean appreciated having Carrie in class; she was a model student and helped Dean by contributing much to the class.

Dean decided to have a quick cup of coffee after school in the faculty room before football practice. He picked up sandwich paper wrappings and a banana skin left on the table and put them in the wastebasket. Glancing over the front page of the newspaper, he noticed the headline: "German military 'Blitzkrieg' swarms over Poland. The country is to be divided between Germany and Russia." He skimmed past the article and found the sports page just as Russell Wagner burst into the room, doubled over with laughter.

"What's so funny, Russell?" Dean asked, looking up from his paper.

"Dean, your big tackle, Clarence, met his match in last hour study hall. When I was walking through, I saw Berniece grab him by the ear. She pulled him out of his desk and marched him up to the principal's office. Even principal Rogstad couldn't help but smile. Some of the kids thought it was funny. I waited to see what would happen. When she came back and glared at them..... they all shut up, fast."

"I'm glad to hear that," Dean said smiling. His fear of how the diminutive Berniece would cope with the big farm boys had been extinguished. "Sounds like Clarence will have to do extra laps at practice. I told the team they can't get into trouble because we need everyone."

Noticing the newspaper headline again, he asked, "Russell, here's an article on the invasion of Poland by Germany. Do you teach anything about this in your social studies classes?"

"We talk about current events every day. The students have to find out what's going on in those occupied countries. It's been terrible for them-especially for the Jews."

Dean replied, "Yah, I understand that many people are buying maps of Europe to follow what's going on."

Dean's football coaching career didn't start out to be an average football season as the main street sports enthusiasts predicted. Even with two weeks of practice before their first game, the previous year's conference champions trounced the team. The winner that week was Bill Bradford. The custodian was popular with some of the smokers on the staff when he passed out cigars labeled, 'It's a Boy!'.

"What did you name him?" Dean asked.

"Sally and I decided on Lucas because that was her grandpa's name."

"Hey, that's nice! The doctor was right in predicting a boy!"

The football team improved the next two games, but the result was the same. The Applegrove Eagles lost 21-7 and 21-14.

Warming up Dean's coffee at the Applegrove Cafe, Bruce Strong, the cafe manager, who Dean now considered as one of his friends, remarked, "This week's game with Benton is a big one. They've always been our rivals. Some of the locals think they stole the county seat and the courthouse from Applegrove, and they still talk about it. If you beat Benton, you've had a good football season, no matter what else happens."

Dean smiled, "Anything you can do to help would be great, Bruce. Especially yelling with your sergeant's voice."

Carrie stayed after class on Tuesday. "We like cheering for the team, Mr. Brandum. They're really scrappy." Dean nodded in agreement, as Carrie continued, "Would you give a talk at Friday's pep fest?" she asked.

"Sure, I'll be glad to give a pep talk, Carrie."

Carrie smiled happily and said, "Homecoming week is extra special for me because today's my birthday."

"Congratulations! Are you doing any celebrating?"

"My home economics class is making a cake. They call me the 'old lady' because I'm 19 and the oldest one in the senior class."

Dean said, "By the way, we finally got more chemicals and equipment. Could you come in at noon some day next week and help me unpack them and put them on shelves? I need someone that knows what they're doing."

Carrie, blushing, said, "Thank you, I'll come in Monday right after we eat."

The Homecoming game with rival Benton added to the excitement. Dean saw splashes of red and white colors on the floats parked near the field. Dean had helped the seventh graders with their float and one of the girls had tugged on Dean's arm after the parade and proudly informed him that their float got third prize.

Dean smiled and said, "That's great." He was feeling good.

Watching the team warm up before the game, Dean felt the contagious excitement of the cheerleaders. The music from Mrs. Collins Applegrove band filled the balmy, afternoon air.

The Applegrove offense caught the Benton team off-guard and they were able to get two touchdowns for a 13-7 halftime lead. Both teams struggled to score in the second half, but time ran out with Applegrove having the ball at mid-field. Not only had the first win for Dean and the team been over the county seat rivals, but he'd also cemented his position as the football coach.

The players and cheerleaders jumped up and down and the fans rushed on the field to congratulate the team. In the excitement, Dean got several hugs and hugged back. Later he remembered an extra special one from the cheerleader captain, Carrie. She was happily hugging everybody and, either by accident or design, didn't realize she'd given Coach Brandum a big hug. What neither one of them noticed was that the local newspaper reporter had taken a photo at that opportune moment.

STREETS OF HONOR

Chapter 5

"Wasn't that an exciting game, Mr. Brandum?" Carrie gushed as she entered the science lab on Monday after lunch.

"The team played together really well," Dean replied graciously.

"It was fun to cheer," Carrie bubbled. "The fans were great."

"It was our defense that won the game. For a tenth grader, your brother Pete tackles well. I'm going to give him some time at quarterback. Ed will be graduating."

"He'd like that."

"We better get this stuff unpacked. I appreciate your coming in during your noon hour to help me. We can put it right on the shelves in the storeroom."

As Carrie unpacked the chemicals, glassware, Bunsen burners and scales, Dean checked them off his list. "We can do more experiments now, Carrie." Dean made several trips into the supply room and Carrie arranged the chemicals, test tubes and beakers on the shelves. "I'll bring in the equipment, you use the step stool and put them on the upper shelf," Dean said.

Carrie put the last of the equipment on the upper shelf and started to step down. Her foot slipped off the side of the stool, her arms flailing, grasping the air; she fell. Dean reacted quickly and grasped her in his arms before she could hit the floor. Just as she caught her breath, a figure appeared in the doorway. Turning with his arms still around her, Dean was startled to see Supt. Grafstrom.

"I...I...just caught Carrie as she fell off the stool. She's helping me store the chemistry equipment." Dean released Carrie from his embrace.

44

Carrie, a rosy blush on her face said, "We're done, Mr. Brandum. I've got to go and get my chemistry book." She left the storeroom, and without another word or glance, hurried out the classroom door.

"Thanks, Carrie," Dean said to the retreating Carrie, regaining his composure. "She's my best student, and I needed some help."

"That's why I stopped, Mr. Brandum," the superintendent said, a little more blustery than usual. "Principal Rogstad said you were checking in the equipment and I wanted to see if the order was right."

Walking out into the lab, Dean picked up the packing slip and purchase order from his desk. "Here's the packing slip and the original order. Everything checked out all right."

With a suspicious look on his face, Supt. Grafstrom took the papers and left for his office.

Dean conjured up images of the school board looking over the policies. This, he knew, must have looked bad. However, if he was called on the carpet, he'd explain that she might have sprained an ankle, or worse, if he hadn't caught her.

Tim, the tease, standing in the hallway with his buddies, wondered what was going on when he saw Carrie's beet red expression. He was even more mystified when the superintendent burst out of the lab with a deep frown on his face.

Ignoring Tim, Carrie hurried down the hallway to the washroom to compose herself. Seeing Louise getting her books out of her locker, Carrie beckoned her cousin to follow her into the washroom. Carrie told Louise in a hushed voice what had happened. "I don't know what to do, Louise!"

"You can say you're sick and have to go home," Louise offered.

"I haven't got a way to get home, so I have to go to chemistry class," Carrie said with a deep sigh.

"There's the bell. You didn't do anything wrong, so just

act like nothing happened."

Easier said than done, Carrie thought, as she hurried to her locker for her chemistry book. She felt conflicting emotions of her sudden close relationship to her teacher and her fear of the school superintendent's reaction.

When she entered the room, Dean gave Carrie a reassuring glance, but this did little to set her at ease.

The other class members took their seats. Dean began by asking Carrie a routine question. "What are the elements in sulfuric acid?"

When Carrie had to ask for the question again, the class was surprised. Carrie always responded quickly and with the right answer.

Both student and teacher were relieved when the bell rang. Carrie relaxed somewhat in her next class, as did Dean. Fortunately, neither one was aware of the bigger surprise they would be in for later in the week.

Wednesday noon, Bill Bradford gave Dean a big smile and said, "Nice write up about the game in the paper, Dean. Nice picture too." The Applegrove Press routinely came out on Wednesdays and contained local news, city council activities, the past week's weather observations, current school activities and editorials. Dean had planned to send a copy of the article about his first coaching win to Ma and Eric.

"What picture?" Dean asked in a puzzled voice.

"You and Carrie Swenson both made the Sports page. You'll have to see it," Bill said with even a bigger grin.

Dean ate quickly and told Berniece, with whom he occasionally ate lunch, "Bill said there's a picture in the paper that's got my curiosity up. I'll have to check the school's copy in the faculty room."

Russell Wagner gladly relinquished the paper to Dean when he saw Dean's quizzical look. The caption under the picture of Dean and Carrie read, "Coach Brandum gets special winner's hug from Cheerleader Captain, Carrie Swenson."

Dean put the paper down in front of him and looked at Russell. "Now what, Russell? I suppose I'm in real trouble with the school board."

"I don't think so. I saw some of them after the team beat Benton and I think Stan Shopfer, the school board chairman, would have hugged you if you'd have been there."

"Just the same, I better stay out of the limelight for awhile."

Seeing Bill Bradford in the hallway as he went to chemistry class, Dean said, "Bill, I've had pay day now and I should get over to Willmar to get some new clothes and get the oil changed on my Studebaker."

"Did that picture make you nervous, Dean?" he asked, changing the subject

"Not really, but I need to get out of town for awhile. Would you, Sally and the kids want to ride with me to Willmar on Saturday?"

"I think we could. Lucas is old enough to travel and the weather's nice. Sally's folks haven't seen the baby since he was born. But I'll check at home."

Carrie thought Mr. Brandum acted naturally all week. Some of the students and the other cheerleaders mentioned the picture to her, but it was Louise who was most descriptive. "Don't you remember it, Carrie? Boy I sure would. You must have been really excited."

"I was hugging everybody," Carrie said defensively.

The football team, going on momentum gained from their big Homecoming win, won their next game, 21-0. Pete Swenson, Carries brother, was able to quarterback for several plays and showed real potential as a passer.

Bill Bradford told Dean, "I checked with Sally and we'll go to Willmar with you on Saturday. She thought it would be better if we didn't have to leave until 8:00 in the morning."

"That sounds good. I'll come by shortly after 8:00," Dean replied.

Dean wanted to talk to Mrs. B. The events of the past week had bothered him. Seeing she was busy in the kitchen when he walked down the hallway to get upstairs, Dean manufactured a loud, "Hello, are you busy."

Mrs. B said, wiping her hands on her apron, said, "Why don't you sit a minute. I've just made some fresh coffee and we'll have a cup. I haven't seen much of you, but I've been following things in the newspaper."

Dean was relieved that she had brought this up. He took his usual seat at the kitchen table and gladly accepted the cup of hot coffee. He took a sip and said, "I suppose you saw the game write-up and the picture. I was going to send it to my mother, but now I'm not so sure if I should. She might not understand about my hugging the cheerleading captain. Ma's a conservative Scandinavian."

"I don't know why not. I think she'd like that. I thought the picture was real fitting. It captured everyone's feelings."

Dean was relieved to hear that. Sticking his legs out under the table, he put his hands behind his neck and said, "Tomorrow, I'm going to drive to Willmar, Mrs. B.. Bill Bradford, the school custodian, and his family are riding with me."

Mrs. B. said, "It's nice to have someone to talk to. They just had a baby awhile ago, so you'll have a car full. I know his wife is from Willmar."

"Thanks for the coffee and for visiting with me. I really do feel better now." Could I dare to send it to her now? he wondered.

The next morning for breakfast, Dean went to the Applegrove Cafe. He knew Carrie was working at The Corner Cafe and didn't want to talk to her in public for fear of what people would think. After breakfast he stopped at Bradford's small, one story house on Second Street, three blocks from the school. The two Bradford kids were still asleep so Sally held

Lucas in the back seat and Bill held Bridget in his lap.

Carrie, whose folks couldn't afford the paper, didn't see the article or picture until she came to work at The Corner Cafe on Saturday. Carrie thought, It seems like I just get involved with Mr. Brandum even when I don't try. I wonder where he is this morning? He usually comes in for breakfast. She rubbed an imaginary spot on the booth's tabletop ambitiously, not wanting to admit to herself that she missed him.

"When we get to Willmar, Bill, I'll drop you and your family off at Sally's folk's place and then I'll make an appointment to get my oil changed and shop for some clothes. I'll come by after I eat and maybe you could come with me to the Studebaker dealer."

"Sounds good, Dean."

"Bridget, you can't sit on Mr. Brandum's lap," Sally scolded her as the little girl, now wide-awake, squirmed away from her dad.

"Can you say, Hi Dean," Bill asked?

Trying to grab a handful of his blond hair, she said, "Hi, Dean."

Dean smiled and thought how lucky Bill was to have a nice family.

"You'll have to give me some directions, Sally."

"Willmar's an old railroad town," Sally said. "My folks live near the railroad depot. Just follow the railroad tracks into town. I'll tell you when to stop."

Dean deposited the Bradford family at Sally's folks, did his errands and after lunch returned to pick up Bill.

Dean and Bill stopped by Studebaker dealer and Dean told the mechanic who came out, "If you could check it over and change the oil and filter, I'd appreciate it. I should take a couple filters along with me, too."

"If, later, you need to change oil you can use my garage," Bill offered.

The owner came over while Dean and Bill were looking

over the used cars. "I noticed your car. I haven't seen one of those models around for awhile."

"Why's that?" Dean asked surprised.

"It's a Rockne Model 10. It's named after Knute Rockne, the famous Notre Dame football coach. Studebakers were built in South Bend, Indiana, where Notre Dame is located."

"I didn't know much about this car," Dean explained. "I bought it at a farm auction in North Dakota. It's a '33."

"With the spare tire in the front wheel fender, I think it's a '32. It's an L-head six. They only made 23,000 in the early 30's. If you ever want to sell it, let me know."

"No, I need it, but thanks for telling me about it."

On the way back to Sally's folks, Dean chuckled and said, "It was strange to hear my car is named after a famous football coach. I wish I could be a famous football coach someday."

Bill said, "You're famous now. You've got a two-game winning streak going. By the way, have you thought any more about joining the Guard? It's a good way to earn some extra money."

"Maybe this next summer or fall. I'll have to see," Dean answered.

It was almost dark when Dean and his passengers started back to Applegrove. Dean was happy. He was confused about his feelings for Carrie, but the talk with Mrs. B. and the trip had helped him unwind and erase some of these thoughts. Things will have to take their course, he thought. Maybe I should go out some evening with Berniece.....if there is time before basketball season starts.

Returning to school on Monday with the impression that enough time had elapsed that the incidents with Carrie were over, Dean was surprised to find a memo in his mailbox. It read:

Monday, October 16, 1939

"Mr. Brandum, please stop in my office tomorrow during your noon hour."

Supt. Grafstrom

Now what? Dean thought, imagining the worst.

STREETS OF HONOR

Chapter 6

Tuesday noon, Dean felt apprehension as he approached the superintendent's office. "Come in and sit down, Dean," the superintendent said. Dean chose the chair closest to the desk where he could look directly into the superintendent's eyes. "How's practice going this week?" Grafstrom asked, and then paused and looked directly at Dean. "The team seems to be playing well, Dean."

"Yes, they're playing together like a team. I'm proud of them," Dean replied. But he was puzzled, wondering what this was leading up to?

Leaning back in his chair, Grafstrom said, "The basketball season will soon be here. Applegrove has had some excellent basketball teams in past years. The school board's decided to pay expenses to send you to a coaching workshop at Concordia College in Moorhead. It would be beneficial to both you and the team. What do you think?"

Dean felt a wave of relief wash over him. He managed to say, "Well, ...uh, yes. I haven't even been thinking basketball yet."

Glancing at a brochure, the superintendent added, "It's on a Saturday, November 4. It's about 200 miles round trip. You could go up and back the same day."

Coming out of his daze, Dean said, "I would like to go." He pointed to the brochure with his finger, "That's the same information I got. There are some good sessions being offered."

Opening the brochure, the superintendent said, "There's a registration form that I'll send in for you."

"That would be great. And, Mr. Bradford said if I was

gone on a Saturday morning he would be willing to open up the gym for the players to shoot baskets. Would that be all right?"

"If he stays in the gym with the boys, that's okay."

"I'd give him my keys for lockers and ball storage. Thanks, I'll plan on that then." Feeling a great deal of relief, Dean left the office.

Even though he tried to think he had only a teacher-student relationship with Carrie, Dean could not suppress his growing attraction for her. He noticed how well she got along with other students, dressed neatly, always poised, stood straight and carried herself gracefully. In fact, Dean thought she was beautiful. And in addition to being the best student in his class, as cheerleader captain, she was his most ardent supporter.

And on Carrie's side, she wanted to be Dean's best student, but she too had a feeling of being pulled to him. Neither seemed to have any control over what was happening.

Parking his car in Mrs. B's driveway after football practice on Wednesday, Dean let himself in. The letter from Ma was waiting for him on the stairway landing leading up to his room. Dean opened the letter as soon as he got to his room.

> *Auburn, North Dakota*
> *October, 1939*

Dear Dean,

> *I just got your letter and thought I should answer right away. Everything is fine here. The weather has been good and Eric has finished the fall plowing. We're getting ready for winter.*

> *Be sure you eat properly and get rest so you don't get sick.*

> *Thank you for the newspaper story. It sounds like you have many friends and that the Bradfords and Mrs. B. have*

been so nice.

    I was surprised and confused about the picture of you and the cheerleader! Does this happen after a game? You have to be careful so you don't lose your job.

    We are waiting for you to come home at Thanksgiving. Skriv snart.

Love,
Ma

    Dean smiled as he read the letter and knew he had to write soon as the 'skriv snart' meant just that.....write soon. He would be seeing this many times in the future. I'll have to write and explain to her about the cheerleader picture. She shouldn't have to worry about me anymore.

    Saturday, as Dean packed the football gear away after the team ended the season with a win, he was already thinking about next year's team. Remembering Ma's letter, he vowed to answer it immediately.

    On Sunday he wrote to Ma and Eric, hoping the letter would ease their worry. He told them the hugging incident was an emotional reaction and the cheerleader, Carrie, was nineteen and was in one of his classes. There was nothing going on between them and not to worry, he wouldn't lose his job.

    On the following Saturday, Dean planned to leave at 6:00 a.m. for the coaching clinic. Quietly walking down the hallway, he smelled bacon. Mrs. B. said, "Come in, Dean. Thought you could use a good breakfast before you travel," she said, setting a plate of bacon, eggs and toast in front on him. He had told her the night before he would be leaving early but had no idea she would get up.

    "That looks so good, Mrs. B.!" Dean exclaimed. A steaming cup of coffee followed and Dean told Mrs. B. he would be home late that evening. "Thank you, Mrs. B. That should keep me awake on this cool morning." Anxious to be on the road for Concordia, he hurried out the door, grateful to have someone like Mrs. B. to watch out for him.

Driving down the highway lost in thought about basketball, Dean failed to notice the trees shedding their fall colors. Only when he saw the fields black with plowing was he reminded of the farm. He realized how thankful he was to Uncle Eric for his loan and how fortunate he was to have his own car.

At Concordia, Dean sat on the outside row near the front. The day was devoted to drills, formations, presentations by several coaches of last year's state champions, and a basketball game, included in the registration, was scheduled for that night.

Suddenly, at the noon lunch, he remembered his house key was on the key ring he gave to Bill Bradford and he would be locked out of the house. Scolding himself, he'd have to leave the ball game early to pick up his keys from Bill. He didn't want to wake Mrs. B. after she was up so early to make him breakfast.

Dean was happy to see the lights were still on at Bill's. Good. They must still be up. Glancing at his watch, he saw that it was 10:30. Dean was shocked when Carrie answered his knock.

"Oh, I... Mr. Brandum!" Carrie was equally surprised. "Mr. Bradford said you had gone to Moorhead today."

"What are you doing here, Carrie?"

"I'm baby-sitting. They went to Benton to see the second show."

Regaining his composure, Dean explained, "I just stopped to pick up my keys. I left my house key with Bill by mistake and I didn't want to wake up Mrs. B."

"If you want to come in and wait, they should be coming home soon."

"Looks like I'm going to have to."

"The kids went to bed real nice. I've been reading my library book."

Making himself comfortable on the sofa where Carrie had been sitting, he kicked off his shoes and said, "I'm weary, Carrie. I think I'll rest a bit."

"Sally said I could have a snack. Would you like a cookie and some milk?"

"That sounds good."

After getting the snack, Carrie set it on the coffee table and sat down on the sofa. She asked, "How was your trip?"

"It was worth it, but awfully tiring. Left at 6:00 this morning. Um-m-m, this is a good cookie."

Carrie said, "I had to be to work at the cafe early this morning too."

"You're a busy girl.....going to school, working at the cafe and baby-sitting."

Carrie blushed and didn't say anything.

Dean reached for John Steinbeck's, *Of Mice and Men* resting on the coffee table. "I didn't have to read this book until I was a senior in college," he remarked as he thumbed through the pages.

"The movie just came out and if it comes to Benton, our English teacher said we're supposed to see it. I'm to the part where George and Lennie are hired to work on a ranch."

"Well, I won't tell you how it ends." When he handed the book to Carrie their hands touched. Dean held her hand and she made no effort to withdraw it.

Carrie looked down and said nothing. They didn't hear the door open.

"My, this is a homey picture."

Hearing Bill's voice, they stood up embarrassed. "Hi, Bill and Sally," Dean said. "About time you got home. I can't believe it, but I forgot my house key with you."

"How were the kids?" Sally asked.

"They were wonderful," Carrie responded.

Bill, seeing Carrie holding her book, said to her, "The movie, *Of Mice and Men* will be showing the week after

Christmas. It looked interesting.....according to the poster in the lobby."

Sally said, "I'd rather see, *The Wonderful Wizard of Oz*, that's coming in a few weeks. Carrie, thanks for baby-sitting. Bill, you'll have to take her home."

Dean said, "If you get me my keys, I can drive Carrie home."

As he opened the car door for Carrie, they were caught in the glare of lights from a passing car. Much to his chagrin Dean recognized Mr. and Mrs. Grafstrom.

Oh, oh. Now I'm really in hot water, he thought.

Leaving town, he glanced over at Carrie. She had not seen the Grafstroms. He noticed how pretty she looked as the street light occasionally lighted her face. "You'll have to tell me where to turn when we get closer to your place."

"It's nice of you to give me a ride, Mr. Brandum. The folks had our car tonight."

"You can call me Dean, when we're away from school. Is that okay?"

"Okay, Mr. Br...I mean, Dean. But maybe I'd better not. What if I say that in school?"

The street light illuminated the dimpled smile that failed to hide her embarrassment and delighted Dean.

They rode in silence. Dean was worried and Carrie was concerned that Dean's long silence reflected on her someway. Breaking the silence, Dean said, "Bill thought that movie, *Of Mice and Men*, looked, what did he say, interesting."

"We'll be done studying it soon, but Louise and I might go to it anyway."

"I noticed you and Louise are close friends."

"We're cousins," Carrie stated as if that would explain everything. Carrie added, "Turn right at the next crossing and then it's the first driveway to the left. You'll have to come sometime during the daylight."

Dean was quiet as he followed her directions up to her

house.

"Good night, Mr. Brandum. Thank you for giving me a ride home," Carrie said, as she slipped out.

"Good night, Carrie. I'll see you Monday."

Dean was alone again with his thoughts. It's ironic that if I were a student I could go with a girl to a movie, but because I'm a teacher, I can't. If I do get involved, it's like Ma said, I could lose my job. I wonder what the superintendent thought?

Monday morning, Dean had another memo in his mailbox identical to the one he received before.

Monday, November 6, 1939

"Mr. Brandum, please stop in my office tomorrow during your noon hour."

Supt. Grafstrom

Dean thought, Oh, boy, this time for sure I'm in trouble.

"You ask him, Pete, please." Carrie begged.

"Why should I ask him? He's your teacher!"

The three were standing at the end of the driveway, waiting for the school bus. Their breath made small puffs in the cold morning air. "I'm sure not going to ask him," Dawn said, kicking a small rock for emphasis. "The kids in my math class would never stop teasing me."

"Pete, you have him for gym and sports both," Carrie encouraged.

"Well, I'm not going to ask him, and that's that!" Pete said emphatically.

"You were there when I asked Mom, and remember what she said, 'Being you all have Mr. Brandum for a teacher it's okay; but you're going to have to help clean up the house and cook.' She said, 'all'!"

"No, you talk to him. It was your idea," Pete said over his shoulder as he climbed into the school bus.

Fred, the bus driver, raised both eyebrows with a quizzical look, "Are you kids arguing on such a nice Tuesday morning?"

Carrie saw Dean in the lunchroom at noon, but it wasn't an opportune time to talk to him. Besides, he appeared worried.

Dean had admitted to himself that this memo from the superintendent made him much more apprehensive than the first. As he entered the office, the superintendent said, "Sit down, Dean." Dean sat in the same chair as the last time.

"How was your coaching workshop?" the administrator asked.

"There were some good speakers and I'm going to try some of the plays and formations." Dean worried what would come up next?

"You can leave your mileage claim with Maybelle and she can make out a check." Frowning, he put his fingers together just as he had at their first interview and said, "I saw you coming out of Bill Bradford's late Saturday night, so I knew you were back."

"Yes, I had to get my keys. I forgot to take my house key off the ones I gave Bill."

Dean didn't have to wait for the inevitable allegation, one that came altogether too soon.

"I'm curious. I saw Carrie Swenson leaving the house with you."

"Oh! She was baby-sitting for Bill and Sally when they went to the movie. I offered to give her a ride so Bill didn't have to take her home."

"Well, Dean," the superintendent said, his eyes drifting up to the ceiling. "I want to remind you about board policy that staff should avoid socializing with students."

"Yes, Sir. I understand." Dean pictured Ma behind him ready to give him a poke if he wasn't polite.

"You're not aware of this as I failed to mention it in the preschool workshop. Two years ago the Continuing Contract Law of 1937 extended tenure to Minnesota teachers. Termination requires a majority vote by the entire school board, but school boards don't have to give a reason for dismissal if done before April 1."

"I see," Dean nodded.

Superintendent Grafstrom continued, "I want to remind you that teacher personnel policies are related to teacher tenure."

Dean swallowed hard.

Superintendent Grafstom, noticing Dean's discomfiture added, "I hope you learned something at our teacher workshop."

"Yes, I remember hearing the policy, but I wasn't aware of how a school board could terminate a teacher. I appreciate your explanation. Thank you."

As he left the office, Dean thought, April first is a long time away and I don't want to lose my job.

Carrie had fretted all morning. "Thanksgiving's only two weeks away. I've got to ask him today, otherwise he might make other plans."

Carrie waited until all had left the chemistry room. When the room was finally empty, she approached Dean, who was preparing to leave for his gym class. "Mr. Brandum, if you don't have other plans, my mother said it would be all right for you to come to our house for Thanksgiving. That is if you're going to be in town," Carrie added feeling her blush rise up across her face.

"That sure is nice of her," Dean said.

"It's not for a couple weeks," Carrie said in a rush, but it's a week earlier than what it's been. I read in the papers that President Roosevelt moved Thanksgiving one week earlier. He wants to help business by lengthening the shopping period between Thanksgiving and Christmas."

In spite of the remonstration from Mr. Grafstrom, Dean didn't hesitate, "Yes, I'll be glad to come, Carrie. I was undecided about going home for Thanksgiving, but now I can write them."

"If you want to come out about 11:00, that's fine."

"Tell your mother, thank you. I appreciate being invited."

Hurrying down to the locker room Dean rationalized his response noting that it might be considered socializing; but then he reminded himself the whole family, not just Carrie, would be there. Ma and Eric and their big Thanksgiving meal intruded for a moment, but then his strong attraction to Carrie, had made the decision easy for him.

Dear Ma and Eric:

I'm sorry but I won't be coming home for Thanksgiving. You probably heard it's one week earlier this year. I've been asked out to the Swenson farm for Thanksgiving.

Three of their children are students in my classes. Their son, Pete, played on the football team.

It's the end of the six week's marking period so I have to correct tests and mark report cards.

Enclosed is another car payment for you, Eric. I don't drive the care much, as I walk to school.

I'll be coming home for Christmas. School lets out on Wednesday, December 20, so it's not too far away. I'll tell you more about school then.

                    Love,
                        Dean

Dean decided not to tell Ma one student in this family was the cheerleader in the photo.

STREETS OF HONOR

Chapter 7

Thanksgiving Day, Dean easily found Swenson's farm in the daylight. The long driveway wound around the old red barn and up to the small white house. Dean parked in the well worn area in front of the house and climbed out of the Studebaker.

Carrie, who had been watching for him, met him at the door with a welcoming, "Hi." She had chosen to wear a white blouse with an aqua vest and dark skirt.

"Come in. This is my dad, Carl, and my mother, Sophie, Mr. Brandum."

Dean shook hands with Mr. Swenson and nodded politely to Sophie, who was busy at the stove. She smiled at him and said, "We're glad you could come." Dean noticed her sticking a fork in one of the potatoes boiling on the stove just like his Ma did.

Carrie's dad, said, "Carrie, you'll have to introduce Mr. Brandum to the others."

Carrie led Dean into the small living room. "Mr. Brandum, this is my older brother, Joe. This is my sister, Delores and her husband, Eddie. Their baby's name is Anita. You know Pete and Dawn." Dean shook hands with Joe and Eddie, nodded politely to Delores and smiled at Pete and Dawn.

Carl and Sophie followed them into the living room. Carl explained, "We usually rotate Thanksgiving among our families. This year it was Uncle Ray's family's turn. He was so disgusted when FDR changed the date that he's not having anyone over until next week. So this year we're celebrating Thanksgiving twice."

Dean laughed heartily, breaking the tension. "I have an

uncle like that too. Once he gets something in his head, it always has to be that way."

Sophie sticking up for her brother added, "I agree with Ray. I don't think the stores need to put out all their Christmas things so early."

Dean noticed that the living room was much like his mother's home. The overstuffed sofa and matching chair were covered with the same wool mohair material but of a different color. Three wooden chairs sat in various openings in the perimeter of the room. Swirled patterns of gray and burgundy linoleum covered all but the edges of the wooden floor. Even the picture of the young girl sowing grain was identical.

Ma, returning to the kitchen and glancing at Delores and Carrie, said, "You girls help me for a bit and you men folk go outside for awhile if you want to."

The men trooped out to inspect Dean's Studebaker. Carl was sharing a story about a horse-drawn wagon made by Studebaker that they'd owned down in Iowa that had four high wheels, a place to sit and put your feet, and a big storage box behind, when Carrie's voice carried across the yard, "Come and eat!"

Two more leaves had been put in the kitchen table. All nine would fit around it. As the last words of grace died away, Dean felt a oneness with the family. Soon everyone was busy talking, passing food and filling their plates from steaming bowls of vegetables, potatoes, dressing and platters of chicken and ham. Carrie was pleased. Dean fit right in.

Joe, Pete, and Eddie, even on full stomachs, decided to pass the football outside. Dean decided to join them, and soon he and Pete had handily disposed of Joe and Eddie in a game of touch football. The granary, pump house, corn crib and the house determined the side lines after a few cars were moved.

Dean did not want to overstay his welcome so he excused himself after the game was over by saying he had to do some schoolwork. Shaking hands with the family, he gave

Mom a hug and a thank you. He saved Carrie until last and held her hand a little longer, causing the color to come to her face and the familiar dimple to reappear in her cheek.

Carrie's got a real nice family, Dean thought as he drove back home. It was nice of them to invite me. Her mother and my Ma are a lot alike. He wondered how things had gone back home, but was glad he had stayed. It felt right.

The basketball season got underway. The four returning senior lettermen, which included a tall center and a good ball handling guard, helped the team to win their first three games. Then, John, the big center, sprained his ankle in practice three weeks before Christmas.

"I've got to figure out how we can score without John," Dean was confiding his basketball woes to Berniece over the school's noon lunch. "We've lost two in a row."

Berniece shrugged her shoulders and said, "Don't look at me; I don't know anything about basketball."

Dean, remembering his thought that he should be more friendly to Berniece, said, "Say, how would you like to go to the movie in Benton tonight? The theater has a special showing of *The Wonderful Wizard of Oz*. It's Thursday, no tests, no papers to correct and I need to get away from school and basketball. How about you?"

"That sounds good to me, Dean. My Mom used to read me that story when I was a little girl."

"The show's at 7:00. I'll pick you up at 5:30. We'll stop for a sandwich, okay?"

Berniece nodded, a pleased look on her face.

After practice, Dean showered and picked up Berniece. Though not an exceptionally pretty girl, she had long dark hair and dressed attractively.

Stepping up to the concession stand to buy popcorn, Dean did not see Louise, Carrie's cousin. She had bought popcorn and disappeared into the crowd finding their seats.

"Carrie, you'll never guess who I saw," she said to her waiting cousin. "Mr. Brandum is here with Miss Wright, the business teacher. I saw them out in the lobby."

"Oh," Carrie said, not trusting herself to say more. She slid down in her seat and hoped she wouldn't be noticed. Thankfully, the ads for area businesses came on the screen followed by the previews of coming attractions, so Louise did not notice Carrie's eyes close and the trace of sadness that slipped over her face. What she hoped would be a treat, the musical, *The Wonderful Wizard of Oz*, had lost its luster.

She sat quietly during the newsreel, which showed President Roosevelt solemnly telling the nation that America was officially neutral in Europe's war while Britain and France had declared war on Germany. Only when scenes of Nazi atrocities on the Jews and non Jews in Germany at Buchenwald, as reported by the British Government, showed on the screen, did she let out a deep breath and a large sigh. Carrie noticed Louise glance over at her, but the movie quickly drew Louise's eyes back to the screen.

When they came out of the theater, they were surprised by the intensity of the early December snow. The flakes had become larger and thicker, blown by the brisk northwest wind. The girls hugged their coats tight around them. "We better head for home quick," Carrie said, anxious about the weather but wanting to get away before Dean and Miss Wright saw them.

Halfway to the farm, Carrie, her face pressed closer to the windshield, said, "Boy, it's getting bad. I can hardly see the road. It's a good thing you're staying at our house tonight, Louise." About that time the wind blew the snow into one white wall, the highway disappeared and Carrie drove into the ditch.

"Now what?" Louise asked.

"There's a flashlight in the glove compartment. We'll have to try to stop someone and catch a ride. It's a good thing it's not so bitterly cold."

Dean, too, had suggested leaving right away for Applegrove. He proceeded cautiously down the highway, peering through the windshield at the snowflakes that seemed to be blowing directly into the headlights.

Berniece, who'd been quiet, finally exclaimed, "Dean, I see a flashlight up ahead! It looks like someone wants a ride."

Rolling down her window, Berniece recognized the girls from school. "Hi, it looks like you need help!" Dean was more than surprised to see Carrie and Louise standing at the side of the road.

Carrie leaned down to the window. "Hi, Miss Wright. Hi, Mr. Brandum. Could we get a ride with you? I just drove into the ditch."

"Of course, pile in."

The girls climbed into the back seat and soon comments were being exchanged about the happy musical. Carrie didn't feel happy at all and said very little, for she was lost in her own thoughts about how badly the evening had turned out. Berniece, she thought, would look better if she cut her hair and curled it under at the ends.

The snow squall and wind had weakened allowing Dean to easily drive into the farmyard. Louise jumped out first and said, "Thanks for the ride." Carrie, following slowly, still upset over the evening managed a polite, "Thank you, Mr. Brandum. Dad and Joe will have to pull the car out in the morning." She slammed the door and followed Louise into the house.

On the way back into town, Berniece was quiet for awhile, then curious, asked, "Dean, how did you know where to go without them telling you?"

"The family invited me out to the farm for Thanksgiving." There's nothing to hide, he thought.

Dean saw Berniece to the door at her place, gave her a hug, and said, "Thanks for going to the movie. If there's school tomorrow, I'll see you then."

Dean drove slowly back to Mrs. B's thinking that
Berniece was okay to be with. She had moved closer to him
and became possessive after they picked up the girls. It was a
relaxing evening, except for that peculiar storm. Came up
quickly then it was gone. The thought of Carrie and her cousin
needing a ride penetrated his thoughts and pushed Berniece
aside. It's so coincidental I keep meeting Carrie when I least
expect it.

Back at the farm, Carrie's usual bed partner, Dawn, was
asleep on the sofa downstairs. Louise, who had taken Dawn's
place, slept beside Carrie. Carrie lay awake recalling Berniece
sitting next to Dean. She stifled a sob into her pillow and
resentment and anger came over her. I'll show him, she
thought.

The next day Carrie was determined to not let her
feelings show. She continued to be Dean's best chemistry
student. She cheered even more enthusiastically that night at
the basketball game.....even though the team lost again.

Saturday morning when Carrie got to work at The
Corner Cafe, she told herself, I shouldn't let it bother me that
he's dating Miss Wright.

When Dean arrived for breakfast, Carrie did not appear
any different. She could not control her true feelings, however.
Dean was surprised when she clattered his breakfast plate and
silverware noisily in front of him. The team's loss must bother
everyone, thought Dean, but wondered if there was more to
Carrie's behavior than that.

As a money raiser, the senior class served lunch after the
basketball game before Christmas vacation. The team had won,
so Dean was in good spirits when he joined the noisy crowd in
the lunchroom.

Carrie and Tim Thoreson were working and laughing in
the kitchen. Dean noticed how attractive Carrie looked in her
white sweater with the large red A and her short cheerleader
skirt. Again, he thought to himself.....she's beautiful.

Later when he locked up the gymnasium area and prepared to leave, he met Carrie and Tim leaving the building together. They greeted each other, then Carrie and Tim drove off in his car. Carrie was glad Dean had seen her with Tim. Dean hadn't thought of Carrie as having a boy friend. He felt a suppressed longing. A sense of loneliness came over him as he drove away.

School let out at noon on Wednesday. Dean then took the opportunity to stop at the A. J. Johansson Co. Flour Mill in Applegrove, well knowing that he must confront the thought that had bothered him the last few years. The small farm - home to Ma and Eric - was sufficient for them, and Dean was not needed. It was time for him to find another job when not teaching. Bill Bradford and Russell Wagner, Dean's school friends, wanted him to join the National Guard. Dean reasoned that with the extra pay from the Guard and working at the Mill he should have enough income.

Walking among the tall elevator buildings and wheat storage tanks that huddled close to the Pomme de Terre River, Dean felt insignificant. For years the mill had used the rapid fall of the river for power to grind its wheat. Now electrical transmission lines supplied the energy.

When he inquired about work, Dean was directed to Walt Larson's office by one of the workers. His office contained business related items; but, curiously out of place in a showcase behind his desk were some interesting artifacts: A dress form proudly displaying a dress from Johansson's flour sacks, a fancy pillow also made from a sack, a pattern book and a Scandinavian cookbook, all produced by the mill.

Mr. Larson recognized Dean as the high school coach. "What can I do for you, coach?" he asked.

"We got out early from school today for Christmas vacation and I wanted to see you before I left for North Dakota. Would there be work for me here this summer?"

"That's five months away yet, but I can find work for

you. You might have to start out bagging flour at minimum wage. You're a husky fellow and could handle that. Some weeks, we work seven days a week so your wages will add up. Stop and see my secretary for an application and leave it with her."

"Thank you. I appreciate this very much."

"If you're going to North Dakota, take a couple of pattern flour sacks and a pattern book with you. Your folks might like to see them."

"My mother likes to sew. She'll like that."

By the time Dean drove into the farmyard near Auburn, the winter sun had already dropped below the horizon. Stepping into the house, Dean was welcomed with a big hug from Ma, "It's been so long since we've seen you," she said, her eyes moist. "We missed you when you didn't come at Thanksgiving."

They spent a lot of time chatting about Dean's new job, and the farm; but, one day Ma surprised Dean with an unexpected question. "Swenson's, where you went for Thanksgiving, was that the same family with the cheerleader in the picture?"

Dean, realizing that he hadn't fooled Ma, confided, "Yes, and you know, Ma, I was surprised how much their home and the meal were a lot like ours."

She was pleased. "You're old enough to make decisions for yourself, Dean. I trust you. I know you have to spread your wings and leave the nest. But I just don't want you to get into trouble."

Saturday night Dean and Charlie, his neighbor and friend since high school, drove to Valley River to the movie. Neither one cared that it was an old Tom Mix cowboy show. On the way home, Dean told Charlie about his plans to work at the flour mill in Applegrove next summer and to possibly join the National Guard unit. "Don't tell Ma or Eric about this yet," Dean cautioned Charlie.

"I should join a Guard unit too," Charlie said thoughtfully. "I know there's one here in Valley River." Reverting back to his usual amiable self, he teased Dean, "You better watch out! This year coming up, 1940, is Leap Year. Some young woman from Applegrove will end your bachelor days."

"You never can tell, Charlie." Dean couldn't shake the image of Carrie's smiling face that had crept into his thoughts off and on all evening.

"And, if you've meet an extra rich school marm, tell her there's a poor farmer from North Dakota that's eligible," Charlie said, laughing."

Christmas Eve was quiet for Ma, Eric, and Dean. Ma had cooked up another delicious meal and they laughed and hugged as they opened presents. They played a few hands of Widow Whist, but they were glad to be together quietly. Dean struggled to stay with his original plan to wait until later or to tell them now about the job at the flour mill.

After supper, the next day, Dean brought the items from the flour mill and put them on the kitchen table.

"What's that?" Ma asked.

"It's another present Santa couldn't get in your stocking."

Dean explained about the flour mill and how they did extra things to market the flour. Ma stopped in the middle of turning a page in the pattern book when Dean announced, "I applied to work there when school is out."

Ma and Eric both started talking at once. "What did he want to do that for? He could work on the farm? How they would miss him?"

Dean's arguments were definite and made sense. He reminded Eric he still owed him payments on the car he had helped him buy. Both Ma and Eric became resigned to the fact Dean had made up his mind. Dean said, "And also, some of my friends have been encouraging me to join the National Guard."

Ma's worried look pinched her face. "Why do you want to join the Guard?" she inquired.

"I haven't decided for sure, but it's another income for me. I've met lots of nice fellows and it's the patriotic thing to do."

Ma's expression changed then. He can't fool me. There's one big reason for him to stay in Applegrove and that's the Swenson girl. She acknowledged a feeling of resentment for someone that might take her son from her. Then she reminded herself that Dean, soon to be twenty-three, was entitled to a life of his own. It would be different not having him here after he had been such a big part of the family. But it was just another step. Her heart was heavy at the thought.

Dean interrupted her melancholy, "I'm going back to Applegrove tomorrow, Ma." Dean's announcement was of no surprise to either Ma or Eric as they both noticed how restless he was. "I told the basketball team that they could come to the gym on Thursday and Friday afternoon after Christmas," he explained.

The next morning, Ma packed up some goodies to send back with Dean. "I hope they're as good as Mrs. B's," Ma said shyly.

"Ma, no one can top your cooking," Dean said, giving her a pinch on the cheek with one hand and a kiss on the other cheek. Dean shook hands with Eric and headed for Applegrove, what now seemed to him like his home. He had a strange feeling of transition.

Dean had decided to stop in Fargo on the way home to buy a sport coat and he decided to bring a box of candy out to Swensons, a thank-you gift for Thanksgiving, but he really wanted to see Carrie.

Driving into Swenson's farm Friday evening, Dean met Carl heading for the barn. "Pete's in the house, he's had a bad cold the past 3 or 4 days," he said.

"I wondered about him when he wasn't at the gym; but I

really came to see Carrie and Mom," Dean said smiling.

"Oh, well, they're home," Carl said with a slightly surprised look on his face.

When Carrie saw Dean's car drive into the yard she rushed into the bedroom, brushed her hair, then ran to the door.

Dean presented the box of candy to Carrie and Sophie explaining, "This is for taking in a hungry school teacher."

Carrie's face was flushed. Both of them taken aback by the unexpected gift thanked him again and again.

"There's one more thing I want to do," Dean announced. "I came through Benton on the way back from North Dakota and noticed that movie *Of Mice and Men* is showing tomorrow night. I want to take you both to it."

Surprised and flustered, Sophie said, "Well, land sake, I haven't been to a regular movie for years. I don't think I should go."

"You have to go," Dean stated. "You need to be a chaperone! I could lose my job according to school board policy if Carrie and I went. If you want to ask Louise to go along, too, that's fine."

"Well, I suppose I could," Sophie agreed. "I don't want Supt. Grafstrom to have a reason for you to lose your job." She thought, I better talk to Carrie before this gets out of hand.

"It's settled then. I'll come by at 6:00 tomorrow evening," Dean said as he went out the door.

Carrie felt a happy glow throughout her body.

Mom said, "Carrie, you can't have your head in the clouds about Mr. Brandum."

Carrie replied, "He's been so nice, and a friend that I'm happy to be with."

"It seems you have a crush on him and nothing might come of it. Remember it's against school policies."

"Oh, Mom, you worry too much."

"What's the movie about?" Sophie asked on the way to Benton.

Carrie explained, "We had to read the book in English class, Ma. It's not a happy story, but it's a story of life for many."

Dean said, "It was one of the more involved books we read in our college class." Then he added, "This is my treat tonight." He bought tickets and popcorn for his three guests.

A newsreel segment boasted the movie, *Gone With The Wind* with Clark Gable and Vivian Leigh had premiered in Atlanta to a cheering audience.

Louise whispered to Carrie, "I would like to see that!"

On the way home, Dean teased Carrie, "Well, we shouldn't have to worry about a snow storm tonight, Carrie."

Mom was strangely quiet, lost in thought. "I wish those people in the movie hadn't died. I liked that big, gentle Lennie."

Carrie explained to Sophie in a reflective way, "It showed how we can, or should, take care of each other. Lennie said, 'But not us! And why? Because...because I got you to look after me, and you got me to look after you, and that's why.'"

Dean didn't say anything, but appreciated Carrie's insight. "I'll leave you off at your place, Louise, if you tell me where to go."

Subsequently Dean stopped to let Sophie and Carrie off and decided to accept the invitation for ice cream and cookies. Everyone was still up at the farm and curious how the 'date' with the three went. Mom said, "I like being a chaperone. We had a good time, but I'd rather go to a happy movie next time."

Carrie, full of happy thoughts, fell asleep with her arms wrapped around her pillow.

On the way to Mrs. B's, Dean recalled Carrie's quote: "I got you to look after me, and you got me to look after you, and that's why."

What more could anyone want? Dean mused.

STREETS OF HONOR

Chapter 8

The first day of school after the holidays, Principal Rogstad saw Dean in the hallway between classes and asked him to stop in his office during the noon hour.

Dean was surprised to find Berniece already there, seated opposite the principal.

"Come in and sit down, Dean. I was just telling Berniece that I need two advisors for the school carnival. It's the third Friday in January. It's a money raiser for our school activities.....sports, music, class plays, Future Farmers, etc."

Dean said, "I don't know much about the carnival. What do we do?"

Rogstad said, "Each organization has the same event each year and they know what to do. I was hoping you two new teachers would be in charge and work with the students."

Berniece asked, "Is there anything written down about our responsibilities?"

"No," Rogstad answered. "But Russell Wagner and Mrs. Beal had it last year and they will help you." After hearing this, the two agreed.

The next morning before classes, Dean and Berniece found Russell, who answered their questions, "It's in the gym and there are spaces set for booths like the cake walk, basketball shoot, fish pond, lunch, etc. One thing that needs to be done right away is to order prizes, decorations and confetti. We've been ordering the same thing every year."

Dean had to work closely with Berniece to see that each event had space, equipment and workers. This caused considerable talk among the students when the new young teachers were seen laughing and talking together. Dean's car

74

was seen several nights at Berniece's house. This was made even worse for Carrie when Louise felt obligated to keep her informed.

Carrie's reaction was, "That's interesting." not wanting to betray her true feelings which were deep down, tense, and troubled.

In early February, Dean found yet another memo in his mailbox.

Monday, February 5, 1940.

Mr. Brandum, please stop in my office tomorrow during your noon hour.

Supt. Grafstrom

Once again, Dean took his customary seat across from the superintendent.

"The team's been doing better lately. What are you now, 8-4?" Grafstrom asked.

"Yes. If we win the remaining games, we could be seeded directly into the district and not play in the sub-district," Dean answered.

Supt. Grafstrom lost no time and looked keenly at Dean. "Each year we send our senior basketball players, coach and cheerleaders to the State Basketball Tournament."

Dean's eyes widened. He knew the state tournaments were in Minneapolis-St. Paul but hadn't realized that the team and coach would go, much less the cheerleaders. When the superintendent mentioned cheerleaders he was relieved this meeting wasn't about Carrie.

"We've always stayed at the Andrews Hotel in Minneapolis. The games are at the St. Paul Auditorium on March 28, 29 and 30. This year we're sending four boys and the two senior cheerleaders. I still need to find a chaperone for the cheerleaders."

Dean, at the mention of chaperone, thought of Sophie, Carrie's mother. "Does the chaperone have to be from the school staff?" he asked.

"No, no. That's not necessary."

"When Pete Swenson was sick with a cold, I stopped to see him. Mrs. Swenson acted genuinely interested in school activities. And then, Carrie, her daughter, is a cheerleader, so maybe she would do it."

Grafstrom thought a moment. "That might work out. I've been thinking of having Fred Meyer take our small bus to the Cities. Why don't you ask Mrs. Swenson to chaperone? If she can't go, the school district will hire a substitute teacher, so Berniece Wright could chaperone. I'll order tickets and make hotel reservations."

Dean couldn't help but smile as he left the superintendent's office. The best strategy would be for Carrie to ask her mother. After class, he explained the situation to her. Carrie, still perturbed and jealous, brightened up when she heard the senior cheerleaders would be going to the tournament. She knew they went in past years, but hadn't heard about going this year.

When Dean asked, "Do you think your mother would be a chaperone?" Carrie smiled, recalling the trip to the movies and her mother's vigilance to be a good chaperone. Dean didn't dare tell Carrie that Berniece would be the alternate, for he sensed Carrie's coolness toward her.

When Carrie asked her mom, she exclaimed, "Goodness sakes, Carrie, why do they want me? I've never been to the Cities."

"You're the mother of one of the cheerleaders. Mr. Brandum said the hotel requires chaperones. Please, Mom," Carrie pleaded.

Sophie was reluctant. "I don't think so, Carrie, but I'll talk to Pa." On the other hand, she thought it might be good for her to chaperone since she was worried over Carrie and Dean.

After being seeded into the district tournament, the team easily won the first game over one of the sub-district winners. In the next game, the eventual District champions eliminated Applegrove by four points. On Sunday, March 17, after the District Tournament, Dean had his 23rd birthday with no one around to help him celebrate.

After watching the District and Region games, the seniors climbed on the bus for the trip to the Cities. He was disappointed that Mrs. Swenson had decided not to chaperone. Dean noticed that Berniece was exceptionally pleased when she told Dean over the noon lunch that she would chaperone. Dean thought, Berniece and Carrie will just have to get along.

Berniece made sure she sat next to Dean on the way to the Cities. Carrie was relegated to the back of the bus where she kept a wary eye on Dean and Miss Wright. Fred, who had driven the teams there many times, drove right to the hotel and reassured Dean he knew the way to the St. Paul Auditorium.

Dean talked to the players about the teams and who would be favored. "Breckenridge is in the tournament. One of my friends from college is from there. He's teaching in southern Minnesota someplace but he should be at the tournament." They laughed when Dean added, "I've got your meal money, so you'll have to stay close to me."

Dean fussed the first night, worried about the boy's behavior and his responsibility. But Fred's reassurance that John, Charlie, Ed and Richard were 'good country boys' proved true when he looked in on them and found them sleeping.

The girls were no problem either. But then the inevitable happened.....rather innocently. Everyone had started into the auditorium for Friday evening's game. Dean was excited to watch Breckenridge play in the last semi-final game. Carrie suddenly exclaimed, "I left my jacket on the bus and my ticket is in the pocket."

Dean told the rest, "You all go ahead and I'll go with

Carrie. We'll find you in the same place as last night." Fred had given Dean the key for the rear exit door. Opening the rear door, Dean said, "I'll boost you up, Carrie, and you can get your jacket." Dean easily lifted her and she scrambled in.

"I found it, Mr. Brandum, and my ticket's here."

When she went to jump from the bus, Dean caught her and his desire to hold her couldn't be suppressed. He gave her a spontaneous hug and said, "Thanks for being such a good cheerleader, Carrie. You're a very beautiful person. I miss you and your family."

The rosy color highlighted her cheeks and her eyes sparkled. As Dean continued to hold her she said, "You'll have to come and visit."

Just then Berniece came around the corner of the bus. She stopped abruptly and said, "I thought I'd better check to see if you needed help. Did you find your ticket, Carrie?" she said coolly.

"Oh, yes," Carrie answered with a glowing smile.

Dean found Jim Foley when he wandered over to the Breckenridge fan section at half time. They had a few minutes bringing each other current on their lives and friends. Busy with their teaching duties, neither one had been back to Valley River, not even for Homecoming.

Jim said, "Either team could win this one. If Breck can win this game they would play Red Wing in the finals tomorrow night."

"It sounds like I'll have to cheer for Breckenridge then. Come by Applegrove some time, Jim," Dean said, as he started back through the half-time crowd.

Berniece cornered Dean in the hallway by the concession stand. "What was that all about?" she asked.

"What do you mean?"

"When you were holding Carrie back of the bus."

"Well, I ...uh, finally had a chance to tell her what a good job she did as cheerleader captain and gave her a hug."

Dean felt his face get warm as he blushed.

Berniece looked long at Dean, one eyebrow arched and said, "It appears to me that you're more than her teacher."

Dean said, "Berniece, Carrie is a wonderful young lady, but there hasn't been anything between us. I've been out to their farm a couple of times when the family's been there. That's all."

Berniece said, "I don't want to have to report you to Grafstrom, but that sounds like it's against school policies!" and left him standing there. Dean had a hard time concentrating on the game after Berniece's remark and her rebuff.

As it turned out, Breckenridge and Red Wing were in the finals with Breckenridge winning 43 to 40. Still Dean worried over what Berniece might say or do. But everyone else was pleased, tired out, and anxious to get back to Applegrove. They left early on Sunday morning as planned.

Carrie's folks were waiting after church to meet the bus and give Carrie a ride home and find out about the tournament. Dean offered to drive Berniece home, and after he stopped the car she said, "I've kept my feelings to myself, Dean, but I'm frankly disappointed. I was hoping we could do things together more and get to know each other. We started to with the school carnival. But it seems like all you think about is Carrie. I could see the way you two looked at each other, and the smiles you tried to hide from everyone else."

Dean was stunned by her confession. "I like you, Berniece, but I won't mislead you either. You're right, my feelings for Carrie are strong and I have to see how things work out."

Dean saw Berniece's eyes narrow. Her cheeks pushed upward in a forced smile that quickly disappeared. Dean thought he saw something akin to hate spread over her face and loosened her lips. "So that's the way it is," she said, slamming the car door and hurrying into her house.

Tuesday morning Dean found a memo in his mailbox.

Tuesday, April 2, 1940

Mr. Brandum, please stop in my office tomorrow during your noon hour.

Supt. Grafstrom

Grafstrom wasn't smiling when Dean entered the superintendent's office. Dean's concern increased when he said, "Sit down, Mr. Brandum."

Dean quickly took his usual chair. Grafstrom's face was stony.

"I've been told by a reliable source that you've been socializing with Carrie Swenson. This in spite of the fact I've warned you that this is against school policies."

That source has to be Berniece, Dean thought. I better be honest as Ma has always preached, "Sir, you were aware I gave Carrie a ride home. The only other times were when I was invited for Thanksgiving and I returned the favor by taking Carrie and her mother to see a movie in Benton."

"It's hard for me to believe that, when this reliable source said you were romantically involved," Grafstrom persisted.

Dean now knew Berniece had told about the ticket incident, so he readily explained this situation to the superintendent.

"You would place the school district in an awkward position, if you had to be released," Grafstrom said.

Dean bit his lip and said, "I'll follow the school policies."

Grafstrom said, "I'm going to accept what you say and expect you to keep your word."

Dean shook the superintendent's hand, said, "All right," and quickly left the office.

The conversations between Dean and Berniece during the noon lunch hours were fewer.....formal and stiff. She announced to Dean one noon, "I'm not coming back to Applegrove next year. I've applied to schools near the Cities and have some interviews already."

Dean said, "You did have a tough schedule here." But he knew this wasn't the only reason for her decision.

With only part of April and May of the school year left, Dean felt the pressure of school and his personal life mounting. Prompted by this, he asked Carrie after breakfast on Saturday at the Corner Cafe if she would be home around 7 o'clock that evening. He was taking a chance, but he had to see her.

"Yes," she replied, without hesitation. She was curious why Dean wanted to see her.

It was the end of April, the baseball season half over and the farmers already disking last year's plowing, when Dean drove into the yard. Dark clouds along the western horizon brought the threat of rain and the assurance that darkness was not far off.

After greeting Carrie's family, he asked Carrie if she could go for a drive. "Sure," was her immediate response. "I'll tell my folks."

"Don't stay away long. There's an east wind and it's blowing up rain," Carl cautioned.

Driving down the country road with Carrie, Dean confided, "My minds in a whirl and I wanted to let you know what I'm thinking." He had decided to not tell her that the superintendent had talked to him. "I plan to stay in Applegrove this summer. I'm not needed back home and I can work at the Johansson Flour Mill."

"That's wonderful, Dean." she replied. "I'm not sure what I'll do when I graduate. I've been thinking about applying at the bank. Principal Rogstad said I missed being salutatorian by a few percentage points. He said a college would help with some expenses if I wanted to go."

Lightning flashes lit up the darkening sky and raindrops started to splatter on the windshield. "You'll do well in college." Dean hurried on with what he wanted to tell Carrie. "The other thing, Carrie, is that Bill Bradford and Russell Wagner want me to join the National Guard, and I think I will."

"Why do you want to join the Guard?" Carrie asked, puzzled.

"I need the money. I also know a lot of the guys already and the local Guard unit needs more men and, besides it's the patriotic thing to do."

Reaching over and touching Dean's hand, Carrie said, "I don't want anything bad to happen to you." As if to emphasize her words, a huge lightning bolt lit up the night sky and immediately the thunder rolled around them.

"That was close." Dean said. Suddenly the rain came down in sheets and Dean pulled over to the side of the road and stopped the car.

"Let me hold you a while, Carrie." She turned and lay cradled in Dean's arms. Pulling her close to him, Dean kissed her long and tenderly on the lips. She answered his kiss, sighed, and settled into his embrace. Dean held her and said, "I'm going to say something that shy Norwegians have a hard time saying. I love you, Carrie."

She said, "I love you too, Dean. It will be wonderful if you'll be here all summer and it was selfish of me to discourage you from joining the Guard."

"And, Carrie, you'll be graduating next month. You know what I'd like to do?"

"No, what?" Carrie stared up at Dean with wide eyes.

"I'd like to go on a picnic with just you and me after graduation."

Carrie sat bolt upright. "That's a wonderful idea. Let's do it!"

"I suppose you thought I was going to say something else. Charlie, my friend from back home reminded me this is Leap Year and I have to be careful."

Carrie was glad the darkness hid her flush and chuckled.

"I didn't realize that, but it's something I'll have to keep in mind."

"I'd better take you home," Dean said. After kissing her once more, Dean started up the Studebaker and squeezed Carrie's hand, "Thanks for helping me sort things out."

"I didn't do anything, Dean. Things are what they are."

The rain was still coming down as they drove into the farmyard. They were shocked to see Carrie's family in the yard looking at a still smoldering, charred, cottonwood tree. Dawn said excitedly, "You should have seen the lightning and heard the loud noise!"

Dean said, "We knew it was close but we were in the car."

Pete added, "We smelled the smoke and ran outside. It's a good thing it's raining. It helped put the fire out."

Dean gave Carrie's soft hand a firm squeeze that sent electric waves through both of them as he said, "I need to get back to town."

As he left the farmyard, Dean enjoyed a warmth and happiness when he remembered how kissing Carrie seemed so natural and right. Then, trying to imagine their future together, it didn't occur to him that unpredictable storms and fires might be a part of their lives for a long, long time.

STREETS OF HONOR

Chapter 9

Monday morning Dean walked uptown. He wanted to be sure he was at the Applegrove Cafe early; he wanted to talk to owner Bruce Strong.....Sergeant Strong of the Applegrove National Guard Unit.

After the usual pleasantries, Dean asked, "Say, Bruce, what do I need to do to join the Guard?"

"I can get a form for you to fill out, Dean. We have drill every Monday evening from 8 to 10 p.m. You aren't going to get rich, pay is only $1.00 per hour. Captain Monson always wants to interview new men; but you won't have any trouble getting in. A number of the fellows already know you and can vouch for you. Besides that, we're short of men," he smiled.

"Where is Captain Monson from and what does he do?"

"He's a local dentist. If you come tomorrow morning, I'll have the form for you and I can see that Captain Monson gets it. Then you can come to drill a week from today. Come about 7:30, and you can meet with Captain Monson."

"Thanks, Bruce." Dean said as he finished his breakfast and hurried to school.

On Saturday, after an uneventful week, Dean was eating breakfast at the Corner Cafe when Carrie invited him out to the farm for her post-graduation lunch. "Graduation is still two weeks away," she said, "but I wanted to let you know." She also hinted they needed to make more plans for their picnic.

Monday evening when he arrived for his first National Guard meeting, Dean felt confident and happy. He was immediately impressed with Captain Monson's bearing: his looks, his strong handshake and his shiny Captain's insignia.

"Sit down, Dean," Captain Monson said. "I've looked

over the information on the form you completed and we can use someone of your caliber in the Applegrove Unit. It will require considerable dedication on your part, as we have weekly drills one evening a week and a two-week summer camp. Are you willing to do this?"

"My Mondays are usually open for me and I plan to be in Applegrove this summer. It would be good training, and I can use the money."

Captain Monson continued, "The Applegrove Guard Unit is an institution in this community. There has always been an extremely large amount of pride in the unit by the soldiers and the people of the area. During the Depression we had numerous fellows depend on us for money for their families, even though it was only a dollar a day. Don't feel bad about supplementing your income. You'll have to get a physical, which you can do on your own. I'm going to leave it to Sgt. Strong to assign you to your duties. It may be to a rifle platoon or a light machine-gun unit. Do you have any questions?"

"No, but I've never had much to do with guns before," Dean admitted.

Dean's first guard drill was lost in a whirl of uniform fitting and marching. When he was issued an old model 1903 Springfield bolt-action rifle that had been used in the last war, the corporal in supply apologized, saying, "Some day we're supposed to get new Garand M-1's."

Dean met his friends from school, Bill Bradford and Russell Wagner, in the Armory. Bill said, "I hope you get assigned to my platoon. We can use a husky guy in our machine gun unit."

Dean replied, "I sure wouldn't mind that."

Sgt. Strong called the company together and after putting them at ease, welcomed Dean and two new men from the rural townships, Burt and Maynard. "I'm assigning Dean to the light machine gun unit and Burt and Maynard to the rifle platoon. I want to announce that the date for summer camp at

Camp Ripley is Saturday, July twenty-one to Sunday, August fourth. So please clear these dates with your employer. For your information, we'll be traveling by truck this year. Does anyone have any questions?"

Dean stood with the others as they considered their families and their calendars. No one spoke up. "If there are no questions, you're dismissed until next week." That was it.

Next morning at breakfast at the Applegrove Cafe, Bruce asked Dean how he felt about his first Guard drill.

"It reminded me of my first day of football practice when I started college.....how to wear my uniform, different drills, and then meeting a lot of nice fellows. Next week I plan to take my physical," he added.

Principal Rogstad stopped Dean as he was about to enter the teacher's room at noon on Tuesday. "Dean, this is short notice, but would you be a faculty chaperone for the senior trip to Willmar on Saturday? It's not so much as a trip, but more of an outing. It's been a tradition in Applegrove for years. Berniece will be out of town, but Mrs. Beal said she would chaperone."

"I can do that. I don't have anything planned for Saturday," Dean said.

Principal Rogstad said, "That's great. We take a bus to the Country Club north of Willmar. It's a last get-together for the seniors. It involves a meal, short program and afterward a movie. The girl's trio will sing and Tim Thoreson will play his accordion. And, Dean, I've been meaning to ask you, but could you make a few remarks?"

Despite his busy week, Dean said he would make some comments.

The Senior Trip started on a happy note when the baseball team won their Friday game. Dean was tired after his busy week but soon the closeness and happy interchange with the graduating seniors buoyed his spirits. It didn't even bother him that Tim Thoreson gave Carrie an inordinate amount of attention.

Principal Rogstad and the senior class president welcomed everyone. The principal was applauded when he announced the name of the movie they would see, *Gone With The Wind*. After the musical numbers, Dean was introduced.

Dean complimented the class on their leadership and excellent behavior, and then encouraged them to carry this into the future. When he said he was glad that he got to know them better, a hearty laugh went through the group. Obviously, his association with Carrie had not been as discreet as he had hoped. He wished the seniors well and sat down amid genuine and affectionate applause.

The stormy love story of Scarlett O'hara and Rhett Butler set in the south during the Civil War closed out the evening. It did little to ease Carrie and Dean's growing need for closeness, or their fears, which were now related to the fermenting of the war in Europe.

The senior baseball players were disappointed when the team was eliminated on Thursday, the first game of District play. The next night, May 17, was graduation.

Several bouquets of flowers decorated the graduation stage where the chairs had been neatly arranged. The bleachers and the chairs on the playing floor were filled with parents and friends. Dean did not have any special duties for graduation, so he stood in the audience when the seniors entered the gymnasium to the strains of *Pomp and Circumstance*. Dean felt a glow of pride knowing he had helped some of those seniors achieve their first major life goal.

However, it was Carrie who Dean focused most of his attention on. He noticed how she carried herself, smiled at others and remained attentive during the lengthy program. He was surprised when she made a short address as one of the honor students. Her sensitivity showed when she asked for everyone's help and prayers when they, the seniors, assumed their place in the world. Encouraging her fellow seniors, she entreated them to believe in themselves and to always believe in miracles.

When Dean drove into the farmyard for the graduation reception, he felt right at home. Judging by the number of cars in the yard, he knew he would be meeting some of Carrie's relatives for the first time. Carrie greeted him as he climbed out of the car on the warm May evening. He gave her a big hug and said, "I was so proud of you, Carrie. I didn't know you were going to be a speaker. You were great."

"I don't have to tell you everything," she said charmingly as she led him to the house.

"Where's your diploma? I want to see if you really graduated," Dean said teasing her.

"My diploma, tassel, and my school activity awards are on my upstairs dresser," she said haughtily, responding to his teasing.

Dean was introduced to a few of Carrie's aunts, uncles and cousins. Sophie told Carrie and Dean they should dish up first. They helped themselves from the heaping bowls of hot dish and beans and stacks of sandwiches. Dean was hungry and his plate was heaped full in contrast to Carrie's. Still excited about the evening, she had barely covered her plate with cake, and a little bit of hot dish. "I should have taken an extra sandwich for you," she teased Dean as she looked at his full plate.

After eating and making polite conversation for awhile, Dean took Carrie aside and asked if she'd like to go for a walk. Carrie smiled, nodded, and said, "Mom, Dean and I are going for a walk down by the creek in the pasture." Sophie hesitated then nodded at her daughter. With graduation came the wisdom and maturity to make sensible decisions, and Sophie was glad she no longer had to worry about the problem of a troublesome student-teacher relationship.

Dean and Carrie, still in their best clothes, carefully climbed through the barbed wire fence and made their way to the creek. Rex, the part-collie family dog, raced around scattering up red-winged blackbirds. The sounds of the nighthawks reminded them that night was closing in.

Dean held Carrie's hand as they went out of sight of the farm house. He pulled her to him then gave her a hug and long kiss. "When are we going on our picnic, Dean, and where?" Carrie whispered.

"I'm not sure," he admitted, holding her close and enjoying the fresh smell of her hair. Resuming their walk, Dean continued, "I wanted to go to Lake Itasca up by Bemidji and see the source of the Mississippi, but I checked the map and it would take so much gas and time. Do you have any suggestions?"

Carrie folded her arms in front of her to ward off the cool breeze and suggested, "When we have our family picnic on the fourth of July, we go to Lake Minnewaska near Glenside, South of Alexandria. But, we've talked about going to Lake Carlos, north of Alexandria. That's only about eighty miles from here."

"Eighty miles sounds about right. Then we won't get so hungry before we eat," Dean said smiling. "What can I bring for food?"

"I'll take care of the food, if you drive."

The cool evening breeze grew stronger. Dean put his powerful arms around her again and held her close. "Let me warm you up," he said. "Could we go on the Wednesday before Memorial Day? School will be out and the Guard is going to march in the Memorial Day parade on Thursday, the thirtieth."

"I'll be working at the Corner Cafe. But I'm sure I can get off. Let's go!"

Dean and Carrie, holding hands and accompanied by the chirping of crickets and the croaking of frogs, headed back to the house. Rex, sensing the hunt was over, ran excitedly after the pair.

Dean noticed the dish towel cover on the battered picnic basket was made from a flowered flour sack from Johanssons Flour Mill. He lifted a corner and peeked inquisitively into the basket. "It looks great, Carrie. I've been waiting for this day ever since we planned it two weeks ago!" Dean exclaimed.

"Mom helped me," Carrie admitted. "She told me that old saying - 'The way to a man's heart is through his stomach.' I think that's true in your case," she teased.

On the drive through the lake country to Lake Carlos, Carrie bubbled about the beautiful spring scenery. Carrie read the map and directed Dean as they wound their way around Lake Minnewaska, through the streets of Alexandria, stopping only for gasoline. Once they came to the picnic area by Lake Carlos they decided to walk in the woods by the lake. Hand in hand they strolled over the hills sheltered by maple, basswood and aspen-oak. "I had hoped to see more pines. There aren't any pine trees from where I'm from," he remarked.

Carrie found a restful spot on a large grassy knoll overlooking the lake. "Pa says the pine forests are further to the east," she explained to Dean. The musical sound of the fresh breeze in the trees and the smell of the new greenery surrounding them heightened Dean's feelings as he stared at Carrie. Sitting on the grass with the trees bordering the sparkling water behind her, Carrie made an image that would forever be etched in his mind.

Today, he had decided, I will ask Carrie to marry me. The questions though, were how and when should I ask her? He knew in his heart that Carrie loved him, but the possibility of a "No," added to his growing anxiety.

Dean had been sitting on the grass off to the side of Carrie. He twisted around and stood up. The question was whether they should eat first and then ask her or should I ask her, then eat? Dean wanted with all his heart for Carrie to marry him; but, he held back and the words were those of the North Dakota farm boy, "Let's eat, I'm hungry."

Dean's anxiety diminished when Carrie handed him a plate with a fresh bun, thick slices of roast beef bursting out the sides, beans still warm from the blue bowl wrapped in the dish towel and a glass of lemonade from the thermos.

Their picnic table was in the secluded area of the park and on this Thursday afternoon, there were few visitors. When they were through eating and while Carrie was putting the dishes back in the picnic basket, Dean retrieved a blanket from the car and spread it under the large oak tree. They sat together on the ground facing the lake. Carrie leaned against Dean and he wrapped his arms around her. "Carrie, there's something I have to ask you." There was a long pause before Dean could get it out. "Carrie, will you marry me?"

Carrie looked up into his face. "Yes! Oh, yes! Dean. I'm glad you asked me. Otherwise, I would have had to use my Leap Year option!" Pulling his face to hers, she sealed their words with a long, lingering kiss.

"We have to figure out when I can take you to North Dakota to meet my family."

"Oh, I thought we had to figure out when we were going to get married!" Carrie said mischievously.

"That too," Dean said. "Sometime this summer, I suppose."

"Can we wait until this fall, after I'm 20? That's only October 3rd."

"That long?" the disappointment heavy in his voice.

"And I'll have to talk to Mom," she said wondering what her mother would think. Then she added, "The first Friday night after my birthday, okay?"

Dean gave her a big hug that almost left her breathless then said, "We have a football game that day. Can we make it on Saturday?"

"We'll have to check with the church," Carrie said thoughtfully.

They sat there for a long while talking, enjoying each other's company and the warm afternoon sun. Dean finally glanced at his watch, breaking the spell that had been cast over them. He said, "Maybe we should start back. We can look around Alexandria. There seemed to be a lot for us tourists to see. When I put on gas the station attendant said we should be sure to see the Kensington Rune Stone in the museum. Do you know what that is, Carrie?" Dean asked.

Carrie said, "A farmer near Kensington, Minnesota, found the stone when he was clearing timber. It was dated 1362 and told of an exploration party of Swedish and Norwegian Vikings."

"Wow! My relatives must have been here over 500 years ago," Dean said.

"That is if you can prove it's not a forgery," Carrie replied.

"I'll have to talk to Ma and Uncle Eric. They can read Norwegian. Speaking of them, when can we go to North Dakota?" Answering his own question with another question, Dean said, "How about the weekend before the fourth of July? We'll be marching in the fourth of July parade and we'll have Guard on Monday night again."

"You sure have Guard a lot! It seems like you'll be spending more time with them than with me."

Dean replied, "Okay, so let's visit North Dakota on the last weekend in June. I'll have to let Ma and Eric know, so they can expect us."

"That would be all right. I'll talk to Mom tonight, but ask her not to say anything about us getting married just yet."

"I'd like to tell everyone. But that's fine with me, Carrie." Dean agreed as he put their picnic things into the car.

Their hearts and minds filled with plans for the future, Carrie and Dean left the park and started back to Applegrove.

STREETS OF HONOR

Chapter 10

Between the work at the flour mill and his weekly Guard drill, the month of June flew by for Dean. He would often stop at the farm to play cards or board games with Carrie's family. Dean and Carrie would go to a movie, or on long drives, but mostly enjoyed just being together.

At the Johansson's Flour Mill, Mr. Larson recognized Dean was a willing worker and moved him from the flour bagging room into the flour warehouse where he was put in charge of loading trucks, keeping a tally and recording the destination of each load.

On Monday, the last week in June, Dean drove out to the farm after work. "Guess what, Carrie! Mr. Larson said I could have Friday off when I told him I wanted to visit my folks in North Dakota."

"That's good, Dean. I'm sure I can get time off from the cafe too, but I'm a little worried about meeting your family."

Dean smiled, "Ma and Uncle Eric are probably more nervous than you are. I wrote to let them know our plans were to come the Saturday before the fourth of July. Now I'll have to let them know we'll come on Friday."

Dean was right about that. Ever since Dean had written and said he was bringing Carrie to meet them, Ma had been cleaning house and deciding what to make for meals. Eric finally told her, "Don't fuss so, I'm sure she's more nervous than you are."

Dean was nervous too. He hadn't told Carrie, but he had driven over to Willmar one Saturday and bought an engagement ring and put a down payment on a wedding ring. He planned to give it to her that weekend.

In North Dakota, Carrie observed the flat, far-away horizon commenting, "Looks like we could drive off the edge." As they drove into the farmyard, Carrie was unprepared for the simple arrangement of the farm and the lack of trees. The small, white house, the large red barn, granary and tool shed were all she could see. The barn and a small grove of cottonwood and box elder hid the blacksmith shop.

Ma and Eric met Dean outside when the car pulled into the yard. She gave Dean a big hug, then turned to Carrie who opened her arms to her even before she was introduced. By that simple act, Carrie endeared herself to Pauline who knew she would love this farm girl from Minnesota. Dean said, "This is Carrie," his only introduction and watched with love as Carrie became a part of his home and family. Carrie shook Eric's hand warmly. Although Eric seemed almost shy, Dean could tell he was captivated by Carrie's friendliness.

At the kitchen table with steaming coffee and homemade cookies, Dean and Carrie relaxed. Carrie had brought presents for Ma and Eric. A crocheted doily delighted Ma. "It's made by my Aunt Mabel," Carrie explained proudly. She had splurged on a pocket knife for Eric. He was overcome with her generosity.

"By the way, Dean," Ma said, "Charlie called and wondered when he can get together with you and Carrie."

"I'll call Charlie later on. We might go to Valley River Saturday night and look around. Right now we're going for a walk. I want to show Carrie around the farm."

Walking past the barn and blacksmith shop and out into the pasture, Carrie said, "I like your mother and Uncle Eric."

"They like you too, Carrie," Dean said, leading her to a large rock in the corner of the pasture. "Will you sit on this big rock a minute? I have something I want to show you."

Carrie sat down and looked up at Dean quizzically.

Dean took a small package from his pocket and handed it to Carrie. She noticed Dean's hand trembling slightly. "This is for you, for being you," he said.

Carrie opened the little box slowly, hoping it contained what she thought it might. She was not disappointed. It was the engagement ring, simple and elegant in a gold setting. Tears sprang to her eyes. "It's beautiful, Dean," she said, sliding off the rock and into his arms.

Taking the ring from her, he slipped it on her finger and gave her a kiss. "There aren't as many diamonds as I would have liked but it was all I could afford."

As she held her hand out to look at it, the diamond sparked in the sunlight. "I'll be happy and proud to wear this ring," she said.

They walked back to the farm hand in hand. Ma was busy making supper. Carrie tried to keep her new ring hidden, so Dean could announce the surprise. Ma figured Carrie would feel more at home if she helped, so she asked, "Will you set the table if I tell you where everything is?"

"Be happy to," said Carrie.

When Carrie was reaching in the cupboard for the plates, Ma noticed the ring. "Dean, you haven't told us about your surprise."

Dean, who was sitting in the front room talking to Eric, strode into the kitchen. Noticing the blush on Carrie's face, he put his arm around her. "We can't keep any secrets from you, Ma. We're going to get married in October," he said proudly.

Ma hugged Carrie. "I noticed the ring and I didn't want to ignore it."

Uncle Eric hurried into the kitchen and pumped Dean's hand. Reaching into his billfold, Dean took out a check and handed it to Eric. "I didn't spend everything. This is the last payment on the Studebaker loan."

"You don't have to pay me if you're short of money."

"No, I want to. We'll always be short of money."

Carrie was happy that their engagement was no longer a secret. All through supper she kept stealing glances at her ring.

Late Saturday afternoon, Dean and Carrie drove to Charlie's farm to pick him up to go to Valley River. Still bashful around girls, Charlie was charmed by Carrie. Likewise, Carrie could see why Charlie, with his good humor, was Dean's friend. When he heard of the engagement, he clapped Dean heartily on the back, "Good for you, Dean, you lucky man!"

Dean said, "I want to drive around the campus of Valley River to show Carrie. After that, any suggestions?"

"We should do something different, like go bowling!" Charlie said enthusiastically.

"I've never bowled," Carrie admitted.

"I've only bowled once, when the physical education class from college went to the Valley Lanes," Dean confessed.

"I've gone a few times lately, and I've learned how to keep score," Charlie said proudly. "You can rent shoes at the bowling alley."

Halfway through the first game, Carrie caught on, quit throwing gutter balls, and nearly had the same score as Dean. Dean used the alibi, "Getting engaged threw me off my game."

Charlie, besides being a good scorekeeper, got a good score. He was elated. "I finally found something I can beat you at, Dean."

Afterwards at the cafe, they laughed at some of the things that happened. Especially when Carrie had rolled her ball down the alley before the boy setting pins was ready and he had to quickly hop up to his perch and get his feet out of the way.

Dean and Charlie had both played basketball at Auburn High School. They recalled the night he was offered the scholarship to Valley River Teachers College. "That was funny," Dean said. "You fed me the ball and I turned for the lay-up and knocked down those two Haystown players."

Charlie chuckled. "I think the ref wanted to give you two fouls."

"Coach McLear came all the way from Valley River to

see us play. Remember he looked at me in the locker room after the game and said, 'I can't give you a basketball scholarship, but I can give you a half a football scholarship if you play center and linebacker for me.' I told him Auburn didn't have a football team, and I'd never played football."

Then Charlie interrupted, "That's when you asked, 'What's a linebacker?' All of us guys nearly died laughing."

"Yah," said Dean, "and I nearly died from embarrassment."

Charlie had kept one piece of news until they were going home. "I've joined the National Guard Unit in Valley River. After you were home for Christmas and said you might join, I thought about it and joined in February."

Dean was surprised. "What did Oscar think of that?"

"You know my Dad, Dean. As long as I'm going to Guard in Valley River, it's okay. If the Guard were ever called up, he'd miss me, and I'd have to sell off some of my livestock."

Carrie's eyes widened, "I hope the Guard won't have to go anywhere."

"I'm going to make private first class before you, Dean, and then I can boss you around."

When they dropped Charlie off that night, he agreed to come to Applegrove on October 5 and be Dean's best man.

When Carrie and Dean finally drove into Swenson's farmyard Sunday night, they were both exhausted from the excitement and the trip. Even though it was late, Carrie begged Dean to go in with her. "Mom said she would wait up for us and I think Pa is up too. Would you come in? I want to let them know we're engaged. Is that all right with you, Dean?"

"Okay, I'll bring your bag and come in with you."

Carrie told Carl and Sophie about North Dakota, Dean's family and Dean's friend, Charlie. Dean sat quietly listening in amusement to Carrie's observations.

Finally Carrie, who could not contain herself any longer, said, "But, the biggest surprise for me was..." and she held up her hand for them to see her ring.

Sophie gave her and Dean big hugs and said, "I'm so happy for both of you."

Carl shook Dean's hand and hugged Carrie. Dawn came down from upstairs, awakened by the noise. After Carrie showed her the ring, Dawn gave her a sleepy hug and went back to bed.

"Hey, you two, good luck!" Pete's voice bounced down the stairs as he had heard the excitement and the news.

"I better be going," Dean said. "I've got to be at work early in the morning."

Carrie saw him to the door and gave him a hug, kiss and a thank you for what she thought was a perfect conclusion to their family weekend.

STREETS OF HONOR

Chapter 11

After four weeks of hearing Sgt. Strong's marching cadence and maneuvers, Dean felt confident about marching in the 4th of July parade. Sympathetically, Bruce had put him on the inside ranks in case he missed a command. With the band playing the march music, Dean found it easy to keep in step and a had a feeling of pride in his unit and his country.

Carrie sewed the private stripes and the insignia of the 34th Infantry Red Bull Division on Dean's uniforms. Dean noticed Carrie seemed pleased to do this for him and appeared proud when she saw him in his dress khakis and highly polished, new, combat boots. Some of the old timers had told Dean he should have belonged to the unit when they had to wear britches and stockings.

Mr. Larson's patriotic spirit as the local American Legion Post commander, allowed Dean to get two weeks off for Guard Camp. Dean adjusted to Camp quickly. Besides being in excellent shape, he was used to a strict school schedule. Even getting up at 5:00 o'clock didn't bother him.

However, he did encounter two problems. One was with his stiff felt campaign hat that was designed like the Canadian Royal Mounted police with a small band around the outside. Unless it was pushed down firmly on his head, his blond, bushy hair would ease it off into the wind. He was also used to sleeping alone. The six men slept in pyramidal tents with tall center poles. Their snoring and heavy breathing kept him awake. By the third night he was so tired from the regime of marching, inspections and maneuvers that he fell asleep with the light bulb on over his cot and didn't hear a thing.

Private First Class Bradford occasionally reminded

Dean that over the last five years, Company M had won the machine gun trophy.

Dean was responsible for a .30 caliber, water-cooled, machine gun that he had to maintain and have ready for inspection. He also had to learn how to handle the bigger and heavier .50 caliber gun weighing about eighty pounds. It wasn't long before he had mastered both, including setting them up on the tripod. It was a nice break in routine when they could sit and load the long ammunition belts to be ready for the next time.

Sgt. Strong informed Bill and Dean, "You will have the responsibility to fire live ammunition with tracers over the men as they crawl through the night infiltration course. Make sure your ammo is loaded properly and the gun is in perfect working order. We don't want any accidents."

"When are we going to get the newer Browning air-cooled guns?" Bill asked.

Sgt. Strong answered, "Maybe you don't want one of those. You could be in the regular army if you do."

The company learned the reality of why they were training when in the middle of the second week, the company was called together on the parade ground. Captain Monson strode to the head of the assembled men to give them a message that would change their lives forever. "At ease, men. Congress has passed a bill where National Guard members can be inducted for one year of federal service under the limited national emergency declared by President Roosevelt. I'm going to read the following notice to you so there isn't any confusion."

> "Notice: All members of National Guard Unit, Company M, 3rd Battalion, 135th Infantry Regiment, 34th Division should have their affairs in order to leave in October for a year of precautionary training."

Startled gasps and loud "Oh's" went through the company at this bit of unexpected news. Although they had been following world events, they had not anticipated anything like this so soon.

Captain Monson continued, "I know this is a surprise to all of us. We will continue training this week and with our regular weekly meetings until we get further notice. Sergeant, you can take over."

Sergeant Strong, who had been standing ahead of the men in ranks, did a smart about face. His voice boomed out, "Company, attention! Right face! Forward, March!"

Dean, like many of the other men, was not only surprised but also shocked and uncertain about the suddenness of events. There wasn't anything that could be done right now and he did not want to worry Carrie. But he knew if he didn't let her know, she would hear the news around town.

The rain beat incessantly on the roof and windows of the administration building where Dean waited his turn with others to call home. Dean called late in the evening to be sure Carrie would be home. When she answered, Dean said, "Hi, sweetheart."

"Dean, I was just thinking about you. I was sitting in the kitchen sewing on a dress that I might take on our honeymoon."

"That's why I called, Carrie." Dean told her about the orders the Company had received and that the men should have their affairs in order to leave in October.

Carrie was silent for a long time, then asked, "Surely, we can still have our wedding on October 5, can't we?"

"For now, let's not change our plans," Dean encouraged. "I hope we can learn more soon. Guard Camp will be over this weekend and I'll come and see you as soon as we get back." To change the subject and to get Carrie thinking about something else, he asked, "Is it raining there? It's raining hard here now. You said in your letter the corn crop needed rain."

"We had a nice rain all day that stopped before supper. Pa was so relieved."

"There are other fellows wanting to use the phone so I have to get off the line. I love you and can't wait to see you."

"I love you too, Dean," Carrie said, hanging up quickly so Dean didn't hear the catch in her voice.

Carrie told her mother and dad about Dean's call. "I don't feel like sewing anymore. I'm going to get ready for bed." Carrie knew she wouldn't fall asleep right away. She took Dean's framed picture of him in his National Guard uniform and put it under her pillow. She hugged the pillow close to her and said a prayer.

When Dean returned from Guard Camp late Sunday afternoon, he drove out to the farm. He had been reassured that the Army moved slowly since there was much organizing to do. He wanted to pass this reassurance on to Carrie. Dean again held her close. "Carrie, I hear the Army has a lot to do before October. Let's not change our wedding plans." He was rewarded with one of Carrie's smiles.

Dean stopped at school to talk to Supt. Grafstrom. The superintendent had heard the news about the Guard call up and had contacted colleges for replacements for Dean and Russell Wagner. "Dean, there are a few candidates graduating at mid-year from college I can hire. We might have to use some substitute teachers for awhile, if we have to. There's a man from town that could help with the coaching."

"Has Bill Bradford been in to see you?" Dean asked.

"Yes, in fact, with so many local men gone, it might be hard to find a custodian. The school board may have to hire a woman."

Dean smiled when he thought of Bill's reaction on being replaced by a woman.

Carl appreciated Dean showing up at the farm when he wasn't working at the Mill to help him with harvesting. Dean in turn was happy to immerse himself in farm work.

One day in August Mrs. B. asked him to stop for coffee. "Mr. Sherve, who manages the grain elevator, has been renting the other downstairs apartment. He informed me his company is transferring him the first of September. I know you and Carrie will want more room after you're married. Would you be interested in renting this apartment?"

"Sounds great, Mrs. B., but I'll have to talk to Carrie, of course."

Dean and Carrie looked at the apartment the following weekend. Carrie loved the spacious kitchen and adjoining living room. Dean was intrigued with the leaded, stained glass in the upper portion of the living room window facing the porch. "Yes," Dean said. "We want it. I'll move in on September first."

Dean settled back into the school year routine. This year, he felt like a veteran on the first day of the 1940-41 school year. With the same classes as the previous year except for physics class with nine students, he found his classes easier than he expected. What pleased him most were the players returning from last year's football team. They had developed physically, and there was a sense of confidence about them. The winning attitude of the previous year's team carried over.

Pete, Carrie's brother, had practiced passing during the summer and it was evident the first week. Dean was able to change plays to allow for his passing ability and running.

It was the first week of September that Company M got word that the camp in Louisiana was not ready yet and they would leave in November. Everyone was relieved especially Carrie and Dean.....their wedding could go on as planned.

When Carrie and Dean were out for a drive, Dean said, "At Guard drill on Monday, I learned from Sgt. Strong the 'Draft Bill' passed Congress. He told me the Selective Service and Training Act is the first peacetime compulsory military service program. I would have been drafted if I hadn't joined the Guard. This way I can be with my friends."

Carrie was quiet for awhile. "I hope you don't have to go to war."

He did not respond. He hadn't thought of Carrie alone when he would be away in the Army. He wondered, would she have the strength to deal with personal problems by herself? Of course, she would be able to take care of things, he reassured himself.

Carrie occasionally would stop at Mrs. B's and look in on the apartment where Dean now lived. One day she said, "When we both live here, I wonder if Mrs. B. would let me change the curtains and get some different rugs." Dean smiled, realizing it was going to be quite a change to live with a woman.

During July and August, and now into early September, Carrie, Sophie, Delores and Dawn, who was now in the tenth grade, had excitedly worked on wedding plans. Sitting around the kitchen table writing out wedding invitations with Mom and Dawn, Carrie had told them that everything was done that they could do, including the dresses for Delores, Dawn and Louise. Dean's attendants, Pete, Charlie and his college friend, Jim Foley, will wear their own suits. "Joe consented to be one of the ushers. I'm not sure where he'll get his suit," Carrie said.

Dean had gotten to know Tim Thoreson when they worked together at the flour mill. Dean knew Tim was always singing around school and at the job. Dean had asked Carrie, "Do you think Tim Thoreson would sing at our wedding?"

Tim was surprised when Dean asked him, and said, "Yes, I'll be glad to." Dean got the feeling, Tim was very pleased and proud they considered him their friend.

"Mom," Carrie said one afternoon, "Dean and I confirmed the times with the minister. Friday will be hectic with the afternoon football game, and wedding practice on Friday night, and then the wedding Saturday night. Oh, my gosh! It's coming so fast!"

Believe it or not, Sophie had actually told Dean that they should change the football game to another day.

In response, Dean said, "Wedding or no wedding, the

football game has to stay as scheduled."

Dawn, who had been quietly listening said, "Carrie, you were lucky to borrow your wedding dress."

Carrie said, "That's for sure." Carrie had realized they couldn't afford to buy an expensive dress. Julie, one of Carrie's friends who was also a waitress at The Corner Cafe, and lived in a neighboring town, had been married in June. She had asked Carrie one day if she wanted to borrow her wedding dress, saying they were about the same size.

Carrie said, "Oh, yes, thank you. You're an answer to my prayers."

"I'll bring it on Saturday and you can try it on."

Carrie tried on the white satin dress as soon as she got home. It fit her perfectly. She loved the V lace yoke and pointed satin collar. The sleeves were long with the upper lace coming to a V above the elbow. The train that was attached to the back of the long gown had three triangular lace inserts at the hem. Happily, she hurried to show Mom, whose eyes filled with tears before agreeing that the dress fit perfectly.

Friday afternoon, the day before the wedding, the football team traveled to Benton. Dean told Charlie, who arrived Thursday night and stayed in the apartment with Dean, "You can ride the team bus with us over to the game." Charlie was impressed with the team: their sharpness and physical conditioning.

The Applegrove team had easily won their first three games and both Applegrove and Benton were undefeated. Dean told his players, "Remember, this game could decide the conference champion." The noisy excitement and the colorful crowd added to the tension in the air. The team played good offense and defense and came home with a surprising 19-6 victory.

When the team bus arrived back in Applegrove, Dean told Pete, "You had a great game, Pete, I'm proud of you. I'll see you at the church for wedding practice tonight."

"What time is the real wedding?" Pete asked.

Smiling, Dean said, "We have to be dressed and ready by seven o'clock Saturday night."

Ma and Uncle Eric drove from North Dakota on Friday, the day before the wedding. They each had a room at the cozy and clean Applegrove Motel. Dean left Ma and Eric at Swenson's farm during the wedding practice on Friday night to get acquainted with Carrie's folks. Later Ma confided to Dean she had a good visit with Sophie, and they traded recipes. Uncle Eric and Carl talked farming all evening. Ah, these two families might even get along, Dean thought.

The minister kept the practice short and Carrie, who had a lot left to do, was glad. She told Dean, "I have to fix Delores's and Dawn's hair and Delores has yet to do mine. Then tomorrow at 2:00 o'clock we have to be in Benton at Barnes's Photography for wedding pictures. Will you help me to remember to bring all the wedding clothes and bouquets tomorrow?"

"How can I refuse my soon-to-be bride?" Dean said happily.

Dean invited Charlie and Jim to the Applegrove Cafe for noon lunch. When Bruce stopped at their booth, Dean introduced them, explaining that they were his wedding attendants. "This is Bruce Strong. He owns the cafe and is our sergeant in the Guard."

"Hi, fellows. Dean won't need you to make sure he gets there. He's firmly hooked," he laughed.

Jim told Dean, "I hear from Winnie out in Montana occasionally. I told her I was to be an attendant at your wedding and you know what?"

"No. What did she say? I said I'd write, but I never did."

"She was not at all surprised since she hadn't heard from you." She said, "Tell him, the best of luck."

They both laughed when Charlie, listening to the

conversation said, "Hey, Dean, if you have any left over girl friends, I'm available."

That evening the church was packed for the wedding. Dean stood in awe as he watched Carrie walk down the aisle on Carl's arm. Never had he seen anyone so radiant and beautiful. Looking at her a feeling of total happiness overtook him. As they held hands and repeated the promises to be faithful until death parts them, feelings of warmth and love and completeness passed between them.

Afterwards in the reception line, everyone could see the bond the two shared. Handshakes, hugs and kisses were in large supply. Supt. Grafstrom's only comment to Dean was, "Good luck to you now." Mrs. Grafstrom was very genuine when she told them, "I'm very happy for both of you."

Dean had told Carrie earlier that he hoped they might leave soon after the wedding. However the reception, lunch and numerous well wishers made this impossible. Carrie's family agreed to pack up the opened gifts displayed on the tables and take them to their apartment. After thanking and paying the minister and Tim for singing, Dean finally took Carrie firmly by the arm and whispered, "Let's go now. We can change clothes at the farm."

As they hurried out of the farmhouse, Dean exclaimed, "Come on Carrie, let's get on with our life together!"

"Dean, you haven't told me where we're going on our honeymoon. I thought you would tell me by now. We've only got tomorrow."

"I've got two surprises for you. We're going to Bemidji and Itasca State Park. Remember I wanted to go there."

"Oh, that should be wonderful!" Carrie exclaimed. "The trees have started to turn color. What's the other surprise?"

"I took advantage of Grafstrom's good mood and asked him to arrange a substitute for me on Monday. So we don't have to be back until 8:00 that night for Guard drill. Hey, let's go!"

The next two days were filled with the glorious excitement of young love. They walked on the rocks across the rippling waters where the mighty Mississippi has its origin in Itasca Park, laughed when Dean slipped in to just above his ankles and strolled along the beach of Lake Bemidji in the shadow of Paul Bunyon and his Blue Ox. They spent nights holding each other wishing this would never end.

After a late breakfast on Monday, Dean and Carrie checked out of the motel and headed for Applegrove to be back in time for Dean's Guard drill. Dean had asked Russell Wagner to supervise football that afternoon, so he had that covered. The captains were to lead practice.

Dean quietly opened the door to the house. Although Carrie had her arms full, Dean carefully carried her across the threshold of the apartment and kissed her at the same time. She whispered, "You know what? This reminds me of the time you caught me when I fell off the stool in the chemistry room."

Dean said, "That was the start of all this."

Even though they expected it, they were taken aback by the wedding gifts covering the dining room table, sofa and chairs. "I'll wait for you to come home from Guard and we'll look at them together before we put them away," she said.

Dean answered with a lingering hug and, "I want to do everything with you the rest of my life."

STREETS OF HONOR

Chapter 12

The month of October, 1940, was, for Dean, one of pleasant memories. Guard units in Minnesota, Iowa, and North and South Dakota were being considered for federal service, but had not yet received word about induction. The Applegrove football team was undefeated with two conference games left. Dean, working hard with the team, told them, "You could win the conference if you continue to play like you have." They were rewarded with an undefeated season.

Dean and Carrie celebrated by driving to Willmar on the weekend for an evening meal and movie. Dean held Carrie's hand before the movie started. She whispered, "Don't you want me to eat my popcorn?"

Dean whispered back, "I'm so happy I don't want these days to ever end, Carrie. You're a perfect wife."

"It's a good thing it's dark, so you can't see I'm blushing."

The peace they were feeling, sitting in the dark theater, was disturbed later by the realities of war, when the newsreel showed the wreckage and death in England. A little girl, holding her doll by her bombed out home, brought a gasp from the audience. A Far East correspondent reported Japan would be joining the Axis pact to link with Germany and Italy. "This military alliance will affect profoundly both the course of the European war and the world in general."

Driving home, Dean said, "I liked the movie. Happy endings make me feel good." He said nothing about the war newsreels, as he didn't want to worry Carrie. Carrie, thinking the same thing, leaned over and cuddled close to Dean.

Carrie and Dean, blissfully in love, did not get involved

in discussions on the November 5th presidential election. Families were divided over the choice between Franklin Delano Roosevelt and Wendell Wilkie. This was also true in the Swenson family; Pete wore his big FDR button and Dawn had been given a "Win With Wilkie" button and a bag of peanuts at the Republican campaign headquarters. Dawn said FDR shouldn't have a controversial third term, and Pete argued FDR had brought the country out of the Depression. Roosevelt earned the third term, Pete said, with a 54.7% margin, but Dawn saved her Wilkie button.

One thing that interrupted their wedded bliss was the weather. Dean had a mercury barometer in his science laboratory that he used in his physics class. Armistice Day, Monday, November 11, 1940, started out bright and sunny. It was a holiday, there was no school. Some of the men at the cafe had asked Dean at breakfast about going duck hunting. Dean answered that he was going up to school to correct some tests and set up a physics experiment. Now, glancing at the barometer after he opened the classroom door this unusually warm November morning, he was shocked to see the mercury in the tube was the lowest he had ever seen. By mid-morning, the temperature at fifty degrees was still well above the average for that time of the year. However, the wind had started to pick up.

He called Carrie at the Corner Cafe. After graduation, Willie, the owner, had asked her to work mornings. "Carrie, there's a storm coming. Better call your folks. I'm going home now. Call me at home when you're done work and I'll come and get you."

Trusting Dean's judgment, Carrie notified her folks. "Mom, Dean called and said there's a storm coming."

"Land sakes, it's nice out now," Sophie responded. "I better tell Carl to get Pete home. He went duck hunting down by the creek."

The Armistice Day storm of 1940 struck with a fury. During the day the wind increased to 32 miles per hour gusting to 60. Temperatures that were in the 50's dropped quickly during the day to six above zero. Rain turned to sleet, sleet to snow, and then the wind. Visibility was down to zero at times. Telephone lines that had become iced over, snapped in the strong wind. Roads became impassable.

There wasn't much activity in town. Dean and Carrie walked home over drifts, glad that they lived close to uptown. She told Dean, "One of the men was hanging on to his felt hat, but the wind blew it off anyway. When he came into the cafe, all he had left was the small piece in his hand."

Carrie, worried about Pete after her mother told her he had gone duck hunting, and waited anxiously for the lines to be repaired. After trying to call off and on for several hours, she had to wait until the next morning to get through.

Sophie answered the phone. "Tell Dean, thanks for the warning. We had a real scare. Carl went down by the creek and hollered and hollered for Pete, but he didn't answer. He heard Rex barking and finally found Pete down by the slough. He was loaded down with ducks and didn't want to stop hunting because the ducks were flying low all over. It was really snowing and blowing by then. They couldn't see a thing! They followed Rex back to the fence line and left the ducks there except for two green head mallards Pete wouldn't leave for anything. They followed the fence back to the house. They're all right but they could've died. Thank goodness for Rex!....and for Dean!"

The next morning, Dean went with Carrie to the cafe. Dean learned there would not be any school until Thursday. A farmer near Applegrove froze to death when he went out in the storm to check on his cattle. Dean read in the paper that many of the 59 that died in Minnesota were duck hunters or travelers in cars that became stalled in the deep drifts. The Minneapolis Tribune reported a record amount of snow in the twenty four hour period of 16.8 inches, 22 inches at Orr and 26.6 inches at Collegeville, near St. Cloud.

Even though it happened on Armistice Day, the storm pushed aside the thought of war for awhile. Dean told Carrie, "There's a dance Saturday night at the Armory, and we should go. The Community is sponsoring it to show their appreciation to the Guard. The snow has been cleared off the roads so people can get out."

Carrie was puzzled. "I didn't even know you could dance, Dean. We've never danced together. I learned to dance when I went to barn dances with Mom and Pa. Maybe we should practice before we go."

"I'll have to tell you about my dancing lessons." Dean laughed, swinging Carrie around the apartment.

The word had gotten out among the football team that Dean had resorted to Homer Engelson to teach him how to dance. Dean had scoffed at the thought when he was a junior, thinking some of the guys that saw them would laugh him off the campus. Now as a senior, the pressure was on. One of the duties of the football co-captains was to be the first ones to dance with the Homecoming Queen. Dean took the ribbing from his football teammates good naturedly. But also, the experience had given him confidence to rid himself of the bashfulness he felt around girls.

Dean stuck his head into Homer Engelson's room and announced, "Here I am, 'teach'!" Homer roomed on the same floor as Dean, played cornet and had his own dance band.

Homer groaned and got up from the chair by what was supposed to be his desk. Piled high with records and sheet music, it bore no resemblance to a college student's desk. "Dean, this is the hardest money I've ever earned," Homer said wearily. Dean had agreed to pay him $2.00 a session. Homer had asked $3.00 but Dean convinced him $1.00 was more fair. But when Dean had insisted that Homer wear a wig, they agreed on $2.00. Homer had found a wig in the Drama Department. This was the 3rd session of four.

"Okay, Dean, let's go over the waltz and the fox trot. Just refuse to dance any polkas. I'm going to put on a waltz. You seem to do better with that."

Homer put on his dark, longhaired wig and asked, "Tell me how you would hold your hands, Dean?"

"First, I take her right hand gently in my left and lead her to the dance floor. Then I put my right hand on her back just above her waist like this and hold her right hand with my left." Taking Homer by surprise, he demonstrated.

"Whoa, Nellie, she's not a hay bale. Do it gently. You show me how to lead." Homer shook his wig and fluttered his eyelashes at Dean. After they bumped into a table, Homer entreated. "Just a minute and I'll find a slow 'belly rubbing' fox trot record."

Startled, his Scandinavian shyness evident, Dean asked, "What do you mean by that?"

"Well, you've got to dance close with Queen Jewel Jensen. But with her big bosom you may not even get close!"

Dean thought, it's been a struggle to get over being afraid of girls. But I can tell I'm actually feeling relaxed around them now.

As the music of Cole Porter's *Blue Moon* filled the dorm room, Homer said, "There you go, Dean! You've got better rhythm. Now swing me around more in a circle."

In his enthusiasm, Dean picked the slightly built Homer up off his feet. "Hey, that's great, but you can't do that to Jewel."

Dean bumped the table. The lamp teetered and fell with a crash. As they looked at the pieces scattered on the floor, Homer said, "You better wait for a waltz on Saturday night."

Carrie giggled all through the story and they were both laughing uncontrollably at the end. Suddenly they stopped and clung to each other with the realization Dean might soon be leaving.

At the Armory Dance in honor of the Guard, Carrie and Dean enjoyed the whole evening. They found it easy to dance with each other and Dean relished every opportunity to hold Carrie close.

The band struck up the popular Scandinavian waltz, *Hils fra mig der hjemme,* "Greet from Me Those That Are Home." To one watching from the balcony that surrounded the armory floor, it appeared that the shuffling figures moving effortlessly became one. Yet each couple had their own private thoughts. It was truly an emotional celebration..... happy, yet sad.

Carrie's parents invited Dean and Carrie to celebrate Thanksgiving with them. The days between Thanksgiving and Christmas flew by. So many warm moments of joy and hope.

But then, coming home from Guard the day before Christmas Eve, Dean told Carrie, "I heard that we'll be leaving the first week in February."

Carrie became quiet and thoughtful. Then she answered sadly, "It's a Christmas present to have you with me during January."

Dean and Carrie spent Christmas Eve together. Dean gave Carrie an aqua wool sweater and she gave Dean a pen and pencil set with a note, "Be sure to write me!" They spent most of the evening talking and holding each other close. Christmas Day they went to Carrie's church and out to the farm for Christmas dinner.

New Years Day was on Wednesday and school started again on Thursday. Dean found yet another memo in his mailbox.

Thursday, January 2, 1940

Mr. Brandum, please stop in my office tomorrow during your noon hour.

Supt. Grafstrom

At least he's not going to fire me. Or, is he? Dean

wondered. He dropped into the now very familiar chair opposite the superintendent.

"I understand the Guard call-up might be the first week in February, Dean."

"Yes, that's what they were saying at the last drill."

"Dean, I've been thinking that the best thing for both you and the school district would be if Friday, January thirty-first, was your last day. A fellow graduating from Moorhead says he'll be able to start on Monday, February 3. He's short a couple of education classes but the State Department said it's all right to hire him if he completes his work this summer."

"That will be fine. I'll help him in any way I can before I leave."

Major Grafstrom was proud of his cadre of soldiers. He shook Dean's hand and said, "I wish you well. You'll be missed. You did a fine job. When you return, check with us. We may have an opening."

The last day of school for Dean, Russell, and Bill, the students made a sign wishing them well and hung it in the lunchroom. The junior high students in Dean's classes especially made him feel he would be missed. They had made cards for him and arranged to bring treats. Dean had to discourage them from making a big celebration.

That evening, the basketball team played together, winning their last game with Dean as their coach.

The order calling Company M, 3rd Battalion, 135 Infantry Regiment, 34th Infantry Red Bull Division into federal service came on February 1, with February 10, 1941 set as the departure date for Camp Claiborne, Louisiana. Starting on Monday, February 3rd, Guardsmen were ordered to sleep in the Armory. Cots were set up everywhere including the balcony. Those who lived close to the Armory could stay at home.

Dean was one who spent his nights at home. As he felt the curves of Carrie's warm body next to him and the smooth, softness of her skin it became increasingly difficult to leave. He loved Carrie more each day.

Every morning for the rest of the week, he donned his GI clothes, bundled into his overcoat, and trudged to the Armory for 6:00 a.m. muster. The company cooks, two brothers, always prepared good meals. Each day the men got their equipment in order to prepare for inspections and drills. Physical exams and immunizations were also completed.

Monday, February 10, 1941, dawned clear and cold. The temperature on the Armory thermometer read 20 degrees below zero. The company assembled with Captain Monson at the head and Sergeant Strong giving the commands, they marched to the Milwaukee railroad depot to board the troop train. The guardsmen from neighboring towns had already boarded the train.

Although the morning was bitterly cold, the townspeople, friends, and relatives crowded the station platform. Carrie was there with her mother. The water pump in the well had frozen and Carl stayed home to thaw it out. Dawn, now a member of the Applegrove High School Band stood off to the side with the other band members and played her clarinet.

Bill Bradford's wife Sally brought her two children, Bridget and Lucas who were confused by the excitement, the sadness and the tears. Bridget insisted on hugging Dean as well as Bill.

Carrie's eyes welled with tears and spilled down her cheeks as she clung to Dean. "Write or call me often, Dean. I'll miss you so much."

Dean, wrapping his arms around Carrie, kissed her on both cheeks and rocked her gently in his embrace. He whispered, "I love you," over and over. As the mournful whistle of the train pierced the cold air, he gave her a final hug, then turned and climbed aboard.

The train with 106 other Company M guardsmen was bound for Camp Claiborne. The guardsmen were to put in one year of service and then come back home. Many, watching the train depart, wondered if the actions of the world would permit that.

STREETS OF HONOR

Chapter 13

The clickity-clack of the wheels of the troop train reminded Dean and the rest of Company M they were being carried far from their home and loved ones. Looking out the Pullman car windows, Dean took in an expanse of whiteness. The numerous lakes with their blanket of snow were indistinguishable from the surrounding fields. The smoke and steam from the locomotive rose straight up in the clear morning air as the train stopped in Hutchinson. The scene on the platform of loved ones saying 'goodbye' was again repeated as more men prepared to board the train.

When the troop train slowed in towns and cities, young and old waved excitedly. Passing through Minneapolis, the train traveled along the Mississippi through Iowa, Missouri, touching Tennessee at Memphis, then passed through Arkansas.

Dean dozed off and on for most of the three days. To relieve the boredom, some of the men played poker. Mealtime was a welcome interlude. The kitchen car was a converted baggage car with a hole cut in the door so the smoke from the stovepipe could join the cold winter air.

The first impression Dean had when he saw Camp Claiborne, was the snake-like path the railroad tracks made through the swamp. Across the highway from the railroad siding, the camp looked barren and lonely. As the men climbed down from the train, they noticed the pine trees on opposite side of the track. The trees brought memories to Dean of the honeymoon trip to Bemidji. His thoughts ended when Company M was ordered into formation along with the others and marched to their assigned area. A light rain had made the grassless streets mucky with red clay.

Sgt. Strong told the men assembled on the street in front of the tents, "This is home for awhile. Five of you have been assigned to a tent. Now count off by squads."

Camp Claiborne, Louisiana
February 22. 1941

Dear Carrie:

I have been away from you for less than two weeks but it seems like years. Did you get my letter I wrote on the train? I miss you so much. When I see someone that reminds me of you, or hear a song, I want to hold you in an embrace so bad it hurts.

The camp is not ready yet and the 34th Division is the first one here. It appears that two hills in the swamp have been leveled off and made into a base. The red clay quickly turns to a sea of mud. Our first assignment was to build wooden sidewalks. Our sergeant said, "Make them just like the Atlantic City Boardwalk."

We're sleeping in parameter tents, about fifteen feet square, like at Camp Ripley. I bunk with four nice fellows. Only one of us snores. You might have guessed who it is ..... Bill! The tent has a wood floor and a natural gas stove for heat.

One day it is warm and humid and the next it's cool and raw. The nighttime temperature which is near freezing is more what we're used to. The first week everyone was issued a size 42 long-johns underwear. Some of the 106 men in Company M are six feet six tall and some are only five feet. You can imagine what we looked like. We had a good laugh over this.

Greet everyone. I will try to write often. I wait for your letters.

I love you, Carrie
Dean

Dean wrote a similar letter to Ma and Eric with the added biased opinion that, "I'll take North Dakota 'gumbo' anytime."

Dean attended each mail call, patiently waiting to see if there was a letter from Carrie. When finally the long awaited letter came, he hurried to the tent to read it.

Applegrove, Minnesota
March 1, 1941

Dear Dean:

I waited for your letter so I could get your address correct. I'm glad you still love me and miss me. I love you more than ever. Your birthday is not for two weeks but I am sending you three different kinds of cookies. Happy 24th!! I wish you were here with me. We'd celebrate together.

The basketball team hasn't been doing very well, so they have to play in the sub district this year. Pete has been playing okay, but is disappointed in the team's record. He says to tell you to wait until next year when he's a senior.

Dawn asked that I tell you that when the band played the morning you left, it was so cold the reed froze to her mouthpiece. She wondered how much warmer it is down there.

We're still busy at the cafe. Mr. Morrison, the bank president, came in for coffee. He told me they will have an opening in the bookkeeping department July first and that I should apply. I know you would encourage me to do this and I think I will.

All this is just stuff, Dean, and I only want to tell you that every moment apart from you is torture. I love you so much, and I need you here. But, I also know you are doing what you need to do for us and our country.

My prayers and love are sent your way, morning, noon, and night.

I love you,
Carrie

A few of the Company members who were over twenty-eight years of age were discharged because of age, including one of Dean's new friends, Sgt. Christensen.

It wasn't long before bars, arcades, photo galleries and the usual camp followers appeared around the camp. The nearby city of Alexandria welcomed the 8,000 soldiers.

Dean and Bill were able to secure weekend passes. A round trip bus ticket to Alexandria cost 55 cents. Dean generously said, "I'll pay this time."

Used to the cold and white of the north, it was a new and different world to them. The tall, green trees with yellow or pink blooms amazed Dean. "What kind of trees do you think they are, Bill?

"We'll have to ask someone," answered Bill.

Company M was designated as a heavy weapons company which consisted of machine guns and mortars. The men trained with real equipment rather than a stovepipe that simulated a mortar or a wooden model of a machine gun as other units had to do. Dean had to take down, clean, and reassemble an old Browning, water-cooled, .30 caliber machine gun.

On one of the first days of April, the riflemen of the regiment enthusiastically received the new Garand M-1, 30-06 semi-automatic rifle. The men who were anxious to try the new weapon readily turned in their .30 caliber 1903 bolt action Springfields. Bill couldn't resist bragging to Dean, "I qualified as a marksman today. Quite a few from our Company did."

Dean replied, "I'd rather have my machine gun."

The 34th Red Bull Division was organized as a square division consisting of the four regiments - the 135th from Minnesota, the 133rd and 168th from Iowa and the 164th from North Dakota. Having come from small towns and farms, the men from the Midwest states worked well together as a unit.

In late April, as Dean returned from morning chow, he noticed a long column of trucks pulling into camp. He'd heard that their load of draftees had been brought down from the Midwest to bring the Division up to strength. Although in uniform, the draftees hadn't much exposure to the military. Mostly from small Midwest towns such as Vergas and Battle Lake in Minnesota and Flandreau, South Dakota, the recruits made friends easily and melded into the squads and platoons of the Company.

Dean felt like a veteran when the new men were assigned to the battalion, and he was to assist them on the firing range. "It's not so bad," Dean told the recruits, "You get plenty to eat, good clothes and $30.00 a month." This brought moans and griping when compared to how they had it back home.

To get prepared for the fall maneuvers, the Company had numerous practice exercises. On these trips the main fear of the men was not the marching, sun or mud, but the poisonous snakes in the swamp. Lt. Marsh told the men, "There are coral, water moccasins, copperheads and timber rattlers in the area. Some of the snakes are five or six feet long. Be sure to shake out your boots in the morning before you put them on." Much to Dean's horror, one soldier did die from snakebite to the neck while on the rifle range. He was astonished when he learned how many others died in drowning accidents or vehicle accidents on and off the post.

Camp Claiborne, Louisiana
May 3, 1941

Dear Carrie:

Hi sweetheart! How are you? It's almost three months since I've seen you and it seems like three years. Would you take the train down here? Some of the wives are now visiting. You could stay in Alexandria. It is a nice town, eighteen miles north of Camp and is about ten times the size of Applegrove.

Why don't you come as soon as you can?

If you could get here on a Friday and stay the week, then leave the following Sunday, we could have two weekends together. I'm sending some money to help you make a decision. You can take what ever else you need out of our savings.

It's starting to get hot down here so if you come, bring summer clothes.

Bill and I played a practical joke on Russell Wagner. We have so many snakes down here. One night on bivouac Russell was asleep in his two-man pup tent with his partner. We got a rope from the weapons carrier truck and Bill reached in from the end of the tent and dragged it across Russell's body. Russell's first reaction was to flail his arms and kick. Then he jumped to his feet and knocked the tent down. His yelling woke up the neighboring soldiers.

Bill dropped the rope when we ran. Burt found it the next morning and told Russell that it was the snake he felt last night. Russell, who's never seen anything but a garter snake in his life, claimed, "No, it felt like a big copperhead was slithering across my chest! I felt the scales and it was real slippery."

We had a good laugh about it, but don't tell anyone because we don't want him to know it was us after all the commotion he made. Russell will be too embarrassed if he knew the truth.

Yes, take the job at the bank. You are good with numbers and keeping our checking account straight so it should be easy and fun for you. Maybe you could come down before you start your new job at the bank.

I'm not going to write any more as it's almost 11 o'clock, lights out time. Besides, I want to go to sleep and dream about you being here for a few days. I want to show you around when you come down.

> *I love you,*
> *Dean*

Sgt. Strong checked promotion orders regularly hoping to make staff sergeant. In mid May he was walking around with a big smile.....he'd made it. He told some of the men in the Company, "There are promotion orders posted on the Headquarters bulletin board. Dean, your name's on there. You were promoted to Private First Class. And I've just got word Capt. Monson is returning from officers training at Fort Benning, Georgia." The men were glad to hear he was coming back and the cooks planned to make a cake for him. He would be Regimental Adjutant in charge of orders, records, reports and correspondence.

PFC Bill Bradford, anticipating a corporal stripe, walked with Dean to check the promotion list. He was disappointed when his name was not on the orders. "Maybe my name will be on the next batch," he said to Dean.

One of the men on the machine gun crew, looking at the list, overheard Bill and told him, "You'll have to get to know Captain Monson better. He might make you a corporal."

Bill retorted, "If I do, I'll make sure he doesn't give you a furlough."

When finally, Dean received a response from Carrie, he sought a quiet place to read it.

Applegrove, Minnesota
May 11, 1941

Dear Dean:

I got your letter about coming to Louisiana. I checked the railroad schedule. If I leave here on Wednesday, June 4, I'd arrive in Alexandria Friday night at 9:10 p.m. I got the money you sent, but it won't be enough so I'll take some from our savings.

Willy said I could get off work at the cafe. When I get back to Applegrove it will be only two weeks and I start work at the bank. It worked out that the girl that will take my place could work when I'm gone.

126

It would be wonderful if you could get weekend passes so we can be together. It's a long way to travel, but I want to be with you so much.

Joe broke his leg in a car accident. He was alone when he ran off the road and hit an approach. It's the same one he broke when he was in grade school. Undoubtedly he won't be drafted, at least for awhile. He's been working on another farm beside mom and dad's and has a farm deferment.

I'll tell you other news when I come down.

Love you so much,
Carrie

Dean had applied early for passes for the weekends when Carrie would be in Louisiana. When he explained his wife was coming, they were readily granted.

Finally the Friday of Carrie's arrival came. He took the camp bus to Alexandria where he nervously paced up and down the station platform. His mind was awhirl with thoughts: Is it ever going to get here? Will she be on the train? Where will the passenger car stop? How long before she can get off?

When Dean saw Carrie step down from the car farther up the platform, he ran over, covered her with kisses, and held her close for so long, she finally said, "You better find my suitcase or I'll have to wear the same clothes all week."

Carrie was happy to see Dean looking tanned and healthy. "I found a room for us in the old hotel uptown," Dean said. "There are so many visitors to the camp that I had to take what I could get."

"Whatever we get, doesn't matter, Dean. I'm just so happy to be with you."

They spent the first weekend getting reacquainted. Carrie, who wasn't at all used to the hot weather, didn't want to spend a lot of time in the blazing sun. In the evenings they walked along the levee protecting the town from the Red River.

Dean, studying the places where the river had washed away the soil said, "They must get a lot of rain, it looks like the river has overflowed its banks in past years."

Monday morning Dean hurriedly dressed and caught the bus back to camp for reveille and roll call. Carrie sat in the hotel room later in the morning after Dean had left for camp, and stared out the two large window panes at the rain that beat rhythmically on the outside walls and windows. She wondered if this would cause the river to flood. The yellow-orange paint had peeled away from the window sill exposing the gray weathered wood. Looking down at the street, she saw the same pattern carried around the balcony that hung over the entrance door. The proprietor had accommodated his patrons by installing two lengths of eaves trough. This drained the rain away from the front step. The depressing sight made her wonder about the decision to join Dean. It had taken most of their savings for a round trip ticket from Willmar to Louisiana. But, as Dean had staunchly argued, "We have to enjoy the time together, when we can." In her heart she knew that he was right.

The rap on the hotel room door broke her reverie. "Maid service."

Carrie opened the door and told the young, dark-skinned maid, "I'm going to be here all week so you don't have to do much."

"Oh, that's okay. I'll change the bathroom linens and see what else is needed."

Carrie had never talked to a black woman and wanting to be friendly asked, "What's your name?"

"My name's Karey," she answered.

Carrie exclaimed, "My name's Carrie too!" She took an instant liking to her and appreciated the chance to talk to someone.

"Where you from, ma'am?"

"I'm from Minnesota and visiting my husband. He's at

Camp Claiborne."

"We have a lot of you ladies from up north come down and they always seem so anxious to get back home." She shuddered. "I don't know why - it's so cold up there."

"It's something you grow up with," replied Carrie. "Have you lived here all your life?"

"Yes, I'm married and we have two little children. I work here and I have a waitress job on weekends - just so we can make ends meet."

"I'm doing waitress work too right now. But, when I get back home again I'm going to start working in a bank the first of July."

"I wish I could work in a bank. But I got married and the kids started coming. You got any kids?"

"Not yet," Carrie answered.

"Well, I better get going. I'll stop by tomorrow and change your linens. I'll bring pictures of my kids."

"Maybe you could tell me how to get to the library. I've got to find something to read or do."

"Sure. Go down this street two blocks and it's on this side of the street." Carrie found it easily. The librarian said she could check out two books, but she also had to put down Dean's name and camp address.

Dean had explained to Carrie how to take the camp bus. Wednesday he wanted her to come out and she could ride the bus back to town after the evening meal. Dean was proud when many of the men gave Carrie appreciative glances. She sat in the mess hall with Dean and Bill Bradford and chatted about happenings in Applegrove. Carrie told Bill she'd see Sally when she got back. Sally had really wanted to come but thought she better not leave the kids.

They were served a delicious meal of baked ham, mashed potatoes and all the trimmings. Carrie looked at Dean in surprise and said, "Dean, I think you're really spoiled. I don't cook this good at home."

"We haven't been married long enough for me to find out," Dean said. "Carrie, let's come out again Sunday for church and the noon meal."

"Is there a church here too?" Carrie asked.

Dean said, "We have one large building that all the denominations use at different times. The services are full. In times like this the men are taking their religion seriously."

Carrie told Dean about going to the library and her friend, the maid. Dean and Bill agreed that the people in Alexandria were friendly, whether they were black or white. Carrie, who never complained, admitted she could not get used to the hot and now humid weather after the rain. She thought she'd spend time in the library and stores to help pass the week.

Dean told Carrie, "As long as you're at the library, ask about the trees with the yellow and pink blooms."

Later in the week, she informed Dean that the librarian told her those were magnolia trees. One could be an evergreen or Southern Magnolia. The pink, she thought, was a deciduous tree called the Saucer Magnolia. Teasing Dean, Carrie said, "You mean I came all the way down here to teach you something."

They had spent their last Saturday night and Sunday morning awake, talking and planning for the future when Dean would get out of service. They took the bus out to camp for church services and the noon meal.

Carrie's train left at 4:00 p.m. They said their good-byes to each other at the hotel and headed out for the depot.

Carrie had told herself she wasn't going to cry, but she felt hot tears on her cheeks as the train pulled away. Seeing Carrie's tearful face through the window, Dean had a difficult time keeping his composure. With the taste of her mouth and the sweet scent of her perfume lingering, Dean turned slowly toward the bus stop, the one with the sign that read for Military Personnel Going to Camp.

STREETS OF HONOR

Chapter 14

Camp Claiborne, Louisiana
July 26, 1941

Dear Carrie:

Hi darling. I wish I were back in Minnesota. It's very hot down here. We could go to Lake Carlos and have a picnic like we did when I asked you to marry me. A wonderful memory for me is you sitting by the lake with the trees making a border around you and the sparkling water in the background.

The entire 34th Red Bull Division is going on an eight-week maneuver exercise. I'm not sure about the mail so if you don't hear from me you'll know we're tramping around the woods and swamps of Louisiana.

I forgot to tell you in my last letter, Charlie Nelson is here. He's assigned to the 164th North Dakota regiment, which is part of our Red Bull Division. He got a delayed enlistment so he could help plant the crops and sell his livestock. I don't see much of him because he's in training with his unit.

I'm putting in for a furlough. We should be back from maneuvers at the end of September. Wouldn't it be wonderful if I could get home for your birthday?

If you could send some more cookies I might get them when we're on maneuvers, but if not, I can always have them when we get back.

When I return, I'll call and let you know if I get a furlough. I'll be praying I can get a leave so I can come home.

Love, and I miss you so much,
Dean

The maneuvers started August 11, and ended Monday, September 29, 1941. During the maneuvers, the 34th Red Bull Division in their eagerness attacked without sufficient reconnaissance. Some platoons became lost because of faulty scouting. But overall they received high praise for their intelligence and ingenuity. The weather-beaten men came back from maneuvers tanned and hardened.

Dean hurried to Battalion Headquarters to check the bulletin board, which provided a list of those granted furloughs. Leave for him and several Company M soldiers had been approved, starting October first. Dean called Carrie as soon as he could that evening. "Carrie, Honey, I can't talk long, but I've got good news! I'm getting a weeks furlough. With travel time it will be thirteen days. Bill Bradford, George Grant, and Harry Schaefer also got leaves. We will leave for Applegrove Wednesday morning so I'll be home late Friday for your birthday."

Carrie, her voice full of tears, said, "That's wonderful, Dean, I can hardly wait to see you."

"It seems like longer than three months since you were here. I get tingles and shivers all over when I think about holding you again. I'm going to start packing right now."

"I'll be waiting for you, Dean."

Carrie sat gazing out the window, reflecting on the happy times they had spent together and anticipating the days ahead with Dean.

After he hung up, Dean realized he needed a birthday gift for Carrie, so he hurried to the Post Exchange.

The foursome rented a car from one of the soldiers and by switching off drivers and stopping only for gas and something to eat, they drove into Applegrove before midnight on October 3rd. Bill, who happened to be driving, left Dean off at his apartment. Not wanting to alarm Carrie, Dean rapped gently on the door. It flew open and Carrie dashed into his arms almost knocking him over. "Hey wait," Dean said, "How did you know it was me? It could have been a stranger."

"I could tell by your footsteps!" she exclaimed.

"Happy 21st Birthday, Sweetheart!"

"You're the best birthday present I've ever had.....ever."

Holding Carrie in one arm and his suitcase in the other, Dean stepped into the familiar apartment, kicked the door shut and closed out the world.

Seated at the kitchen table Saturday morning, Dean glanced at the wall calendar and mentally counted the days. "Let's plan our next seven days, Carrie, so we won't waste a moment of our time together. I have to leave for camp a week from today."

"I'll be working at the bank all week but I can have Friday afternoon off. There's a football game that afternoon."

"I'd like to get out to North Dakota. When you're working, I could drive out there one day, stay overnight and come back the next day."

"That's okay. I wouldn't mind if you went alone, except for the 'gone-at-night' part," she said putting a cup of coffee in front of him and slipping onto his lap.

"If you act like this I won't go anyplace," Dean said laughing and nuzzling her neck.

Carrie slipped off his lap and looked into his dark blue eyes. Holding his face in her hands, she asked, "Why don't we just loaf today? Tomorrow Mom wants us to come out for dinner after church. Is that all right?"

"That's great.....and, oh. I almost forgot your birthday present." Opening the package, Carrie's eyes widened at the sight of the square shaped bottle with a crystal stopper.

"I know you like perfume, Carrie. It's a small bottle, but all I can afford."

"It's wonderful, Dean, but Chanel Number Five? Wow!" she exclaimed. "I'll wear it for special occasions, but especially for you."

Sunday morning, Dean and Carrie went to the country

church where they were married. Many of the congregation knew Dean and were anxious to shake the hand of the tanned, husky soldier in uniform. Finally, the pair escaped and headed for the serenity of the farm.

Sophie and Carl were pleased to have Dean home. Dawn was shy with Dean and Pete proceeded to give detailed explanations of their football season. Joe, who was working as a hired man and lived with that family, came. Also his broken leg had healed. He told Dean that his draft status had changed. "I might be in the service too before long."

During the meal of Sophie's great cooking, Dean talked about army life, the recent maneuvers and his surprise at seeing Charlie Nelson. Carl spoke about the harvest and grain prices. Conversation, laughter and good food made for a warm, wonderful evening filled with gratitude for being together.

When they left, Dean and Carrie drove around the community. Dean, stopping for a moment by the now silent Armory, asked Carrie, "What would be happening to me if I hadn't joined the Guard? I suppose I would have been drafted and in service with men I didn't know." Carrie just squeezed his hand and said nothing. They were happy to return to the apartment, together.

Dean called out to North Dakota that evening. "Ma, I'll see you tomorrow. Carrie has to work and won't be coming." Ma was pleased that Dean had decided to come anyway, especially when he added, "I should be there around noon for dinner and I plan to stay overnight."

Dean left Applegrove early. When he drove into the familiar farmyard he noticed how the shelterbelt to the north of the farm had grown in the last few years. Ma hugged Dean as if she never thought she'd see him again; and Eric pumped his hand vigorously, clasping Dean's shoulder with the other hand.

Over their noon meal, Dean explained they were getting acquainted with their equipment and with each other. He related many small incidents that happened and how surprised he was to see Charlie. Dean said, "I'll have to call Charlie's folks. They will want to know how he's doing."

Ma detected a subtle change in her son: there was a certain maturity and sense of purpose that was new to her. She wished he could stay longer.

Eric shared her wishes and asked Dean, "Do you want to plow for awhile?" It was Eric's way of sharing his love of the farm with Dean. "The flax field is small and you could finish it this afternoon."

"I'd like that," Dean said, wishing that he could have been there to see the blue blossoms blowing in the wind like waves on a lake.

After an afternoon of plowing, Dean came in for supper and called Nelson's. He told them what he knew about Charlie.

That night Dean went to bed in familiar surroundings, his room full of North Dakota air. When he awakened early feeling refreshed, he lay in bed and realized how much his home meant to him and how Ma and Eric had helped him. He recalled the day of the auction sale when he bought the Studebaker.

Dean had come home from college for the sale. The morning of the sale, Eric said, "I plan to bid on a disc and a rake. I suggest you wait and let someone else open the bidding on the car, Dean."

"How much do you think it will go for?"

It's six-years-old. I wouldn't think it would go for over $300. I'll lend you that much, Dean, but that's it."

Dean's lips grew taut. He really wanted that car. Charlie came by and picked him up. Charlie was planning on farming on his own and had been buying up old machinery. On the drive, Dean studied the sale bill announcing the Andrud Auction for Saturday, May 13, 1939. "I see they have a truck and a pickup to be auctioned off too," he remarked.

Charlie thought aloud, "I'd like to bid on the

International tractor, but I better buy the cultivator instead."

They wandered around among the machinery while the household and shop items were being auctioned off. "Charlie, I don't think they're ever going to get to the machinery and vehicles," Dean said. "I'll buy us some bars and coffee. Ma's church circle is serving lunch."

Uncle Eric got the disc, but bidding went too high for the rake. Charlie had the winning bid for the cultivator. Of course, the Studebaker was the last item to be auctioned.

Dean listened carefully to the auctioneer's chant so he would know how to bid. He stood where the auctioneer would be sure to see him - on the inner ring of men in bib overalls, blue denim shirts and a variety of denim caps and straw hats. The bidding on the car opened at $100.00. Dean bid at $150.00, then a few times more, stopping at $225.00.

Dean was getting nervous. He took off his cap and rubbed the sweat off his forehead with the back of his hand. The price was getting close to $300. Dean made up his mind to keep bidding. The auctioneer continued to chant so Dean said, "250."

"You've already got the bid, son. I'm calling for $250.00."

To Dean's surprise, the two neighbors quit bidding. They were sympathetic toward Peter Andrud, but they didn't want to go any higher. Besides Peter had told them he had paid $600 for it new, so it wasn't only generosity toward Dean that made them stop.

"Sold to that blond haired young man for $225.00. You got a good buy, son."

Dean could hardly believe his good fortune. "Charlie, its only got 27,000 miles on it."

As he walked around the car with a pleased expression on his face, Dean continued to expound. "Look, the chrome is still shiny. No rust anywhere." Kicking a tire, he said, "Look at that rubber! The inside's dusty but I can clean it up."

Charlie was excited too. "If we get a trailer hitch, we could pull the cultivator to my place with your car, Dean."

"Oh, no. This is a going to be a town car. It's not going near fields or muddy roads."

"Then you'll have to buy another car, Dean.....one to visit us."

Dean was ready to go after noon lunch the next day. He was anxious to get back to Applegrove. Dean hugged his mother, who stood with tears running down her cheeks, wondering when and if she'd see Dean again.

With as much assurance as he could muster, Dean said, "I'll see you soon, Ma." Dean hugged Eric and shook his hand. In the rear-view mirror, Dean could see them waving as the Studebaker left the farmyard.

Dean arrived in Applegrove in time to pick up Carrie at the bank after work. At the apartment, Dean gathered Carrie into his arms and longingly kissed her as the soft feminine scent of the Chanel #5 perfume filled his senses. Hugging her close to him he said, "I missed you so much." Before she could answer he kissed her again and said, "I wish this moment would last forever."

Dean slept late Wednesday. After fixing himself breakfast, he looked up a couple of the friends that had been discharged because of age, one of them included Sgt. Christensen, who had rank over Sgt. Strong but worked in the Company Headquarters office. Another, Corporal Kline, had joined the Guard when he was older and had been in charge of a rifle platoon. Both men conjectured about being recalled. In both cases Dean sensed they wouldn't mind going back in as they missed the sense of camaraderie that came with being a part of the Red Bull Division.

Dean had time on his hands so the next day he visited with Bill, Bridget and Lucas. Sally was working and Bill was watching the children. Dean, on his hands and knees playing with Lucas, said, "I remember Lucas was born the day we played our first football game in Applegrove."

Bill, shaking his head, said, "It's hard to imagine that was over two years ago." Before Dean left, they agreed to leave at 5:00 a.m. Saturday. Bill said he would let the other two men know of their pre-determined plans.

Dean decided not to stop at school since most of the boys he coached had graduated and the new man had established himself as their teacher and coach. Friday afternoon at the football game, Dean said, "Let's sit way up in the bleachers, Carrie, and be one of the fans." Students and parents greeted him enthusiastically as they climbed to the top. They enjoyed watching Pete at quarterback. Both Dean and Carrie cheered wildly when it turned into an exciting game, Applegrove winning 21 to 13.

Friday evening, they drove to Willmar to shop and see a movie. Dean disliked the portion of the newsreels devoted to the war. This time was no exception as they watched the Nazi attacks on Russia and Hitler's plan to starve Leningrad. Dean wondered about his future in the army and with Carrie. He reached for her hand, gave it a squeeze and held it for the rest of the movie.

As the end of his furlough approached, Dean promised to make the most of the year on active duty in the military. Suddenly, he felt like his two friends, Sgt. Christensen and Corporal Kline, and missed the camaraderie of his buddies.

That night, when they returned to the apartment, they were both thoughtful and quiet.....not wanting to say, 'goodbye.' Dean said, "We're leaving at 5 a.m. in the morning so I'll slip out quietly. We'll eat breakfast later in the morning."

Dean woke up around 4 o'clock. Carrie laid with her back to him. Dean's arm rested on the curve of her hip. Pulling her close to him, he felt the softness of her skin. She woke and snuggled close.

"I lied to you," he said.

She raised her head and said, "What?"

"I said I would slip out quietly."

"I forgive you, Dean."

"I want to love you forever," he said, as he held her in a lover's embrace. He felt a tear from Carrie on his cheek and heard a muffled sob in her throat. Pulling her even closer he said, "Don't cry, darling. I'll call or write whenever I can. Soon enough, we'll be together again."

STREETS OF HONOR

Chapter 15

For Thanksgiving Day, the cooks had prepared a turkey dinner with all the trimmings. Captain Monson and his wife Phyllis were invited as guests. Sgt. Strong, standing by the mess hall door, saw Dean come in. He said, "Now that you've made Private First Class you can sit next to Mrs. Monson."

Dean found her to be a charming and vivacious person. She laughed when Dean told her about Carrie's uncle who wouldn't accept the one week earlier Thanksgiving date. They both laughed when she said, "The president did that to help business, but Congress ruled that after this year, Thanksgiving would be the fourth Thursday. Your wife's uncle was right after all."

After Thanksgiving, word came from Headquarters that the men who played in the Company band were to ship their instruments back home. This increased the growing anxiety as to what was planned for the regiment.

At church on Sunday morning, one of the corporals from Headquarters came in and spoke to the chaplain in a hushed tone. Dean watched as the chaplain's face turned pale. He then stood up and announced to the men, "I have just received the news that the Japanese attacked Pearl Harbor. The United States Fleet has been devastated and there are many casualties."

The silence of the church was broken as the reality of the words set in. Shock and disbelief were followed by fury. Some men jumped to their feet and left the church. Others sat quietly as if they had anticipated involvement in the war-torn world. Dean's thoughts turned to Carrie. What would become of their plans for the future?

The service ended quickly and the remaining men left to

find radios. The radio announcer reported, " Japanese torpedo bombers have attacked eight battleships on 'Battleship Row' in Pearl Harbor near Honolulu, Hawaii and approximately one hundred cruisers and destroyers in or near the harbor have been damaged. Wheeler and Hickman airfields were also attacked, and shore-based navy and army aircraft have been destroyed."

Dean listened to President Roosevelt addressing Congress and the Supreme Court. "Yesterday, December 7, 1941, is a date which will live in infamy. We will gain the inevitable triumph, so help us God." The next few days the radio carried the news of a Declaration of War on Japan and on the l lth of December, American leaders voted to declare war on Japan's Axis partners, Germany and Italy.

Dean wondered what this would mean for Company M? He saw a renewed purpose and morale rising to a new high. The men were energized; even those who had been discontented and threatening to go AWOL (Absent Without Leave) had changed their tune.

The 34th Red Bull Division was given orders to protect the Gulf of Mexico from sabotage. Dean's Third Battalion was assigned to guard the Port of Texas City, Texas. Other battalions would protect the coasts of Louisiana and Florida.

Dean learned that Charlie's North Dakota, 164th Infantry Regiment had orders to be detached from the Red Bull Division and be sent to San Francisco. Dean hurried over to Charlie's tent and found him packing. Dean said, "It appears we won't be going to war together."

"The rumor is we're being sent to fight the Japanese. This is what we're training for, Dean, but it does scare a person," Charlie said.

"I'll bet you five dollars, Charlie, if the Red Bull Division is sent to Europe, we can finish the Germans faster than you can finish the Japanese."

Charlie scoffed, "It's a bet, but who's going to hold the money?"

"Why don't we meet in North Dakota and settle up after the war?"

The two friends shook hands, then embraced. Dean, overcome with emotion, quickly left the tent, saying he had to get packing too. Dean returned to his tent and took in the activity going on around him.

The next day, the mail brought a letter from Carrie, and Ma's letter soon followed.

Applegrove, Mn.
December 7, 1941

Dear Dean:

This morning, Pa called me with the news about the attack on Pearl Harbor. I wasn't listening to the radio, so I didn't know anything about it. I'm so scared, Dean. The first thing I did was to get dressed and go to church and pray for you and for our country.

I've been listening to the news reports all day and it sounds bad. I have to admit that I'm glad that you aren't over there and I hope you don't have to go.

One of the ladies at church has a son on the Battleship Arizona in Pearl Harbor and she is worried about him. I wonder if she has heard from him yet.

Write me or call and let me know what is happening.

I miss you, worry about you and want to hold you.

I love you more than anything. Please take care, my darling.

Carrie

Auburn, North Dakota
December 9, 1941

Dear Dean:

We are worried about you. Pearl Harbor was such a shock. So many men and ships lost.

Eric and I are worried about our nephew in Norway, too. We heard he had joined a resistance movement against the Germans after Norway was invaded last year. We haven't had news from our relatives in Oslo for a long time.

I am sending you some Christmas treats - lefse and fattigmand. It will be after Christmas before you get them, but they still should be all right.

I hope you don't have to fight in the war.

Skriv snart.   *Love,*

         Ma and Eric

Dean smiled, remembering the morning before Christmas when he was home from college. He heard Ma reciting as he came into the kitchen for breakfast,

"Bake, bake kake! Hvem skal kaka smake?
Det skal far, og det skal mor, vesle soster, store bror."

When Ma smiled and lapsed into Norwegian, Dean knew something special was happening.

"Do you know what I said, Dean?" Ma enjoyed quizzing Dean on his Norwegian.

"Something about who'll taste the cake, father, mother, sister, brother?"

"Yes, I'm going to send some fattigmand and some krum kake with you to college."

           Texas City, Texas
           December 17, 1941

Dear Carrie:

I miss you so much. It will be different to be away from you and home this Christmas. I won't be sending any Christmas presents home and you shouldn't send me any either.

The Army didn't waste any time in bringing us here. We are warm and dry as we've been quartered in warehouses, railroad roundhouses and shacks.

We might be back in Camp Claiborne after New Years. Guard duty is keeping us busy but many of us feel nostalgic and a little homesick. We're still angry about the sneak attack on Pearl Harbor. I don't think I'll do much celebrating this year.

The Texans are real friendly and have invited soldiers to their homes after church services in town and are inviting us for Christmas dinner.

Thanks for all your letters. It makes me so happy when I get one from you.

I Love You,
Dean

Dean was right. After New Years they were loaded on trucks for the return trip to Camp Claiborne. When they were given a new mailing address, APO, New York, it meant only one thing; they might be scheduled for overseas duty. This premonition increased when they were issued mittens, hoods and other winter clothing. The winter gear was appreciated when on January 6th, the regiment boarded Pullman cars. Three days later they arrived at Fort Dix, New Jersey.

Fort Dix, New Jersey
January 12, 1942

Dear Carrie:

I'm getting farther and farther away from you. I'm not sure for how long we'll be here. You will have to use the APO address when you write now.

The temperature is below zero and about sixty degrees colder than Camp Claiborne, but more like what we're used to back home. Remember how cold it was when our troop train left Applegrove? Next month it will be a year. If it weren't for this war, our year of duty would be over.

With the passing of each day, I love you more and more. I've saved all your letters. I've got quite a bunch, but I'm afraid I can't keep them much longer. I might send them all back to you. It depends on where we go.

We traveled through quite a few states on our way here. I plan to do some sightseeing around here and in New York, If Headquarters issues us passes.

The scuttlebutt around the Fort is the Red Bull Division performed so well during the Louisiana Maneuvers that it will be the first US Division to leave for Europe.

Thank you for the cookies. Ma sent some Norwegian treats too.

I miss you and send you my love.

Dean

The day after mailing his letter to Carrie, Dean received a letter from her and retreated to the squad tent to open it.

Applegrove, Mn.
January 8, 1942

Dear Dean:

Our letters may be passing each other but I wanted to let you know the exciting news.

You're going to be a father!!

Dr. Midthune thinks the birth will be around the 4th of July. I must've gotten pregnant when you were home on leave during my birthday. I feel fine and will work until the baby's due.

I'm anxious for you to come home safely. I'm not going to tell your mother and Eric about the baby. You can write to them.

I wait for the mail and your letters. When you call, I can tell you more.

I Love You,
Carrie

Fort Dix, New Jersey
January 16, 1942

Dear Carrie:

I had to hurry and write to you again. I'm so happy to hear we're going to have a baby! I bragged so much, some of the guys told me to shut up.

It was nice hearing your voice when I called you, even though the connection was poor. You take it easy now and don't do any heavy work. I wish I were there to help you.

Like I told you on the phone, you'll have to name this one and I'll name the next.

Not too much is new here. We've been getting lots of different training and the officers impress on us how important this is.

I love you and want to hold you close to me.

Love,

Dean

Toward the end of January, speculation ended when news reports said General Hartle, the Red Bull Division commander, had arrived in Ireland with regimental troops to plan for the remainder of the Red Bull Division to come to Ireland.

Dean read in the Fort Dix military newsletter that a guardsman from Hutchinson, Minnesota, represented the Thirty Fourth Red Bull Division as the first soldier of the American Expeditionary Forces to set foot on foreign soil in the European Theater.

Company M realized something important was happening when, February first, orders came down promoting Captain Monson to Major. He endeared himself to the men when a truck brought a group of 90-day-wonder second lieutenants. When they came up to the head of the company, Major Monson told them, "If you think you know more than my troops, you can take your own bags to your tent."

Dean's 135th Regiment spent the next three months in training and expectantly waiting for orders to leave for Ireland.

Fort Dix, New Jersey
April 26, 1942

Dear Carrie:

I hope you are feeling okay. Please do what the doctor says.

This is the last letter that you'll get from me written 'stateside'. Company M's regiment, the 135th, is the only regiment of the Red Bull Division left here at Fort Dix. The other two regiments are in Ireland so it's no secret that we'll be going there too.

The 'old boys', twenty-eight years or older, were recalled and joined our outfit this month. Maybe you remember me telling you about visiting Sgt. Christensen and Corporal Kline when I was home on leave. We've added new recruits and our regiment is now up to full strength.

By the time you get this letter, I will have called you. I want to hear your voice again and want to tell you how much I love you.

Love,
Dean

The 135th Regiment left Fort Dix by rail on April 29, 1942, for New York harbor and boarded the *Aquitania*, a converted British ocean liner that had carried troops during the First World War and now could transport six thousand men.

Seeing the Statue of Liberty emerge from the mist, Dean felt a chill. He would, he thought, die for his country in order to protect its freedom. But on the other hand the thought of Carrie holding their baby made him want to be with her. The conflicting emotions left him unsettled. He hurried down the stairwell to his bunk. He wanted to live to be with Carrie again.

Protected by a convoy of destroyers and led by the

battleship, *New York*, the ship sailed across the North Atlantic to Belfast, Ireland. After the trip of twelve days, the big ship couldn't dock in the shallow water. The men were transferred to coastal steamers. On the night of May 12, 1942, they disembarked at Londonderry, Ireland.

The mail call brought a letter from Carrie. Dean especially appreciated the end of her letter:

I'm sending you this to your APO address. Maybe you'll get it soon after you get to Ireland.

I went to the doctor today. Dr. Midthune said everything is all right and there is a strong heartbeat. He's guessing it will be a boy. He's usually right.

I'm getting my exercise helping Mom with the garden on the farm. We've been encouraged to plant 'Victory Gardens.' Mom and I planted a bigger garden. We should be able to can quite a bit this fall.

Everything is fine. We are busy at work and time goes by fast, but I miss you terribly.

Love you more than ever,
Carrie

Dean reported to Bill, "Carrie said that Dr. Midthune says it's going to be a boy. You told me once he's never wrong. I hope so. I would like to have a boy and play ball with him."

Camp Cranmore, Ireland
May 14, 1942

Dear Carrie:

I got your letter. It was so nice to get mail so soon. It would be nice to have a son; but little girls are nice too. Especially if ours is like you. I'm glad you're getting exercise and fresh air working in the garden. I never liked to pull weeds.

We're glad to be on solid ground again. We were on the

ship for twelve days and I never got seasick.

Ireland is an Emerald green island. It is a romantic place and I wish we could be here together.

Our billets are small-corrugated steel huts. I had a smell of North Dakota threshing when we were issued a mattress cover and had to fill it from a straw pile. It felt better than the bare cot.

They must be expecting us to stay awhile. I've never seen such a monstrous pile of coal; but, we were issued one bucket daily for each hut.

Our camp is on the estate of the Montague family. The little farms around the area are cut up into small fields surrounded with hedgerows so training is a real problem. Farming here is different. I look forward to telling Carl about it.

Be sure and write and let me know how things are going. I'll pray for you.

If I only wrote I love you, my letters couldn't be censored. I love you.

       Love,
       Dean

      Brookeborough, Ireland
      June 6, 1942

Dear Carrie:

How's the future little momma? It's getting closer to the time. I wish I could see you and hold you, and help you.

We've moved again. This estate is much larger and battle training has gotten tougher. We've been working with the British and the Irish Home Guard.

The Irish brogue is nice to listen to, but the troops are having a difficult time with shillings, pounds, etc.

If you were listening to NBC radio, our regimental swing outfit, "Ambassadors of Swing", played over the Trans-Atlantic short wave program. Many of the men in Company M are good singers and word of our expertise has spread throughout the Battalion.

I hope you like the military's new V - mail. A picture is taken of a letter and put on this smaller, lighter paper. It's not as easy to read after all the photography is done. Keep writing.

I miss you. I look at your picture in my wallet when I get lonesome.

Love,

Dean

The Division became involved in maneuvers that took them away from camp for several weeks. When Dean returned to camp, he was pleased to get one letter from Carrie and another from his friend, Charlie. He anxiously opened the letter from Carrie.

STREETS OF HONOR

Chapter 16

Applegrove, Minnesota
July 7, 1942

Dear Dean:

You're a father!! Dr. Midthune was right. It's a boy. Spencer Dean Brandum was born Tuesday, July 7, weighed 7 lbs. 5 oz. and is the cutest little baby. He has blond hair too.

I admire Winston Churchill and one of his middle names is Spencer. I like that name so I chose it for our son. I hope that's okay with you.

I started having labor pains after I came home from work on Monday. They kept on all evening and when they got worse I called Mom and she took me to the hospital in Benton. He was born a little after five a. m. this morning.

Labor was a lot more painful than I thought it was going to be. I kept wishing you were here to hold my hand.

I want to get this out in today's mail. I will write more later.

Love you so much,
Carrie and Spencer

Dean dashed out of the tent with Carrie's letter in hand. When he heard Bill and a few of the others had gone off the camp to a nearby pub, he hurried over. "I'm buying a round fellows! I've got a son. Carrie says he's so cute. He must look like me." After some good-natured kidding, one of the men said, "Now you've got someone else to fight for." That quieted the boisterous celebration, but only momentarily.

Only later when he was back in his tent did Dean remember the letter from Charlie that he had tucked away in his pocket. He quickly opened it, eager to find out what had happened to his good friend.

APO San Francisco
July 1, 1942

Dear Dean:

My mom got your APO address from your mom. I can't write too much other than to let you know we have been in New Caledonia since January. Our regiment was merged with a regiment from Illinois and one from Massachusetts to form the Americal Division. They created the name for the Division by combining parts of America and New Caledonia.

Our insignia is four stars on a bright blue background in the form of a Southern Cross Constellation indicating the Southern Hemisphere. Maybe you'll read about us in The Stars and Stripes.

I won't be able to write anymore but I intend to collect on that bet!

Your friend,
Charlie

Before Dean had a chance to answer either letter, he got another one from Carrie.

Applegrove, Minnesota
July 10, 1942

Dear Dean:

Spencer and I are getting ready to go home from the hospital. I thought I better write you because it might get hectic when we go home. He's been a good baby, but he has to eat every four hours, so my sleep is always interrupted. The news is I'm taking three months off from the bank to be with our baby. After that I'll put him on the bottle. Mom has been a great help. There's a lot I have to learn about taking care of babies.

Mr. Morrison said when I come back to work at the bank, I'm going to be a receptionist rather than working in the bookkeeping section. The position opened and he wanted someone that knows the people in Applegrove. It's fine with me as the position is more flexible and will be better for me with the baby.

Have you been drinking a lot of coffee? Coffee is being rationed here. I heard it is being sent to the soldiers for their morale. Gas, rubber, and sugar are also being rationed. With the bigger family, Mom gets a larger sugar allowance. She gives some to Aunt Clara and Uncle Ray's as it's just the two of them. Rubber is needed for the defense plants. Mom says she's willing to give up her girdle. After having Spencer, I should use it. Ha.

Thank you for your letters. I wish you could stay in Ireland. It sounds like such a nice place. Write soon.

I'll write more later. Right now I'm really tired. I'm not used to being a momma.

Love You,
Carrie and Spencer

Sometimes, Carrie's letters came in a bunch and Dean sat and reread them many times. He hadn't realized the amount of work and time involved in taking care of a baby until Carrie described this to him. The joy of having a son offset his sadness of not being with her when Spencer was born.

Brookeborough, Ireland
August 16, 1942

Dear Carrie:

Thank you for all your letters. I'm so happy and proud to be a father. I will always be disappointed that I was not with you by your side, holding your hand and helping you. Perhaps your pain would have been easier. I hope it won't ever happen this way again.

Spencer is a fine name and I want to be there to watch him grow. I think I'll call him Spence. I would have liked to hold him when he's a baby. You'll have to buy him a ball.

I'm glad you're not going back to work at the bank right away. I want you to take it easy. I'll keep sending you most of my pay, as I don't need much money over here.

We've been out on field exercises and some long hikes and I haven't been able to write. The heather is in bloom. It is pretty and it makes me homesick for the fields of flax.

It's quiet here. I'll write again soon.

I love you, I love you, I love you. Give little Spence a hug from his daddy.

> *Love,*
> *Dean*

The first order that brought the reality of war to Dean came on October 18. Dean's platoon from Company M and Companies I, K, and L were detached from the Regiment for special training for the invasion of Africa. The rest of the Regiment remained in Ireland. Staff Sergeant Bruce Strong volunteered along with Corporal Russell Wagner.

Sgt. Strong told Bill, "You're the most experienced with the machine guns and I'd like you to go."

Bill responded, "Okay, I'll go."

Dean had not intended to go on this mission but quickly changed his mind. "If you fellows are going then I will too."

Sgt. Strong, pleased, said, "Our Company M platoon really can use you men."

No administrative personnel were included, so the word around camp was that this outfit was selected for immediate combat duty. The rest of the Battalion would remain in Ireland. Major Monson had taken over the command of the Third Battalion in June and was promoted to Lt. Colonel in early August. Dean realized that Company M, Applegrove, Minnesota, might soon experience their first casualties of the war.

At their briefing, the men learned they would be part of

the larger amphibious landings on the shores of Africa known by the code name, Operation Torch. Their special operation was to attack the port of Algiers. Other units would attack the ports of Casablanca and Oran.

Seventeen men from Company M's platoon were included in the attacking force of six hundred troops, American and some British; it was an American operation. They were sent to Belfast to receive special training. The men sailed from Belfast, Ireland, past the Straits of Gibraltar, to Algiers, Africa.

'Operation Torch' began on November 6 when the six hundred troops were divided between the two British destroyers, the *HMS Broke* and the *HMS Malcom*. Dean, Bill, Russell Wagner and Sgt. Strong were assigned to the *HMS Broke*. (Map 1).

Captain Fancourt, in charge of the men when aboard the *Broke*, briefed the men. "Our orders are to launch an assault on the harbor here at Algiers and secure the port. We have to go ashore and protect docks and installations from sabotage; the port will be used to unload men, guns, tanks and equipment. There's a large boom across the entrance that has to be broken."

Sgt. Strong asked, "How are we going to do that?"

The captain replied, "Our ship's commander told me the compartments behind the bow are filled with concrete and have a steel spike welded to the bow to ram the boom. After the ship's inside the port, the assault party will be unloaded."

"Sir, are we doing this alone?" Sgt. Strong asked.

Captain Fancourt explained, "No, your Red Bull Division's, 168th Infantry Regiment along with British forces are assault parties landing west of Algiers at the beaches coded Beer Green, White and Red. They will advance on the port."

Colonel Blacket, who was in charge of the operation once ashore, received a message at 0220 hours that the beach landings of the combat teams were successful and the ships were to attack the harbor. When they approached the harbor, the lights of Algeria went out; searchlights picked up the two

158

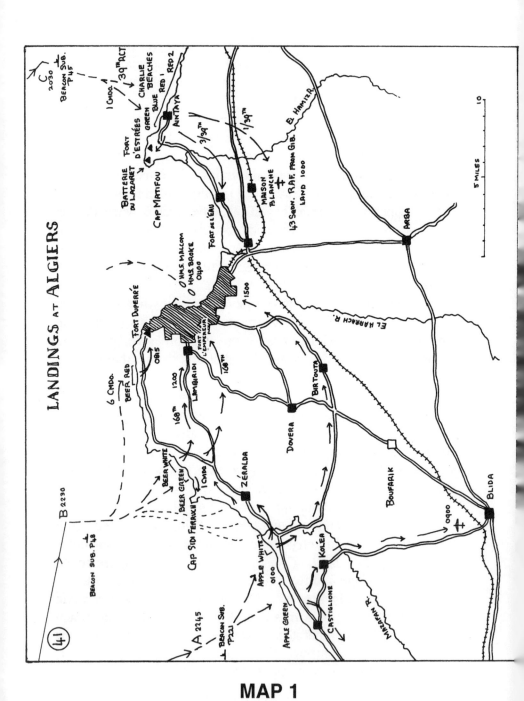

MAP 1

From The Campaign for North Africa by Jack Coggins, p. 89

ships right away, and heavy guns on shore opened fire.

All personnel were ordered below decks. Crowded together below, the men were uneasy as they heard the artillery fire from shore and the rounds echoing around the ship.

"Who's in charge of the port?" Dean leaned over and hollered the question to Sgt. Strong over the noise of the shore artillery and ship's engines.

"The French."

"I thought they were on our side."

Sgt. Strong moved closer to Dean and said, "There's so much political unrest here that the French forces don't know who to support."

Russell Wagner, the former history teacher, said, "It's the French loyal to the German Vichy government in control of France that we're now fighting. We helped liberate them in the Great War of 1914, and now they are firing at us when we want to do it again."

Because of the blinding searchlights and the smoke of the artillery, the ships missed the entrance to the harbor twice. On the third try the *Malcom* was heavily hit. A fire started in the boiler room when the ammunition exploded. She limped seaward, unable to give the operation any more assistance.

It was now about 0500 hours and in the early dawn, the British commander of the *HMS Broke* could see the channel entrance. Ordering full speed ahead, the commander directed the ship to ram the boom of heavy timbers. Dean heard the sound of snapping wood above the noise of battle as the ship entered the harbor. The ship's deck guns quickly silenced the machine gun and rifle fire from the dock. Dean and his fellow platoon members, shaken by the bombardment, disembarked as quickly as they could. Their ears were still ringing from the deafening roar of the shore artillery. The smoke of the artillery and the acrid smell of its ammunition hung heavy in the stagnant, morning air.

Sgt. Strong ordered, "Bill, you stay here by the dock, set

up your machine gun and protect our escape route and the ship. Dean, Russell and the rest of you men come with me. We'll follow Colonel Blacket's orders." The troops moved along the street next to the dock. The bullets from small arms and automatic weapons fire whined noisily as they ricocheted off the buildings.

Meanwhile the *HMS Broke* came under heavy artillery fire from the coastal defense guns. Bill, guarding the dock with his machine gun, heard the whine of the incoming shells and the resounding 'whump'. The ship's commander turned his vessel around for a quick exit and for protection moved behind merchant ships docked in the port. He allowed space on the dock for the troops that would be returning to quickly come aboard.

The ship continued to suffer hits from the mobile artillery. The ship's commander sounded the recall signal. Bill waited in vain by the dock for the men from his platoon to return. A ship's ensign hollered at him and, at the last minute, he reluctantly carried his weapon aboard. Bill and approximately sixty of the American soldiers boarded her.

The ship had a damaged propeller, but by zigzagging was able to get out of range and clear the harbor. Bill stood anxiously at the rail wondering what happened to his friends as he listened to the small arms fire and the crackle of machine guns.

A British seaman brought him out of his stupor. "Hey Yank, help us plug some holes or we're all going to have to swim." Bill, who had never learned to swim, quickly moved to help. Their frantic efforts to plug the leaks and throw the depth charges overboard took his mind away from Dean and the battle taking place on shore.

Dean's platoon and the troops under attack on shore heard the siren recall above the noise of the gunfire. Colonel Blacket refused to let the men go.

"I can't subject you men to the bombardment of the

ship. With no other hope for withdrawal, we'll have to stay and fight. Those combat teams that landed on the beaches should be near the city. Sgt. Strong, take some men and another sergeant with you and organize the outer perimeter so no one can get in hand grenade range. The rest of you men, we'll set up a defense around these piles of sand, wood, and baled straw."

As the sergeants led the men to the outer perimeter and crossed an intersection, Russell Wagner's buddy, Doug Johnson, fell wounded. Russell, seeing this, quickly left the main defense and dragged his buddy to safety. Learning that he would be all right, Russell started back. Dean watched in horror as the machine gun bullets sprayed around Russell. Just when he reached the protection of the straw bales, the bullets struck him. His arms flew upward, his body arched, his rifle clattering to the street.

Dean pulled Russell's lifeless form into the protected enclosure. He sat by the crumpled body, crying. Russell was the first teacher he met in Applegrove. Russell was the friend who was always available whenever Dean needed someone. Russell was the calm influence. Knowing that the others relied on him, Dean crept to his position.

Dean stared down the street. Suddenly he yelled at Colonel Blacket, "Sir, there's three tanks coming." A shell from one of the tanks exploded causing more casualties and setting the straw bales on fire. Black smoke covered the area.

Colonel Blacket, crouching behind the protective wooden barrier, was alarmed when two more tanks covered the other openings and would annihilate his men. Hearing no firing from the land combat teams, he pulled out his white handkerchief and told Dean, "Put this on the end of your rifle and wave it in their direction. We'll have to surrender."

The survivors of the landing party were lined up in the street and then disarmed. The dead and wounded were put in vehicles and taken away. Dean watched carefully, noting that Russell's body was moved safely with the other dead. During the next two days, the prisoners were treated well by the French. Some of the French officers supported the operation and others, loyal to the Vichy government, showed by their treatment of the prisoners they were definitely against them.

Sgt. Strong told Dean, "At the debriefing with the officers, I learned Colonel Blacket is recommending Russell for a Distinguished Service Cross for his heroic actions. The Colonel said he didn't want to surrender, but this way we can fight our main enemy, the Germans, later."

Dean replied, "It's sad. Russell was my friend, but I knew so little about him. I know he was unmarried and came from a small town near Brainerd. He was always so good to help me at school." Dean's thoughts then turned to Bill, who was dealing with his own troubles.

Aboard the struggling *HMS Broke*, Bill felt the ship list as it took on more water. Fortunately the *HMS Zetland*, located outside the harbor, took the ship in tow. Captain Fancourt told the men, "We're going to have to transfer to the *Zetland* and take the wounded with us."

On the afternoon of November 9, Captain Fancourt told the men, "You're going to be put ashore on White Beach, about twenty miles west of Algiers."

The lieutenants told their men, "Our orders are to make a forced march to Algiers and make contact with the rest of the battalion. We've been informed the French captured some of the men that landed in the port. Negotiations are being held to secure their release."

Marching at a rapid pace, Bill and the troops reached Algiers late that day. As they approached Battalion headquarters, the captive Americans were released. The French officers in charge had learned an agreement had been reached to cease-fire. Dean saw Bill's group arriving. As soon as Bill's group got permission, Bill and the others hurried over.

Shaking hands with one and hugging another, Dean was happy to see his buddies again. "How did they treat you?" Bill asked Dean.

"All right. They even gave us Algerian wine."

Looking around, Bill asked, "Where's Russell?"

Dean filled Bill in on the death of their friend and the events of the past four days.

Sgt. Strong said, "We had fourteen others killed and thirty-three wounded. It was a rough way to start the war."

"Is there any other way?" Bill asked. The three friends were quiet then, each lost in his own thoughts and feelings of grief.

The unconditional surrender of the French forces to the Allies was completed on November 10, 1942. The French resistance to the American invasion would prove costly in American and British lives. The Germans were given time to reinforce their troops in Africa.

The heartfelt sorrow Dean and the others in the company experienced would follow them and the rest of the Red Bull Division as they fought the Germans deep into Africa.

STREETS OF HONOR

Chapter 17

Algeria, North Africa
November 15, 1942

Dear Carrie:

Hi, darling. Finally I have Sunday off with time to write you.

Thank you for your letters. The mail finally caught up with us. I really appreciate the picture of you and Spence. I carry it on me all the time. Thankfully, he's starting to look more like you. He's a cute little fellow!

We've had our first combat action with of all people - the French, who were collaborating with the Germans. You perhaps know about Russell Wagner and some of the other casualties from Company M. I miss Russell very much and it's been difficult to get over his death. I don't know how much of my letters get by the censor but I want to let you know how I am.

Things have quieted down so we shouldn't see any more action for awhile. The French have agreed to help fight the Germans. We're doing police duty and protecting the Allied headquarters here.

This will be our second Christmas apart! I wish the war were over. I want to come home to you and Spence.

Remember the day we went on the picnic and I got up enough nerve to ask you to marry me? I relive and treasure all my memories of our times together.

Love you,
Dean

Sitting in the mess tent after supper one evening in late

November, Dean asked Sgt. Strong, "When are we going to see the rest of our regiment and the Red Bull Division?"

Putting down his fork, Bruce replied, "Headquarters said some of the Division, including our regiment, is shipping out of Liverpool and sailing with a convoy to Africa. The rest of the Division will be coming later in December."

"Then what'll happen?" Dean asked.

"We'll have to wait and see." Sgt. Strong seemed lost in thought as he picked up his fork. "I hear we'll be chasing the 'Desert Fox'."

Dean, about to take a sip of coffee, set his cup down and stared at Bruce. "You mean they have fox over here in Africa?"

Bruce laughed loudly. "You haven't heard of German Field Marshall Erwin Rommel, the commander of the German Panzer units?"

"No, in my spare time, I've been catching up on the Applegrove news."

Bill, who had been half-heartedly listening to the conversation asked, "What's a panzer?"

Setting down his fork again, Bruce answered patiently, "The panzer is a German armored vehicle, a tank. The British have been fighting the Germans in North Africa and Rommel, the Desert Fox, and the Africa Korps since early '41. I read in an Irish newspaper before we left that it's up and down or back and forth for Rommel and the British. One wins some territory then the other counterattacks and takes it back."

"Where are they now?" Dean asked.

"About five months ago, Rommel went sixty miles into Egypt. But when British General Montgomery took over, the British defeated the Axis at El Alamein. Rommel was ill and in Germany recuperating at that time. Hitler sent him back to Africa even though he was still sick. Rommel's been withdrawing west towards Tripoli for the last three weeks."

"We don't have to worry about him then," Dean said relaxing.

Sgt Strong smiled slightly. "Oh, yes we do. The officers are talking that we're part of the plan to attack him from the west to push the Germans and Italians out of North Africa."

Dean took another swallow of coffee, "I'm glad we have 'Ike' as our general." General Dwight Eisenhower, affectionately referred to by the men as "Ike" had led the American task force landing in North Africa on November 8.

The next few months, the platoon was kept busy policing the various French factions and dealing with the continued unrest among the Arabs, French and Jews. Much of the fighting was due to political differences. Others battles were fought because of ethnic and religious differences.

Since January 9, 1943, the widely scattered troops of the Red Bull had been gradually assembling in the vicinity of Tlemcen, an historical town in Western Algeria. The soldiers of the 34th Red Bull Division knew they would soon have to face their main foe - the Germans. That day arrived on February 2, 1943, when the Division departed on the long journey of nearly a thousand miles to the east, the place where the Allied forces were positioning for the campaign to take Tunisia.

During the first part of the journey, Dean's regiment traveled through mountain ranges sparsely inhabited by Arabs. Nearing the Tunisian border, the convoy traveled at night in order to avoid the German air attacks. The moonlight, filtering into the trucks, illuminated the determination written on their quiet faces.

After having been briefed by the officers, Sgt. Strong told the men they would relieve a French infantry unit holding a defensive position near the town of Pinchon.

From the bivouac staging area, Dean's platoon was sent up front to the French positions. Dean was stunned at the sight of the French in their old, dirty uniforms. They had been fighting valiantly, with their artillery on old-fashioned wooden carriages drawn by horses, and with outdated weapons and equipment.

Wiggling his warm, dry toes, Dean commented to Bill, "Those are some tough soldiers. They don't even have socks in their boots." Their appearance didn't matter to Dean and the rest of the platoon, who appreciated their advice. In fact, they pointed out some enemy locations and even went on patrol with them.

Pinchon overlooked a wide valley. German soldiers were spotted on the opposite ridge. As the artillery from both sides dueled, Dean and the platoon dug gun pits, fox holes, and awaited further orders.

As the shells from the opposing armies screamed overhead, Bill asked Dean, "Have you figured out which is incoming or outgoing?"

Dean, from the safety of his rocky foxhole, exclaimed, "It's the one I won't hear that bothers me!"

One of the new battalion lieutenants hadn't figured out the difference between the incoming or outgoing shells, and in his haste to protect himself jumped in the garbage pit. The troops nearest him, including Bill, had a good laugh over that. Bill, in fact was still laughing uncontrollably when he tried to tell Dean. When Bill finished the story, Dean chuckled and said, "You'll have to write home about that one."

Dean's battalion was pinned down occasionally by the artillery fire and the German Stuka airplanes that harassed the troops. The .50 caliber air-cooled machine gun had been dug in adjacent to one of the foxholes. One morning before the sun came up, Dean was changing the guards on the gun when a plane came diving for their position. Dean quickly swung the gun around and fired. Shiny red tracers lit up the already red morning sky. Suddenly the plane veered crazily, then plunged into the ground.

Dean felt himself being pulled out of the gun emplacement and hugged and slapped by Colonel Monson and Lieutenant Marsh. They had been watching the plane approach their position. Bruce, at the sergeants' meeting at headquarters, heard about the incident. "Dean, the Colonel is putting you up for Corporal on the next promotion roster. Congratulations!"

The 168th Regiment, one of the infantry regiments of the Red Bull Division, was assigned to defend Faid Pass a few miles from Dean's 135th Regiment. With only the old General Grant tanks against the well-armored Panzer unit, the regiment was encircled by the enemy.

Sgt. Strong told Dean, "Many of them were forced to surrender. I lost some of my good friends." The entire Division felt the loss of their comrades when the 168th had 1,628 men killed, wounded or captured.

The defensive position of Dean's battalion was also fragile. In mid-February, Colonel Monson told the platoon leaders, "We have to abandon this position and move back to the west thirty miles and form a defensive line at Sbiba." The battalion formed up columns and moved out rapidly at dusk on the night of February 16, 1943.

The men heard the clank of German tanks. Sensing they were about to be caught in a trap, they increased their already rapid pace. Suddenly, Sgt. Strong quietly motioned for everyone to get off the road and into the ditch. The ping, ping of ricocheting bullets from the road where they had been, whistled over their heads. The platoon crawled ahead. Dean felt sweat running down his chest despite the cold February night as fear gripped the men. He failed to notice the rocks from the ditch digging into his arms as he crawled along. Bile from his stomach worked its way up into his mouth. Finally they were able to return to the road. When asked about his observation that had saved many lives, Bruce responded, "I don't know. I just had a hunch that we should get off the road."

The noise from the rear stopped. Just before dawn the men were able to rest at their destination, a rocky mountainside near Sbiba. As the morning sun warmed them, they thanked God to have survived the night.

A few days later, Dean and Bill were sitting with their backs to a boulder eating a meal of C-rations. Between mouthfuls of hash, Dean told Bill, "One good thing about this position is we're getting fed. I never thought I'd like C-ration hash again. I hated British kidney and mutton stew!" Dean took a sip of GI coffee adding, "I did learn to like British tea. It tasted good when it was hot."

The next order for the Red Bull Division was to open the pass at Fondouk el Aouoreb. As they hurried across the flats to the assault line, Dean asked Sgt. Strong, "What are we getting into?"

Bruce explained, "Up ahead at the village of Foundouk, held by German, Italian and Arab troops, the pass is only about 1000 yards wide with a shallow river winding through it. We have to open the pass for the British Armored Division." (Map 2).

Things went well until the crossfire from machine gun, mortars and artillery killed some men from the 3rd Battalion, stopping the attack about 2:00 p.m.. After three days of small infantry attacks, General Ryder called the operation off and the weary troops withdrew on April 1st and 2nd.

A week after their first attack, General Ryder told his officers, "We're to attack Fondouk from the south, while the British infantry will be attacking Hill 290 and eventually Fondouk from the north." He added, "The British General Crocker is in charge and thinks that Hill 290 is not well defended but, if it is, we can expect fire on our exposed northern flank"

Dean thought, the 34th Red Bull Division was being committed to a faulty plan, which threatened failure. The 1st Battalion of the 135th, now lead by Colonel Monson, was subjected to artillery and mortar fire from the hill to the north which had been anticipated. The entire regiment had no choice but to seek shelter as the shelling, smoke, and noisy confusion covered the area. Shallow trenches were hurridly dug or men

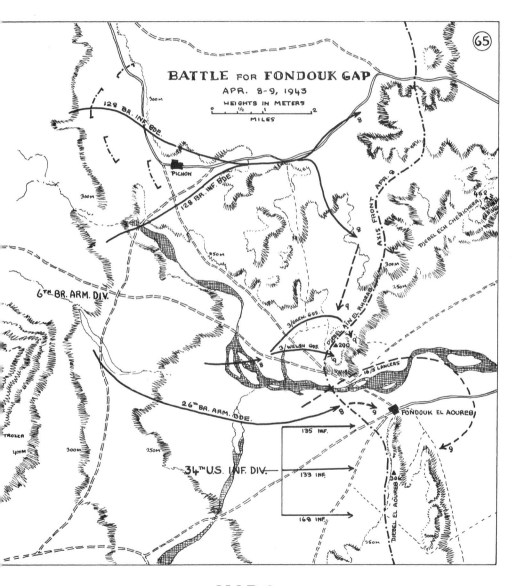

MAP 2

From The Campaign for North Africa by Jack Coggins, p. 147

lay behind hummocks for cover. The fresh smell of April greenery was a sharp contrast to the clouds of dust that rested upon them like a smoke screen.

Dean was surprised when Lt. Col. Monson crept by the depression Dean had carved out and said, "I have to see if we can't direct some artillery fire on those guns." When the barrage let up he hurried on. Later Dean learned the Colonel had been wounded in the face and neck while acting as a forward observer directing artillery fire.

As the shelling continued, one Company M soldier died when a shell made a direct hit on his shallow trench and in the confusion of smoke and dust the regiment lost another soldier.....run over by a friendly tank. Some of the 135th reached enemy positions but could not hold them. There would be no clearing of the hills on their side of the pass by the 34th Red Bull Division.

General Crocker blamed the failure of his operation on the inability to get through the pass promptly and that failure was due to the incapacity of the Red Bull Division. Colonel Monson told the Company officers, "We criticized General Crocker's plan and emphasized General Ryder's predicament when ordered to attack with an exposed northern flank. I understand that General Eisenhower and British General Alexander suppressed the arguments on both sides. Things are being changed so we can work as American units under our own leadership."

The battles at Fondouk cost the Red Bull Division, 1075 men killed, wounded or missing. Among them were twelve casualties from Dean's Company M.

As they pitched their two-man pup tent, Bill told Dean, "I hope our battle plans are better. I hear next we'll have to scramble over a bunch of hills."

Dean didn't reply. Right then, his thoughts were back home. He couldn't shake his fear that there would be more loss of life in attacking the next hill.

To put the American forces into the northern part of Tunisia and the British and French south of the Americans so that each could operate more efficiently as separate fighting units required a massive shuffling. For the Americans, this involved moving 90,000 soldiers and thousands of vehicles and equipment. After their march to northern Tunisia, the 34th Infantry Red Bull Division was inserted between the US First and 9th Infantry Divisions on April 26. (Map 3).

The main obstacle that stood in the path of the United States II Corps in their drive to defeat the Germans in northern Tunisia was Hill 609. It was named such because it was 609 meters high. It was also about eight hundred yards in length from east to west and about five hundred yards wide at its widest point from north to south. When seen from the air, it resembled a crude arrowhead pointing to the east. On the south slope was an Arab village. Surrounding Hill 609 were several other hills also numbered by their height.

The 34th's mission was to take Hill 609. Sgt. Strong told his men, "We have a chance to redeem ourselves and show our fighting ability." Redeem themselves.....they did.

General Ryder discovered that any direct assault on 609 was impossible without first clearing the nearby hills. Hill 490, next to Hill 609, was won and held in spite of numerous counterattacks with hand to hand combat. Dean and Bill, assigned as a team to a .30 caliber machine gun, had fired bandoleer after bandoleer of bullets at the attackers. With sweat running down their faces as the weapon heated up, they held their position and the attacks were repulsed.

Standing on Hill 490 and looking through field glasses at Hill 609, Sgt. Strong told his men, "The ground is ideal for the Germans. If we attack the sheltered side we'll be pinned down on the rocky tops by machine guns from those next hills and fire from the reverse slope.   If we go up the ravine we'll catch mortar fire."

Bill, catching his breath, offered, "It sounds like we

174

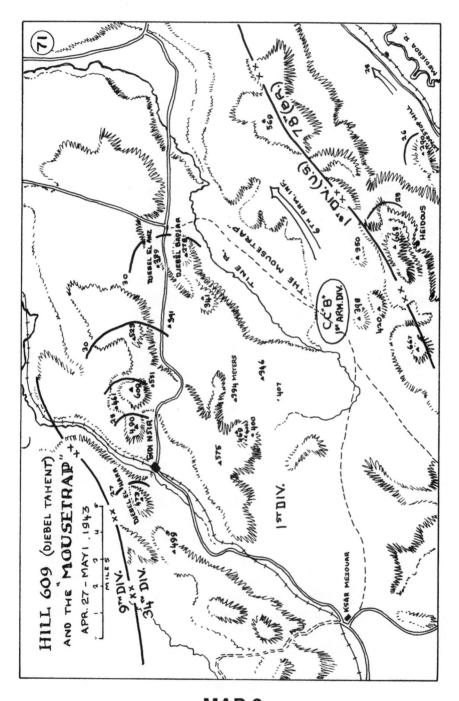

MAP 3

From The Campaign for North Africa by Jack Coggins, p. 159

should stay right here."

The First Battalion, 135th Infantry commanded by Colonel Bob Monson from Applegrove, was to attack Hill 609 from the east and northeast. Colonel Monson remembered the lessons from Fondouk where failure of coordination was disastrous. Meeting with two platoon sergeants, he told them, "I want a telephone line run to the command post of the infantry next to us." Later he was able to direct artillery fire on enemy targets in that area.

Dean and Bill protected the attacking riflemen with consistent fire from their machine gun from a rocky outcrop along a low rise. The buildings of the Arab village lay just ahead. As Bill leaned over to retrieve a bandoleer of bullets, an enemy rifleman waiting for that moment, shot and killed Bill instantly with a single bullet to the head.

Dean stared at the sight unable for a few minutes to comprehend what had happened to his friend. In death, peace had come over his face. Where a few minutes ago Dean had been scared and frightened, now he was mad, fighting mad. He let out an almost inhuman, bloodthirsty cry, the anger welling up in his throat. "You bastards..."

Dean started to pick up the machine gun to storm the village when something in his memory went back to the football game at Valley River when Coach McLear had told him something he didn't understand.

Dean sensed there was something unusual by the second quarter.

The calm, autumn Saturday afternoon belied the tension on the field. Dean felt the punishing blows as hard fists struck his body. In the pile of players after he made the tackle, he could not see the blows but heard and felt them where there was no padding. Some of the visiting Mount Vernon players were trying to get him mad.

Walking off the field at half time, Dean rubbed his sore

stomach. As center and linebacker he had played the entire half. He was tempted to say something to Coach McLear, but decided not to. The coach had told the team members, "To play football you have to be tough." Dean wanted to be known as a player who could take punishment. Besides, Coach McLear might even take him out of the game. With the score 0 to 0 at half time there was a lot of football left to be played. In the middle of the third quarter Dean couldn't hold his temper any longer and shoved the Mount Vernon player that hit him so hard he fell over on his back. As it happened at midfield close to the Valley River bench, Coach McLear saw the incident.

'Lil Buck' Nelson immediately entered the game. "I'm supposed to replace you at linebacker, Dean," he said. Dean saw the player he shoved had a big smirk on his face.

Coach McLear motioned for Dean to sit on the bench. The bigger Mount Vernon team soon wore the smaller Valley River Vikings down and pushed over a touchdown and added the extra point. Dean languished on the bench the rest of the game and watched his team lose 7 to 0.

Jim Foley, Valley River's co-captain and Dean's friend, fell in step with Dean on the way back to the gym. Helmets dangling from their hands, they walked along in silence. Jim spoke up, "They were a rough bunch."

"I shouldn't have gotten mad, but I couldn't take it any longer," Dean responded.

"Coach asked me to tell you to come to his office after you've showered."

"I hope he won't keep me sitting on the bench or kick me off the team."

"Good luck, buddy," Jim said encouragingly after they had taken off their football shoes and turned into the locker room.

Dean showered and took all the time he could getting dressed. The locker room was nearly empty when he slowly opened the door to Coach McLear's office. The coach was sitting at his desk looking at what appeared to be a sheet of game statistics.

"Sit down, Dean." Coach McLear continued to study the sheets. Dean's anxiety grew. He couldn't help but fidget in his chair. He felt his palms getting sweaty. What would be his future on the team? Would his dream of being a successful coach end here?

After what seemed like an eternity to Dean, Coach McLear laid the papers down. " I suppose you wonder why I didn't let you play the rest of the game?" He hesitated to see if Dean would respond. Dean was so nervous that he couldn't think of anything to say. The coach continued, "There are a couple of reasons. I saw you shove that player when you got mad. I also saw them hit you a couple times. I want my teams to be known as those that play hard and not those that fight. Someday, when you become a coach, I'm sure you'll want your team to play hard and be good sports. But most of all I did it for you."

The coach got up and stood looking out the window at the American flag flying in the late afternoon breeze that now blew over the stadium. "Someday you may experience a moment in your life where getting mad will mean the difference between life and death. It is an impulse that you need to control."

"Yes, you're right, coach. I'm sorry that I let you and the team down. I talked to Jim about it already. If I can play the rest of the season, I'll show you I can keep from losing my temper."

"I hoped you would say that. I appreciate your attitude. Okay, I plan to start you next week in our Homecoming game with Minot."

"Thanks coach," Dean said. He didn't realize he was holding his breath until a rush of air escaped his lips.

"However, you must realize that if this happens again you're off the team." As Dean got up to leave, Coach McLear came out from behind his desk and put his hand in Dean's and gave him a slap on the back.

Dean felt better after the talk. As he mulled over Coach McLear's remarks, he thought, "I admire Coach McLear. I want to be like him someday, but I don't see how my getting mad might result in a life or death situation."

Now he knew. Dean, crouching behind the rocky outcrop, retrieved the fresh belt of bullets. Feeding it into the gun, he raked every possible opening. The riflemen continued their attack, despite the bullets riddling the bodies of their buddies. Dean then covered Bill's body with his jacket, picked up the machine gun and ran to the village. Setting the machine gun down Dean grabbed an automatic rifle and grenades from a downed rifleman and hurried after the retreating enemy, the anger still boiling in his body.

One of the enemy turned and thrust his rifle bayonet at Dean. Dean parried his thrust, knocked the German's rifle aside with his, then swung the butt end up and knocked the German unconscious. He threw a grenade well ahead of the running Germans. Several were killed and three turned to fight. Shooting one, he rolled to his side and shot another. The third dropped his gun and shouted, "Comrade" and surrendered.

The soldier Dean had knocked down, staggered to his feet. Taking the two prisoners back, he turned them over to Sgt. Strong who gave them to a prisoner detail. Sgt. Strong put his arm around him and said, "That was a brave thing you did, Dean. Here's your jacket. The medics checked Bill and turned his body over to the Graves Registration Team. I'm sorry, Dean. He was my friend, but I know he was your special buddy."

Dean turned away, his shoulders shaking uncontrollably as the tears rolled down his cheeks.

The attack to take Hill 609 was to continue in the morning. Dean sat with his back to the wall in one of the abandoned stone houses in the village, alone, unable to sleep, distraught over the loss of his friend. He knew his life after this war would never be the same again. Bill's wife, Sally, and his children Bridgett and Lucas would never know the warmth and love of Bill again.

In the morning the Battalion rifle companies occupied the heights and repelled enemy counterattacks as they tried to regain the valuable height. By the afternoon of the first day of May, the 34th Infantry had completed the ring around Hill 609 and was in complete control.

With continued pressure on them, the enemy hurriedly withdrew but were soon trapped between the British and American forces. The Red Bull Division commanders reassembled their 135th, 133rd and the 168th Regiments and gave them the task of corralling the thousands of the enemy who sought to surrender.

On May 10, the German forces to the north of Tunis accepted the terms of unconditional surrender. Dean asked Sgt. Strong, "Bruce, how many prisoners would you say there are now?"

"Headquarters thinks it will total about 40,000."

In the south, the Allies kept constant pressure on the dazed and disorganized enemy. The German and Italian generals surrendered to the Allies on May 13, 1943. In the days that followed the throngs of Axis prisoners reached 275,000. They were moved slowly westward toward ports and eventual shipping to prison camps in North America.

So ended the campaign in North Africa. The American Forces alone had 18,221 casualties and almost one fourth of these were from the 34th Infantry Red Bull Division, many of whom included Dean's friends from Company M, Applegrove.

North Africa
May 15, 1943

Dear Carrie:

Hi, Sweetheart! We're done fighting in Africa. It should be a happy time but I am still sad about losing Bill. I was told those killed were temporarily buried in the Army cemetery in Tunis. I take solace in knowing he is resting in peace.

The one who said, "There are no atheists in foxholes" was right. So far the Lord has been listening to my prayers. We had Easter services among the rocks. The significance of Easter has become more meaningful.

I plan to send a separate V-mail to Sally. I hope she and the kids are all right.

The 135th Infantry Regiment has been selected to represent the Red Bull Division in the Victory Parade in Tunis.

How's our little boy? Tell me more about you and Spence.

I'm sorry for the short letter, but I'm tired. I'm all right and I'll write more next time. Thanks for writing regularly. I miss you.

Love you and am always thinking about you,
Dean

At the Victory Parade on May 20th in Tunis, the men marched in their woolen battle uniforms to the combined 135th and 133rd Regimental bands. Next to the French in their flashy dress uniforms and beautiful horses, the rugged, battle tested men of the 135th received the most cheers.

After the parade, the Division assembled in a field near Tunis to participate in a memorial service. The columns marched to a valley where several days earlier the enemy had controlled the hills to each side. The regimental bands played a hymn and the chaplain held a non-denominational prayer service. The Company commanders read the names of those killed in action. A bugler on a lone hill played taps. As the somber and mournful notes were heard by the assembled men, Dean thought of Bill, Russell and the others from Company M and the tears rolled unashamedly down his cheeks and, he noticed, the cheeks of his fellow soldiers.

That evening, Dean reflecting on the service, said to Bruce, "If I live through the war, I feel a responsibility to those that didn't get back .....like I have an obligation to them. I want to be a better person, husband, father, teacher, and friend. I can take some satisfaction in that the world will be a better place because of Bill and Russell."

The Divisions were assigned to duty along the coast. Much of this time Company M was busy with battlefield cleanup. Dean, bringing some of the weapons to the rendezvous point, commented to Sgt. Strong, " I hope I never see these up close." as he held up two German grenades with wooden handles.

The duty near Tunis didn't last. The Red Bull Division was ordered back the thousand miles to Oran. Most of the men of the Division made the trip by rail. Dean had his first experience with the 'forty and eight' wooden boxcars. One of the lieutenants said, "The French call them 'Quarante hommes ou huit chaveaux', forty men or eight horses."

Dean told some of his friends, "Riding in these boxcars isn't so bad. I'm just glad I don't have to stand up." Makeshift benches along the sides provided some rest and room to stretch their legs. The stifling July heat and the constant noise from the rails made sleep nearly impossible, that is, until they were overcome with exhaustion.

STREETS OF HONOR

Chapter 18

Ushered into the Community Baptist Church for the Memorial Service for Bill Bradford, Carrie sat on the left side behind members of the local American Legion. She was wearing a conservative dark blue suit with a straight skirt and collarless jacket that buttoned down the front. A single strand of pearls offset the plain outfit.

There was not enough room in the small upstairs church or in the tiny basement for the crowd that wished to pay tribute to one of its soldiers. Sally, Bridgett and Lucas Bradford were ushered to the pew on the right side as the assembly sang the verses of *Beautiful Savior*. Sally's parents, who had driven over from Willmar for the Memorial Service, sat beside her. Sally and Bill's relatives filled three-quarters of the pews behind her.

The space around the altar was decorated with bouquets of fresh flowers. The scent filled the air of the small church.

The chaplain from the local American Legion Post read the opening prayer, " *Prayer to a Departed Comrade*."

"Eternal God, Supreme Commander of us all, Lord of the far-flung battle line, to whom the ranks of life report, we bow before you with reverent hearts and in sublime faith, knowing that you lead us on in death as you have in life."

"For again you have ordered a veteran to that realm in the West, beyond the twilight and the evening star, where beauty and valor and goodness dwell forever with the unnumbered multitude."

Then the congregation sang, *"Abide With Me."* The pastor wisely kept his message short with the familiar themes of

"He leads me beside the still waters; He restores my soul; In my father's house are many mansions." Glancing over at Sally, Carrie noticed Sally relaxed as she heard the message.

The Post Adjutant came forward. "Sally has given me a letter to read from Bill's friend, Dean Brandum, who was with him when he was killed," he said.

> *North Africa*
> *May 15, 1943*

Dear Sally:

I thought you would want to know that Bill died a hero, and how he died fighting for his country that he loved so well.

He did not suffer. He was killed instantly. I covered him with my jacket and the medics saw to it he was placed in a transport to the rear. For a time he will be buried in Africa in the military cemetery at Hadjeb El Aioun, Tunisia. Later he'll be returned to Applegrove.

We were able to capture our objective and several of the enemy paid with their lives. I am sorry that you lost your husband, and the children their father. It's true for myself and for all of Company M, we lost a true friend.

If there is anything that I can do, write to me or let Carrie know.

> *Sincerely,*
> *Dean Brandum*

Some of Bill's relatives covered their eyes with their hand and bowed their heads. Stifled sobs could be heard.

The Post Commander, Walt Larson, who had been Dean's employer at the flour mill, presented Sally with an American flag. Carrie watched in sadness as Lucas, now three and a half-years old, tugged on his mother's arm and reached for the parcel. When she gave it to him, he clutched it to his chest proudly. The Commander also presented her with a Gold Star banner to take the place of the Blue Star banner she had proudly displayed in her window at home.

The Legion chaplain gave the *Committal* for the Memorial Service.

"Almighty God, this tender hour of memorial comes, when we can give our moment of affectionate tribute to our comrade who has passed away, but who will never be forgotten. Help us, Our God, so to live, that our lives, by our dreams, by our hopes and by our deeds, we must justify his noble sacrifice and keep our country strong. For all God - loving people everywhere, forever free, in the name of all humanity. Amen.

The far away melodic, mournful sounds of taps played by one of the high school students crept through the church. Here and there sobs were choked back. Glancing across the aisle, a tearful Carrie saw Sally straighten and square her shoulders.

As the congregation sang, the procession made its way down the aisle. Those who didn't have to return to work or other duties stayed for lunch in the church basement.

It was then that Carrie had an opportunity to console Sally. Carrie and Sally wrapped arms around each other and held each other close. Carrie whispered, "Strength to you now, Sally. You were so great during the service. I pray that there will be healing for you."

Sally in turn gave strength to Carrie, worried about Dean far away in a Mediterranean country, his life in danger as Bill's had been. "When you write to Dean, please tell him 'thank you' for sending me the letter."

"Yes I will, Sally. And as Dean said, if there is anything that we can do, please let me know."

The warmth of small town people extending their sympathies, engulfed Sally.

Carrie drove out to the farm to pick up Spencer. Carrie realized he wouldn't understand the service; so she had asked Mom and Carl to take care of him that morning.

186

Sophie held open the screen door for her daughter. When Spencer saw Carrie, he ran to her. Carrie picked him up, held him close and slipped into an easy chair.

"Mom, there were so many people at the church. They even had chairs and loud speakers outside. Sally was so brave. I broke down when little Lucas walked up the aisle carrying the American flag after the service." Carrie nuzzled Spencer's neck, loving the familiar scent of her small son.

"Mom, I've been thinking about all the baby-sitting you've been doing for me. You've been such a help and I appreciate all you've done. Mrs. Bogenrief said several times that she would baby-sit if it would be helpful for you and me. I know how busy you are here at the farm." Sophie nodded her head. "It would save a lot of time not having to drive him out here every day. What do you think?"

Sophie, a little surprised, but realizing the truth said, "Yes, Carrie. I think that would be okay. He's old enough now, so Mrs. Bogenrief shouldn't have any trouble. But don't forget, I can still baby-sit at times."

Carrie got up with Spencer still in her arms and gave her a hug, "Thanks, Mom. I knew you would understand. Now I'd better be getting home." She let herself into the apartment and laid Spencer down for his nap. She decided to write Dean right away about the Memorial Service and let him know that his letter had been read.

Applegrove, Minnesota
June 19, 1943

Dear Dean:

I went to the Memorial Service for Bill today. The Applegrove American Legion took part in the service.

Sally said to be sure to say thank you for the letter about Bill and how he died. She gave it to one of the Legion officers to read at the service.

The religion of a serviceman doesn't seem to matter, as

there have been Memorial Services in all churches in Applegrove. I recently attended a Memorial Service at the Armory for a cousin of a lady at the bank. The Service was for two soldiers killed about the same time in Africa.

Spencer and I have a Blue Star Banner hanging in our apartment window. It is for you, away from home in military service. It was so sad when Sally was given a Gold Star Banner at the service.

Spencer is taking his nap, so I can write a little more. He's outgrowing all his clothes but I finally found a blue romper that fits. Mom watched Spencer when I was at the service. She said he was busy throwing his blocks around and last week he crawled over to the kitchen cabinets and pulled all the pots and pans out on the floor. I talked to Mom about Mrs. B. helping with the baby-sitting, and she said it's okay with her.

Dad has all the crops in and they look good even though he couldn't cultivate as much because of the gas rationing.

I pray for you and ask God to watch over you. Each night I fall asleep holding my pillow and make believe it's you.

Love,
Carrie

It was several weeks before Dean received Carrie's letter. Reading it several times and laughing each time he read about Spencer, he folded it and put it with his treasured possessions in his field pack. The longing to be with his family and watch his son grow overcame him. The laughter and happiness Dean felt turned to sadness.

By the end of July, all of the 34th Division units returned to the vicinity of Oran. After he heard of the assault on the island of Sicily, Sgt. Strong relished his chance to expand on his knowledge of the war. He said, "I heard that Winston Churchill wanted to attack the Axis soft underbelly, as he called it." The island of Sicily fell to the Allies on August 17, 1943, when the City of Messina was captured after nearly six weeks of intense fighting by the American and British forces.

After so many weeks of traveling and training, Dean's Division had more time to relax and the mail caught up to them.

> *Auburn, North Dakota*
> *April 16, 1943*

Dear Dean:

I hope you have been getting our letters all right. It is easier to write now that winter is over and things are starting to turn green.

Eric is anxious to get the field work done. He has to be cautious because gas rationing limits how much he can do. We have other things being rationed now. There are ration coupons for shoes, canned goods, meats, fat and cheese. We're fortunate to live on the farm and have a place to raise cows, pigs and chickens.

The ration book coupons have numbers and little pictures of airplanes, ships or tanks. I guess the rationing board must want to remind us of why we have rationing.

Thank you for your letters. I understand that you have to write Carrie often, so you don't need to apologize. I was happy to be a grandmother. Maybe one day this summer we can drive to Applegrove and see Spencer. Perhaps in July, for his first birthday.

Skriv snart.

> *Love,*
> *Ma and Eric*

Dean was reading an old copy of the GI newspaper, *Stars and Stripes*, when he noticed something unusual, "Sarge, listen to this," he said. "You remember Charlie, my friend from North Dakota? He was the best man at my wedding. His outfit is the Americal Division. It says here, 'Japanese resistance on the island of Guadalcanal has ceased. The victory was won in a long, hard fought battle that began in August and ended

February 9. In mid October the US Marines were reinforced with men from the Army's Americal Division equipped with the new M-1 semi-automatic rifle. This Division was the first unit of the US Army to take offensive action in the war in the Pacific.' Charlie and I've got a bet on who will end the war first," Dean explained.

Bruce, reading his own mail remarked, "Sounds like you're about even right now."

North Africa
July 25, 1943

Dear Carrie:

How's our little family? I was happy to get another picture of you and Spence. You both look wonderful. I laughed out loud when you wrote about Spencer throwing his blocks around and pulling the pots and pans out of the cupboard.

I was pleased that you went to the Memorial Service for Bill. I didn't expect my letter to be read; but, that was the least I could do for Sally and the kids. It's still hard for me to accept he's gone.

The big news is what came over Radio Rome today. Mussolini was overthrown and arrested. Even surrender of the Italians is being talked about.

Right now the biggest headache for us is losing some of our equipment to young Arab boys who are slick at taking our clothes and equipment.

We're quartered near the beach now and may even get time off to go there. Maybe I can learn to swim.

Thank you for all the little things you write about you and Spence.

Miss you and love you,
Dean

On September 2, a ship dropped anchor in Oran and the 100th (Hawaiian) Inf. B. disembarked. The battalion was composed of Japanese Americans from Hawaii. They were assigned to the Red Bull Division's 133rd Inf. Regiment as its 2nd Battalion. The commanding officer told his officers and men, "They are not Japanese, but Americans born in Hawaii and will be fighting alongside the rest of us." Friendships blossomed as the Nisei were integrated into the Regiment. The men could often be seen frolicking in the ocean surf like sea otters.

Dean decided to learn to swim. Cutting off an old pair of khakis, he sauntered down to the beach and proceeded to walk out waist high. Windmilling his arms and rapidly kicking his feet got him nowhere.

That was when one of the Nisei swam over to him. Laughingly, he said, "I'll hold you up in the middle. Keep your legs stiff and kick. Pull with one arm, then the other."

Encouraged by the flashing smile and friendly help, Dean tried again and was amazed to see how far he swam. Puffing he stopped and asked, "What's your name?"

"My name is Taro Takayama. What's yours?"

"Dean Brandum."

Taro asked, "Are you an officer?"

"No, I'm a Corporal."

"I'll call you Corporal Dean. I'm a Private."

"I'm going to call you, 'Captain Nemo'."

"'Captain Nemo' who's that?"

"Nemo was the submarine captain in Jules Verne's book, *20,000 Leagues Under the Sea*. We read it in high school. You act like you live in the sea."

Nemo helped Dean until he was able to swim unaided the length of the roped-off beach area. Puffing and wheezing, Dean staggered to the beach and sprawled out on the sand.

"Are you okay, Corporal Dean?"

Dean sputtered, laughing, "I thought I would die out there, Nemo"

The two new friends lay in the sun and talked. Nemo

offered Dean a cigarette. Dean surprised himself when he automatically accepted it and the light that was offered. Perhaps the days of boredom, the loss of his friends, and the incessant action of combat had compelled him.

Dean told Nemo about life on a North Dakota farm. He took a puff on his cigarette, coughed twice, and turned away so Nemo wouldn't see the tears in his eyes.

Nemo explained what it was like to live on an island, work in the sugar cane fields, go surfboarding, and outrigger canoeing.

Dean told his new friend, "Stop by the barracks sometime."

The Germans had plenty of time now to strengthen their defenses. Newspapers, magazines, radio announcers and government officials indicated the Allied intention to invade the Italian mainland.

Dean's friend, Nemo, came by the barracks when he heard the Division was loading for Italy. With his big flashing smile he told Dean, "I came to seek your advice."

Puzzled, Dean asked, "What do you mean?"

"You're a farmer from North Dakota, right? The ships we're going on are transporting mules to Salerno. You're the expert. What do we do?"

Dean said, "I don't know anything about mules. What are they going to do with them?"

Nemo explained, "They're needed on the mountains to supply the men. Each Division is supposed to have a pack train unit of 300 to 500 beasts."

Dean studied Nemo for a second and realized he was teasing. With a wide smile he said, "If I need a mule skinner, I'll call for Private Taro 'Nemo' Takayama, okay?"

"If you need more swimming lessons, call for me too. I'll see you in Italy" Nemo said with a grin as he scurried out the door.

Much to Dean's relief, the mules, their equipment and

feed had special shipping arrangements. They didn't need to share accommodations.

The 34th Red Bull Division was needed to counterbalance the build up of the German ground forces. Headquarters, by rescheduling, had found enough ships to transport the Division to Italy. Four days after departure from Oran, the ships anchored in Salerno Bay.

Headquarters protected them with an elaborate smoke screen, air cover and barrage balloons suspended on cables to ward off enemy aircraft. The men, who were transferred from the ships to landing craft and unloaded on the sandy beach, were led to believe they had nothing to fear.

It had been far different for the men jammed into the landing craft at the first Salerno landing. Dean, seeing the devastation on the beach.....the burned out landing craft sunk in the harbor and equipment littering the beach, exclaimed to Sgt. Strong, "That must've been some battle!" He was relieved not to have been there.

Colonel Monson had told the men once they were formed up that they were to march to the Regimental bivouac area at Montesarchio in the rear of the 3rd Division, adding that General Lucas wanted to keep their presence hidden from the Germans.

On October 5th, tanks and men of the Fifth Army rolled into Naples to a cheering welcome. The prize of the Operation, the City of Naples, had been utterly destroyed by the retreating Germans.

STREETS OF HONOR

Chapter 19

"Dean," Sgt. Strong's voice startled him. "We've got orders to cross the river." The Fifth Army, which included the Red Bull Division, stood at the Volturno River at the end of the first week of October. Operation Avalanche was brought to an end. The cost was more than 12,000 British and American casualties. As Dean stood on the river bank watching the rushing, dark, water and thinking of his home, he realized that in the coming winter, the mountainous terrain and the disciplined German Army would make things very hazardous.

Dean, the fright evident in his voice, said, "How are we going to do that? Most of us in our battalion can't swim."

"At the staff meeting," Sgt. Strong explained, "it was decided that your Hawaiian friend from the 133rd would swim across pulling a rope to use as a guideline. After that's anchored the rest of us can use it to get across."

Dean, clearly alarmed, asked, "When will this happen?"

"Tonight, at about 2300 hours."

Looking at the swift flowing current and knowing the 133rd Regiment was upstream from them, Dean worried about Nemo. Would he be able to make it across? What if there are enemy soldiers on the opposite bank?

Dean went looking for the quartermaster in charge of the weapons carrier. "I need a BAR (Browning Automatic Rifle) and a hundred rounds of ammunition."

"And who do you think you are? Are you going to take on the German Army?"

"No, I'll just need them 'til morning."

"How am I going to account for a hundred rounds of ammo?"

"I'll bring back what I don't use. Tell Headquarters a patrol was infiltrating by your truck and you had to use it."

That night, Dean hid along the bank, well downstream from where Nemo would enter the water. The moonlight shimmered on the river as the rushing water made small waves rippling noisily along the bank. The rain made the Volturno, over 200 feet wide and over five feet deep, even more formidable. The banks from five to fifteen feet high were steep, muddy and slick. Brush and olive groves lined the hill slopes.

Dean saw Nemo's small dark figure enter the water. He watched as Nemo swam valiantly into the current. As Dean had anticipated, the river quickly carried him downstream, his head barely visible in the rippling water as he swam. When he was about three-fourths of the way across, Dean heard rifle shots and saw the muzzle flashes of enemy guns. Nemo's head disappeared under water.

Dean gripped the rifle and fired round after round toward the muzzle flashes on the opposite bank. The zip, zip of bullets over his head startled him as the enemy returned fire. Dean answered with several quick bursts. Finally, the firing stopped.

He was relieved to see Nemo's head surface and arms move. There were no further shots at his friend.

Several of the engineers that had been guiding the rope appeared on the bank below and anchored the rope. Tying the rope securely to a tree on his side and hanging on to it, Nemo nimbly started back. When he saw Dean standing with the rifle among the engineers, he stopped, flashed his big grin and said, "Thanks for the protection, Corporal Dean. I'm glad you didn't have to swim after me."

"I would've had to wade after you, Captain Nemo."

Just then several of Nemo's Hawaiian friends, puffing from exertion, arrived with their rifles. "We couldn't keep up with you. The brush was too thick."

Nemo smiled again, "It's okay. My friend looked out

for me."

Dean, returning his smile, said, "I didn't want to lose my swimming instructor."

Nemo reported to the engineers, "The river is shallow in places and the Regiment could wade across and hold their weapons above water."

A little after 1:00 in the morning on October 13, the artillery of the Red Bull Division opened fire on the enemy across the Volturno. Fifteen minutes later, infantrymen slid down the muddy banks, some to wade through the water with the aid of the rope and others to paddle across in assault boats. Dean, holding his machine gun over his head in the shoulder deep water, was thankful that he was tall.

The operation almost came to a halt. Whenever the engineers built a bridge for the trucks and artillery, they were destroyed by German artillery. Finally, by patching the pontoon floats and borrowing equipment, the engineers were able to complete a bridge. But it had to be at a new site. The regiment took its objective three miles from the abrupt bend of the River.

A couple of days later, when the Division was assigned to patrol action, Dean and Sgt. Strong were eating their C Rations. "I'm glad we're done crossing that River," Dean said.

"I'm sorry to say, Dean, Colonel Monson told us that when we continue our attack, we'll have to cross the river two more times. Straight ahead of us the River comes down from the mountains."

"Just when I got my boots dried out." Dean said.

Sgt. Strong continued, "After the drive beyond the Volturno River, we'll contact the German Winter line, south of Cassino."

"What's the Winter Line," Dean asked.

"It's a series of defensive lines. The Gustav Line is where the Germans will hold their position. It's based on the natural terrain around the town of Cassino."

That night, under the cover of darkness, Dean's 135th

Regiment made the second crossing of the river. The regiment moved north into the old, walled village of Alfie. General Ryder placed Dean's regiment in reserve at Alfie and sent the 133rd Regiment into the narrowing river valley toward a village five miles away.

The advance of the 133rd had scarcely got under way when the Germans caught the 100th Hawaiian Battalion in the open flats not far from Alfie. The Germans delivered rifle, machine gun, artillery, and rockets (screaming meemies) from the six-barreled mortar, Nebelwerfer, which could fire six bombs simultaneously on the Americans. Shrieking and whining in flight, the mortar shells frayed the nerves of the troops.

Dean was worried about his Hawaiian friend when he learned of the attack. He hurried over to their Regimental Headquarters and asked about him. Much to his relief, the warrant officer said, "His name doesn't show on the casualty reports."

The slow advance against the German defenses cost the Red Bull Division more than 350 casualties in the period of a week.

"We must cross the river if we're ever going to get to Rome," the Commanding Officer decided. This meant the third crossing of the Volturno.

Dean and Sgt. Strong peered through field glasses at the view to the west. Sgt. Strong noted, "Beyond the river I see a highway, a railroad, and farther on rugged mountains."

"I see the bridges have been destroyed and I bet they spread mines below the mountains and are waiting for us to cross," Dean observed.

The Red Bull Division again waded across the swift and icy stream for the third time after an artillery barrage. They struggled forward along with the 3rd and 45th Thunderbird Divisions against the German defenders of the Winter Line. The weather became colder and wetter and the men became exhausted by the unceasing combat.

There was a lull in the fighting. Sgt. Strong asked Dean to help him with the unpleasant duty of compiling records of killed, wounded, and captured friends, comrades and new replacements. Dean, overcome with weariness, saw the faces of each man as he worked. He told Sgt. Strong, "This is the toughest job I've ever had to do."

Sgt. Strong replied, "It's tough for me and Lieutenant Marsh to write letters to the next of kin, explaining what happened. Sometimes grief overtakes me and I have to quit writing for awhile."

On November 15, General Clark sent orders down to Division Commanders to rest the troops for two weeks and prepare for another attempt to smash the Winter Line. The Red Bull Division rested in a small village northwest of the Volturno with the stone houses giving welcome shelter from the weather. Dean, who was sitting with his back to the wall in one of them, was writing a letter to Carrie when 'Nemo' opened the door and yelled, "Corporal Dean!"

Dean jumped to his feet and gave Nemo a bear hug. "Hi. Am I glad to see you! I thought for awhile they'd got you."

Nemo smiled broadly, but his eyes betrayed his sadness. "Yes, I lost many of my friends. You're lucky, Corporal Dean."

Scratching his whiskers, Dean admitted, "Yes, Nemo, I am."

"Corporal Dean, you wouldn't have liked what we did. We had to round up sheep and goats and drive them ahead of us through the minefield. I thought of you on the farm."

Dean answered, "You have to do those things when you don't have any choice. Our mine detectors can't pick up the non-metallic mines."

Nemo said, "At least you're used to cold weather. I have two pairs of underwear on and two pairs of socks, plus all my other clothes, and I'm still cold."

"I'm from the northern part of the United States so I'm more used to the cold."

As Nemo prepared to leave, Dean dwarfed the small figure in his embrace and whispered, "Be careful, Captain Nemo."

"I will. I heard them yell, 'mail call' when I came. The mail has caught up to us."

Dean went out with Nemo and anxiously located the corporal with the mail. He hurried back to the refuge of the stone house and eagerly opened Carrie's letter.

> *Applegrove, Minnesota*
> *September 26, 1943*

Dear Dean:

I'm so glad when I get a letter from you. Much of your letters are censored out, but I don't care because I know you're okay. I'd like to be there with you and follow you around. But, I'd be so scared I'd probably hide all the time. It's a good thing you're big and tough.

The most news I have is that my cousin Louise took a job as a riveter at the Willow Run aircraft factory in Ypsilanti, Michigan. She was clerking at a department store in Willmar, but after seeing the publicity poster for "Rosie the Riveter" and hearing the song over the radio, she decided to take the Michigan job. The government has this campaign going to recruit women to take the place of men called into service. They're saying many millions of women have taken jobs. Louise wrote she's living in a Quonset hut close to the plant. She likes her work and feels she's helping the war effort.

I think I'll help by staying at the bank and raising Spencer to be a good boy.

The bank has a 'Payroll Savings Plan' for employees to buy Series E War Bonds. I've signed up for it. Spencer can use the funds for college. Hah. Dawn is buying stamps at school. She sticks them in a little book. Schools have a 'Buy a Jeep' program. They get to keep the stamps, but the school gets credit toward buying a jeep.

I see Ma and Pa on Wednesdays. That's the day they bring cream and eggs into town to trade for groceries. They know when I have time off at the bank so they buy me coffee.

Ma says she would write, but her spelling isn't very good and she would be embarrassed writing to a schoolteacher. They said to say, 'Hi' and hope the war will be over so you can come home.

Carl says it's the same thing over and over, "Chores and then some more chores."

Spencer can now stand up by chairs by himself. He points to your picture and says, "Da da." He's growing up so fast.

Dawn will be a senior this year. Remember the time when I was a senior and I fell off the stool in the science lab and you caught me just when the superintendent entered the room? Well, I wish I was in your arms now. Miss you so much.

Love,

Carrie

Just as Dean finished reading the letter, Sgt. Strong hurried in from the cold. "Dean, I was looking for you. Colonel Monson said we need to replace squad leaders and your name's going to headquarters promoting you to sergeant. Pick up your stripes at the quartermaster supply truck."

Dean was proud of the promotion but apprehensive at what it involved. "That means I'm going to have responsibility for more men," he said.

"That's right, but you can do it. I've seen you in action. Colonel Monson had some other news for us. He's being rotated back to the States. Along with the Guard time in the States and overseas, he's got enough points to rotate. He's going to be in charge of recruiting in a several state area."

Dean was pensive for a few seconds, then said, "He's

the only CO (Commanding Officer) I've ever had. I'll miss him. Who are we getting to replace him?"

Sgt. Strong replied, "I'll miss him too. It's Colonel Warden. I've met him at Guard Camp. He's a good man."

After the sergeant left, Dean picked up his writing material. The past weeks when the regiment was in combat he'd been thinking about Carrie and Spencer even more. He smiled, thinking about Carrie falling into his arms in the science lab, and how she reminded him of it, when he carried her into the apartment after the honeymoon.

Italy
November 17, 1943

Dear Carrie:

Hi, I've been wanting to write but we've been busy.

Have you had much snow yet? It's been cold here, but not like back home. The bad thing is, it rains and is cold.

I'm getting in increasingly better shape as we have a lot of hiking and climbing.

The mailman just brought your newsy letter. Thank you.

I like when you tell me more about Spence. Can he say "Momma" yet?

I'm glad your cousin Louise found something she likes to do and is helping with the war effort.

We've got a few days rest and it sure feels good. The cooks are going to make something hot, and that will that will be a real treat. The rumor is we'll get turkey sandwiches for Thanksgiving.

Notice my new sergeant rank on the address. I haven't even got my stripes sewn on yet. I'm a squad leader. I'll get paid a little more.

I have a new friend since Oran, Africa. He's a Japanese from Hawaii and is with another Red Bull Regiment. I call him, 'Captain Nemo'. He's got such a big grin that I can feel it down to my toes when he smiles. It's nice to have friends but it really hurts when you lose them in this war.

I've started to smoke now. I never thought I would do that. You would have laughed at me when I just about died trying to keep from coughing and sneezing. Cigarettes are easy to come by here. They include them in the rations.

If you don't hear from me for awhile, don't worry.

Greet your folks and our friends.

Love,
Dean

The two-week's rest ended too soon. Dean and his squad were back on the front line. It was fortunate that offensive operations were halted in mid-November. A heavy rainstorm had started fourteen days of wet weather when the Red Bull was not in combat. Travel by road had become impossible and along the shoulders, the mud was a foot deep or more. The foxholes, the men had dug before falling back, were full of water.

"Sarge, Sarge!" Dean, sitting with his back to a boulder with his eyes half closed, finally realized Andy from his squad was calling him.

Dean, still groggy, said, "Yah, Yah, what's the matter, Andy?"

Dean's new rank, although now several weeks old, had not been etched into his sub-consciousness. They were taking a break, screened momentarily from battle by a large pile of rock loosened from the mountainside by the incessant rain. Andy had his boots off and was wringing water out of his socks.

"My feet are itching like crazy. They're so swollen I can hardly get my boots back on. In Wisconsin, we'd call this frostbite."

Dean bent over and looked closely at Andy's red, swollen feet. In several places the blisters had broken open and bled. "Oh, oh, that looks bad," he said. "When the medics come by, I'm sending you back to the first aid station."

Several days later, Andy returned and reported to Dean, "The doctor said I have trench foot. He said a lot of men are getting it from standing in water and mud. It's a fungus. We're supposed to keep our feet elevated and dry and rub them to keep the blood circulating. We're also supposed to stop smoking."

Dean smiled wryly, and when he told the rest of the squad, they had a good laugh. "How do you keep your feet dry in these conditions?" Burt asked. "I've got two pair of socks, but I can't get one pair dry enough to change."

"A suggestion I heard was to get the extra pair as dry as you can and put them in your helmet." Dean said.

Burt had a quizzical look on his face, but said, "It's worth a try."

Andy added, "At the aid station, I met a fellow who had trench foot and he said some of the guys were putting shaving cream or grease on their feet to keep them from exposure to water."

"Andy," Dean said, "I'm going to put you on the mule, pack-train detail. We have to furnish men for this, and your feet will have a chance to heal."

Dismayed, Dean thought to himself, "I didn't lose anyone as a battle casualty, but I'm losing them to trench foot. Pretty soon I'm not going to have a squad."

STREETS OF HONOR

Chapter 20

General Lucas took the Red Bull Division out of line on December 8, after they and the 45th Thunderbird Division received 800 casualties in a week while attacking along the north shoulder of the Mignano Pass. The Division was given R and R until the day after Christmas.

Italy
December 12, 1943

Dear Darling Carrie:
It's Sunday today and it sure is nice to have a day of rest.
We had church this morning in one of the larger buildings that has been taken over as a recreation building. We have a wonderful chaplain. I don't even know what faith he is, but he's always with us on the front line.
We sang Christmas Carols and had communion. The men sang so well. It helped after being in combat for so long.
I have some swell guys in my squad and we all get along together quite well.
The cooks say that they plan to prepare a complete Christmas Day turkey dinner.
Remember after we were married we spent our first and only Christmas together before I left for service? That was three years ago! I'm happy when I think about it but sad it was our only one. It almost seems that was in another life. I wish I were home to spend Christmas with you.
You'll have to buy a present for yourself and Spence from me this year.
I'll try to write so the censor doesn't black out so much.

If you don't hear from me, don't worry.
                              Love you very much,
                                        Dean

Headquarters didn't waste any time to alert the Red Bull Division. The day after Christmas they were ordered to move back up to their former position.

Andy, who had a break from mule skinning, found Dean and said, "I want to come back to the squad. My feet are much better. No pain that I might suffer will be any worse then what happened to me. Coming down the mountain, I rode the mule part way. A sniper shot the mule right out from under me and the mule and I started to slide down the side of the mountain. If it hadn't gotten stuck between two boulders, I wouldn't be here to tell about it. The next week a mortar shell wounded another mule. Do you know the army has a hospital for mules?"

Andy babbled on and on until Dean gently interrupted him. "You heard we've been losing men in mortar attacks. Our friends dying is hard on a squad. We've had to bury them in the temporary American cemetery on the sheltered slope of the Valley."

"I know, Sarge. But I miss my buddies and I want to come back. Strung out along a mountain path leading a mule is not like being with you guys. It's all right with the sergeant in the mule pool, if it's okay with you."

Dean was pleased and happy to have Andy back with the squad. "All right. Inform the company commander that you're back on duty here."

The fighting during the first ten days of January, 1944, was a continuation of the December operations. The men of the 36th Division, the Red Bull Divisions counterpart attempting to cross the Rapido River, were caught in a trap by the well-dug-in German positions. The two regiments, the 141st and 143rd, which included men from Texas, New York and Pennsylvania incurred 1,681 casualties during the 48-hour assault.

Dean and the men of the Division were glad to hear the Allies had made an amphibious landing at Anzio on the western side of Italy about thirty miles south of Rome on January 22, 1944. They anticipated this landing (code named Shingle) of Allied units behind the German lines would weaken the defenses at the Rapido and the mountain of Cassino as German troops would have to be moved to oppose the landing.

Sgt. Strong told his men, "Now I know why General Clark has been pushing us to attack the Gustav Line here in the Cassino area. I understand our diversion detracted from the landing and the Germans were caught unawares."

Dean asked, "How many men went ashore?"

"Headquarters said there were 40,000 men and 5200 vehicles with light casualties. But we didn't go inland, and now the Germans are racing toward Anzio."

With the 'Operation Shingle' forces safely ashore at Anzio, General Clark urged his commanders with all possible speed to break the Gustav Line, open up the Liri Valley and join the forces at Anzio. Sgt. Strong, who had been apprised of plans for the regiment, said, "To form the Gustav Line the Germans have added minefields, concrete bunkers, pill boxes, booby traps, barbed wire, trenches and machine gun emplacements to the natural terrain."

"You mean we have to attack that?" Dean asked incredulously.

"Yes. On the other side of the Rapido River we'll be in the shadow of Monte Cassino. It's a huge mountain that some call Monastery Hill because on top of its peaks is the Abbey of Cassino. Then there's the town of Cassino at the base of the mountain." (Map 4).

"That must be an historical site," Dean said.

Sgt. Strong rummaged through his things, found a pamphlet and handed it to Dean. "You're right there. One of the officers picked up some of these in Naples."

Dean read the pamphlet carefully. He learned that

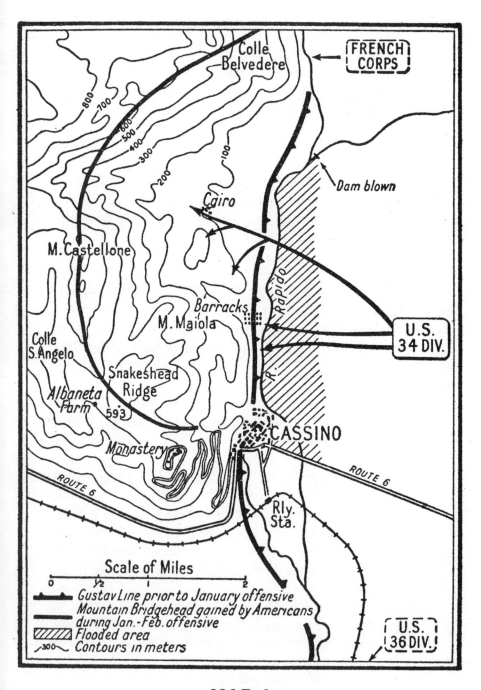

MAP 4

From The Battle of Cassino by Fred Majdalany, p. 79

Monte Cassino is seventeen hundred feet high. To reach the Abbey on top of Monte Cassino, one travels along a five-mile switchback road which winds up the steep slope through hairpin bends. It was on Monte Cassino that the Monk Benedict founded the Benedictine Order. Because the Abbey had historical importance, efforts were made to preserve it as a classical monument. Richly decorated in a heavily ornate Baroque tradition it also contained a large cathedral. Lying on the road to Rome, it had been damaged three times -- by the Lombards in 581, the Saracens in 883, and an earthquake in 1349.

Dean learned in October that the German military had loaded the art from the monastery, as well as the nuns, children and civilian refugees, and moved them to Rome. Left at the Abbey to be moved out later, were the Abbot, five monks, five lay brothers and 150 civilians.

Colonel Warden received word from General Ryder that the Red Bull Division was to apply pressure by a flanking movement to the north of Cassino. The Colonel told his troops, "The German forces have placed the Abbey off limits. But German troops demolished the outlying buildings to create fields of fire, set-up observation posts, and weapons placements."

One regiment was to move down the banks of the Rapido River south into the town of Cassino. Dean's regiment was to strike west across the mountainous terrain. Before they could get there, the Red Bull Division met bitter resistance in the valley bottom of the Rapido. The Germans had diverted the river and turned the valley into a swamp.

Red Bull advanced, yard by yard, fighting in the mud and water. Wet foxholes and freezing nights brought trench foot and illness. Snow and ice made the trails up the mountain treacherous. Dean told his tiring men, "We'll stop here and rest for awhile, but we can't dig in this stuff." He'd learned this lesson in North Africa. "We'll have to pile rocks around us for protection."

Constantly alert for the enemy gunfire and with the January cold turning their clothes and gloves to ice, the men struggled on. Their emotions dipped and plunged. Some whined and cursed the mountain, the weather, and the Germans. Many could be heard praying that they would come through the ordeal alive.

Dean sat with his back to the mountain wall, his head in his hands, resting his body, but not his mind. He'd never forget the agony he felt when the mortar shells landed among his squad. They were now making their way slowly along the mountain pass. The cold was so bitter they clutched their weapons close to them, so their numb hands wouldn't drop them.

A shell hit Wayne, one of the machine gun carriers, disemboweling him. Dean had waved his squad to cover and another shell fragment tore into the neck and jaw of Burt. Dean had caught him as he fell, and eased his comrade into the protection of the mountainside. Cradling him in his arms, Dean felt his warm blood soaking through his jacket and running down his arm. Burt let out a short gasp and died.

Dean called to Art, one of the new men on the squad to help him move Wayne off the trail and into the rocky crevasse beside Burt. Dean and Art averted their eyes from the gruesome scene. The sadness and bitterness on losing their buddies were evident in the faces of the squad members.

"Damn war!" Dean exploded. Burt had joined the Guard at the same time as Dean, trained at Camp Ripley and Camp Claiborne, fought in Africa and Italy. "Another of my friends gone." Dean's sadness was so intense that he almost felt like throwing his body into the line of fire.

The brief rest over, Dean shook his head, brushed his hand over his eyes and scrambled back onto the trail. "Let's go men!" he yelled. The squad moved out, true to the Division's motto.....Attack, Attack, Attack!

To the soldiers that attacked Monte Cassino, it seemed the Abbey atop the mountain had eyes that followed them. With that feeling was the suspicion that the Germans were using it as an observation post.

Dean's squad led the Company through an opening in the rocky slopes and made a sudden advance to about a mile northwest of the Abbey on top of Monte Cassino. Another company attacking along the ridge west of Cassino came to within several hundred yards of the Abbey. They engaged in close fighting with grenades and were driven back.

Dean's squad crouched behind boulders, the bitter cold driven by a harsh wind, penetrated through their clothes to the bone, numbing their fingers. Clinging to their weapons, some barely alive, the men stared at the mountain fortress that denied them victory. Dean's regiment would be remembered as the force that almost succeeded in breaking the mountain defense of Cassino.

The men held on like this for two weeks until the first week in February. The Red Bull Division, seriously depleted, the survivors hopelessly weary, awaited relief. Watching the sun slowly creep down the mountainside, Dean hoped it would bring warmth. It hesitated, then stopped, teasing the men huddled among the cold rocks.

The Allied Command transferred the New Zealand Division and the Indian Division, which were under the command of General Freyberg, to the Cassino area.

"At last we're getting help," Dean told his demoralized squad. "The Indian Division is trained for warfare in mountains like these. We can use them."

Many of Dean's Company were so numb with cold and exhaustion, they needed help to leave their positions. One of Dean's squad members, his face frostbitten and his steps unsteady, leaned on Dean. Together, they stumbled down the steep mountain path.

He felt compassion for his fellow soldiers who suffered

alongside him, yet it was mixed with anger at the war that brought this anguish and death. It made him want even more to be home with Carrie and his son.

Lt. Colonel Sweeney took over for Colonel Warden when he was wounded and told the sergeants, "General Freyberg insisted that the destruction of the monastery was a military necessity. General Clark argued against this stating there is no positive evidence that the Germans are using the monastery. He thought, that for religious and sentimental reasons, it would be shameful to destroy the treasure. If it were bombed it would give the Germans a better defense in all the rubble."

Sgt. Strong told Dean what he heard from the British officers, "Despite what General Clark said, Clark gave the order to bomb the Abbey, but disclaimed responsibility for it. He upset some of the British when he blamed their general for forcing the action on him."

On February 15, at 9:45, Allied bombers attacked the monastery in waves. The Air Command announced flatly that 142 B-17 Fortress bombers and 112 Mediums had by nightfall dropped 576 tons of bombs on Monte Cassino. Added to this was the artillery volleys fired by the Divisions.

Even though leaflets were dropped notifying the Abbey occupants of the pending bombing, the Abbot and a few priests remained in the subterranean chapel of the monastery. Its thick concrete and stone walls protected them. Evacuated by the Germans after the bombing, the Abbot insisted the Germans had not used the monastery for military purposes. Eventually the Germans' persistence to use him for propaganda annoyed him so, that he refused to cooperate.

Dean, Sgt. Strong, and the men of the Red Bull Division reacted with mixed emotions. Even though in awe of the bombing, Sgt. Strong said, "Why didn't they give us that help? Why did they wait until after our battle and until we were relieved by the New Zealander and the Indian Divisions to bomb the Abbey?"

Dean, also bitter, nodded his head in agreement. "Now," he murmured, "they can add the fourth time the Abbey was destroyed.....in the spring of 1944."

When the planes left, observers watched the German troops emerge from their shelters, move down the mountain and occupy the ground abandoned by the Indian units. German troops used the bombed out ruins for excellent defensive positions. As all were well aware, the bombing had achieved nothing beyond destruction, indignation, sorrow and regret. When the Indian Division tried to take advantage of the bombing, the second battle for the monastery on Monte Cassino failed.

Dean learned the Indian Division made a third attempt to capture the monastery after the town of Cassino was bombed. Attacking below the Abbey, they made little progress because of the freezing rain and snow. The Armies remained deadlocked.

Military history recorded after the three attempts that failed by the Allies to capture the monastery, they decided to wait until May to try again when the weather cleared, the ground firmed up, and the troops rested. The Poles, in the fourth and final battle of Cassino, finally seized the monastery. The Poles left many of their dead on Monte Cassino's slopes. A memorial stands in their cemetery on the slopes for all who fought there:

We Polish soldiers
For our freedom and yours
Have given our souls to God
Our bodies to the soil of Italy
And our hearts to Poland.

Bruised and battered, the men of the Red Bull Division were shuttled to St. Angelo Alfie area after being relieved by the Indian Division. Once at the rest area, the men slept in tents, bathed, and donned clean clothes.

Lt. Colonel Sweeney, at the first formation of the Regiment announced, "Orders have been received from 5th Army that our Division is to be transported to the beachhead at Anzio by ship. Our departure date is March 25. Once we're on the beach we'll have further orders. In the meantime, those squads short of men will be getting new replacements to train. Our battalion should soon be full strength again."

Dean mustered some hope and told his squad, "I'm proud of you men. Fighting on this God forsaken mountain hasn't been easy. Anzio is at least flat and it should be warmer. The squads will be getting new men, so help them adjust. They'll depend on you, and you on them."

The Division had been at the rest area a few days when Sgt. Strong took Dean aside and said, "I won't be going with you to Anzio."

STREETS OF HONOR

Chapter 21

Two weeks after Christmas, when Carrie came home from work, she was surprised to find Mrs. B. waiting to talk to her. "I'm worried about Spencer, Carrie," she said. "I finally got him to sleep. He's got a fever and cough and wouldn't take his nap."

Carrie immediately looked in on Spencer. She noticed his flushed face and the dried mucus around his eyes and nose. "Thank you for being so thoughtful, Mrs. B. In the morning I'll take him to see Dr. Midthune."

Carrie sat up most of the night, gently rocking Spencer so he would sleep. Even then, he turned and twisted in her arms. Dozing off and on, she thought, "I wish Dean were here. He would have taken him to the doctor hours ago."

In the morning she called the bank, explaining that Spencer was sick and she didn't know when she would be in. Then Carrie called Dr. Midthune's office. "Bring him right over," the nurse said.

Dr. Midthune let Spencer play with his stethoscope, then listened to his lungs and checked his temperature. "Carrie, Spencer has a cold that is developing into bronchitis."

"Is it serious, Dr. Midthune?"

"It's an inflammation of the linings of the air passages in the lungs. It could develop into pneumonia."

Hugging Spencer, Carrie could hear the rasping sound he made. "What can I do?"

" Boil water for steam. It will help loosen the mucus. Cut an aspirin in half, and mash it into powder, and put it in his applesauce. That way he won't spit it out. This will reduce his fever."

"I'll start right away. Should I come back?"

"If he doesn't get better, I'll prescribe sulfa drugs for him. Would you consent to that?"

"Oh, yes! yes! Anything to have him get better." Carrie was really distressed now.

"There's a new drug that's become available. Its called penicillin. If the sulfa drugs don't work, I'll order some."

Carrie stopped at the Applegrove drug store on the way home and purchased a bottle of aspirin. Laying Spencer in his crib, she said a silent prayer for him, "I wish your daddy were here, Spencer, but he's not. You and I'll have to face this ourselves."

She went to see Mrs. B. and told her, "Spencer is resting now. I'm going to go to work for awhile. After lunch he can have a half an aspirin." She explained what the doctor told her. "If he gets worse call me at work."

On her way to the bank, Carrie thought about trying her mother's treatment when the kids had a cold. In spite of her feelings, she couldn't help but smile. Her mother coated their chests with Vicks Vapo Rub and tucked soft cloths around their chests to keep it from getting on their pajamas. Then, if they allowed it, Mom put a dab by each nostril. It seemed to work back then. But Carrie decided she'd better listen to Dr. Midthune.

Spencer was a bit better by the weekend, so Carrie decided to take him to the farm. She needed some time out of the apartment, too. She'd barely got her coat off and Spencer out of his snowsuit when Mom, her voice shaky said, "Joe got his draft notice. He's going for his physical at the end of the month. Carl and I weren't surprised. It came over the radio that Selective Service is going to double the draft by including fathers of young children."

"Mom, Dean said he would have been drafted, so that's why he went into the Guard."

Sophie added, "The radio announcer said that by July 1,

they want to have eleven million men and women in service. General Eisenhower was made the Supreme Commander in Europe, so something must be happening."

Mom suggested her remedy for Spencer, but Carrie said she felt she should follow Dr. Midthune's prescription first.

At mid-week when Spencer failed to show any significant improvement, Carrie decided to take him to the doctor's office. Dr. Midthune reassured Carrie, "I can tell he's a little better, Carrie; however, I am going to prescribe some sulfa pills for him. If he's not better in a week, bring him back."

Carrie worried continually about Spencer's fever. But by the third day, he was breathing normally. His face was no longer flushed with fever and his body felt cool. Carrie heaved a deep sigh. She hadn't realized how difficult it was to be both a mother and father. Now I can write Dean, she thought.

Dean momentarily stared at Sergeant Strong in disbelief, then asked, "How come you're not coming to Anzio with us?"

Bruce looked off into the snow-covered distant mountains. "Headquarters received orders for me to return to the States. I've got enough points to rotate and they're reassigning me to Fort Snelling to train new inductees from Minnesota. I'll still be in the regular army."

Dean paused. "It will be different without you," he said. "You've been taking care of us for so long."

"That's another thing, Dean. You're being promoted to master sergeant. You'll have responsibility for the platoon now. The company really needs your leadership. Colonel Sweeney wants all units to be organized when they land at Anzio. I'll help with training some of the replacements, but I'm to be ready to go on a moment's notice."

Dean said, "Good, I'll be able to get some advice from you before you go." Dean felt a keen sense of loss. Bruce was the first man he met in Applegrove and Dean had come to appreciate his wise counsel.

A Regimental formation was called to present promotions, commissions, and awards. Dean learned the 100th Hawaiian had moved into the rest area and would be the most decorated of all the units. His pride turned to heartache when it was announced that Taro Takayama would posthumously receive the DSC (Distinguished Service Cross) for his actions when he was killed during the battle for Mount Marrone.

After the formation, Nemo's friends told Dean, "Taro and his lieutenant killed thirty-eight Germans and took two more prisoners. But he was so badly wounded he died on the way to the aid station."

"Thanks for telling me." Dean choked on his tears, saying, "We're all going to miss his happy smile." Afterwards, when alone, he sat for a long time with his head in his hands thinking about his friend Captain Nemo. He felt the sharp sting of tears that he was trying to hold back as they welled into his eyes. He closed his lids tightly but was unable to keep from crying.

The sound of "mail call" brought him out of his melancholy. After fighting on the mountain for several weeks with no mail, Dean eagerly opened one of the letters from Carrie.

Applegrove, Minnesota
January 23, 1944

Dear Dean:
I wished that you had been with me the first few weeks of this year. Spencer's developed a bad case of bronchitis that Dr. Midthune thought might develop into pneumonia. Aspirin and moisture for his lungs helped, but Dr. Midthune prescribed sulfa pills for him. He's all right now. I didn't tell you in my other letters because I didn't want to worry you.

He's growing so much, and his legs are strong. He runs all the time now. So much energy! And he is starting to repeat the words I say. It's so cute.

Joe got his draft notice. He has to go for a physical at the end of the month. Mom just told me. I could tell she was worried already. He's had a bad cold but one of the guys told Carl that if he's warm and can stand up, he'd pass. I think Spencer caught his cold from Joe at Christmas.

I'm so lucky that Mrs. B. can watch him when I'm at work. I don't get out much anymore. Until Spencer feels better and gets older, I'm content to stay at home. I can't think of the last movie I saw.

When I took the Studebaker to Willmar this last time to have it checked and the oil changed, the dealer wanted me to sell it to him for his car collection. I told him I wouldn't do that because you're the one who bought it. What do you think?

Your mother wrote in her Christmas card that she and Uncle Eric might come and visit in July for Spencer's birthday. Just think, he'll be two years old and you haven't seen him! He now says, 'Dad dee' when he sees your picture.

That's all for now. I'll write again soon.

Love and miss you more than ever,

Carrie

Dean's depression grew. His family needed him at home. His friends were being killed. Sgt. Strong and Colonel Monson would no longer be with the unit. He'd been given more responsibility that he was not sure he wanted.

Disconsolate, he walked around the ruined city of St. Angela de Alfie. His mind continually returned to Carrie and Spencer and deepened his resolve to be with them.

Dean stumbled blindly down the road leading out of camp. An MP (Military Policeman) standing guard waved him back. Shutting his eyes momentarily, he prayed, "Lord, help me get through this." His mind and spirit momentarily refreshed, he turned to the company area.

The next few days the Company began training new replacements. Dean, knowing Sgt. Strong would soon be leaving, hung on his every word. Dean noticed the makeup of the Applegrove National Guard Unit was changing, hearing the southern drawls and Brooklyn accents flavoring the Regiment. He now felt like the gristly, old sergeant the new recruits would depend upon.

One morning a truck pulled into the company area. The corporal driving the truck shouted out several names of men that should get aboard for the trip to Naples. A Liberty Ship was leaving for the States. Sgt. Bruce Strong was one.

Dean thought he would have to find him, when suddenly he appeared, his duffel bag in hand. "This is it, Dean," he said.

Dean grasped his sergeant by the shoulder in a firm grip. "I'm happy for you. You've been a good leader for us and I'm going to try to do as well."

"Thanks, Dean. You'll do fine."

Dean gave him a bear hug, shook his hand and said, "If you have a furlough to Applegrove, will you see my Carrie? We'd both appreciate that."

"Yes, I promise I will."

The corporal driving the truck yelled, "If you guys want to rotate, get aboard this deuce and a half and we'll get the hell out of here."

Bruce threw his bag in the back of the truck and climbed aboard. He threw Dean a salute as the truck turned and left.

Even though a month had gone by since the men were fighting on the mountain, it seemed like no time at all when another order was received. On March 18, 1944, the Red Bull Division proceeded to Naples to be transported to Anzio.

The men were unloaded from the trucks that brought them to the port and Dean called his platoon to formation. Marching the men down to the docks for loading aboard the landing craft for the trip to Anzio, Dean could see they had the makings of a tough combat unit.

A week after getting their orders, the Red Bull Division arrived at Anzio. In peaceful times, before war came to this small fishing port and resort town, it was known for its beautiful beaches, quaint buildings, and peaceful harbor. Along with its neighboring city of Nettuno, Anzio was a favorite attraction for Italians and tourists. Roman Emperor Nero, a native of the town, built a large villa there, as did many other Roman nobles.

The scene that now greeted the Division was completely different. The fighting at the beachhead at Anzio had been going on for two months. The walls of bombed out buildings were silhouetted against the night sky. Their rubble, spilling out onto the streets, had been cleared enough for vehicle traffic. Shell craters pockmarked the once beautiful beach. The night air was filled with fumes and smoke from generators. An occasional artillery shell noisily screamed and burst nearby.

At the sergeants' meeting, Colonel Sweeney told them, "Any place on the eleven mile wide by seven miles deep area can be reached by the German artillery. The Germans have a 280 MM. (11 inch) caliber railway gun capable of hurling a 560 pound shell 40 miles. The troops have nicknamed it 'Anzio Annie'. You'll have to instruct your men to protect themselves at all times from artillery and mortar fire."

One of the sergeants asked, "How long before we can break out of here?'

"That's up to the Generals to decide. Right now all we can do is be on the defense."

Defense it was; deadlock had been reached. Dean told Andy his squad leader, "I saw a *Stars and Stripes* when we were in the Rest Area. You know, Andy, I read that Ernie Pyle said, "There is no rear area to rest in, no rear echelon, no safe place. A man was just as liable to get his, standing in the doorway of a house where he slept at night, as he was in a command post five miles out in the field."

Andy paused, then added, "I believe that, the way the

shells are whistling over us."

A few days after landing, the Red Bull Division moved into this stalemate to take over the sector occupied by the Third Division. (Map 5). As they left the beach, the terrain became flat. The soil, a reddish brown color, was foreordained to accept the blood of the courageous soldiers from both sides who would die there. Dean could see the Alban Hills, about twenty miles inland that dominated the southern approach to the Allied goal, Rome.

The Albano road,a large wooded area, and an abandoned railroad track were to the north and northeast. Dean was told the wooded area was called the Padiglione Woods. Tourists traveling to meet the two highways to Rome, the Appian Way or Highway 7 and the Via Castilina or Highway 6, would see sycamore, cypress, evergreens, bamboo and grape and olive groves as they traveled through the area. Dean saw the burned out brush, groves mangled by tanks, trees twisted and crushed, their stalks and stumps protruding from the ground from the continual bombardment.

The weary Third Division had been defending this battle-scarred area. They had gone in the first landing under the leadership of General Truscott and secured the right flank. It was dark when Dean's platoon entered the combat area. The sergeant at the Replacement Depot told Dean, "Don't move around in the daylight unless you want a ride in an ambulance or with the Graves Team." He added, "The Germans shoot at anything that moves."

Dean had been instructed to look up Sergeant Bonner to be briefed on the front line duties. He found him to be easy going with a small paunch that belied his agility and strength.

"We sure are glad to see you guys, " Sgt. Bonner said. "We've been on line since we landed." He pulled out a dirty, battered, 1944, pocket calendar criss-crossed with x's. The barely distinguishable cover said it was from Lubbock, Texas. "This is our 67th consecutive day and we're ready for relief.

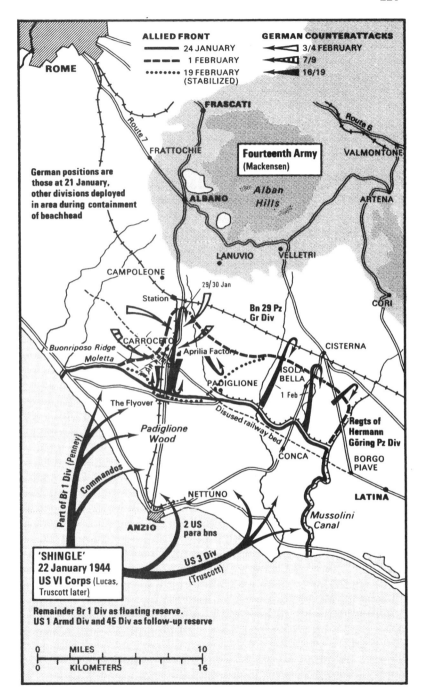

MAP 5

The Battle of Anzio, 'Shingle' From The Rand McNally
Encyclopedia of WWII, p. 15

We fought to get here, fought off the German counterattacks in mid-February when they tried to knock us off the beachhead, and have been fighting holed up here ever since. The Germans brought in their troops from northern Italy, Germany, France and Yugoslavia to drive us back into the sea. But we showed 'em."

"Our Division's been in a stalemate at Cassino," Dean answered. "We thought the Anzio landing would help us break out at Cassino."

Sgt. Bonner grunted, "We've been hoping you'd come through and meet us here at Anzio."

Dean replied, "I'm sure the generals are planning something."

Bonner snorted, "They kicked General Truscott up to be in charge of the whole shebang. General Lucas, who brought us here, was put out to pasture. Some said he should have moved inland when we landed. He seemed to lose his enthusiasm for Anzio. Our Truscott will get us out of here. Here, let me show you around."

Dean followed the agile sergeant as he pointed out the various foxhole defensive positions, fields of fire, and communications. "To the east of us there's a big drainage ditch called the Mussolini Canal. Thankfully it's been a good tank barrier. It was one of Mussolini's public works projects to reclaim the Pontine Marshes from the mosquitoes for farmland."

When Dean asked, "What's that smell?" Bonner replied, "There's a bunch of dead German bodies out there and a dead cow. Nobody wants to remove them. They're hung up on the barbed wire. Tell your boys not to touch that cart behind that farm building. It's been booby trapped and the demolition squad has been too busy to disarm it."

"What else do I need to know?" Dean asked wanting to brief his platoon of all the dangers.

"The British are to the west on the left flank. Don't

worry about them. They kick hell out of anyone trying to break through. Ammo and supplies come in at night. You'll have to bury some to use for the breakout. One thing you have to be careful of is night patrols."

"We've had some experience with those," Dean interjected.

The sergeant grinned and added, "I meant the German night patrols. One of their favorite tricks is to sneak in behind us to probe our lines and set an ambush. They'll throw a few grenades and then take prisoners. It's best if you have a new password each night."

"Thanks a lot, Sarge. You've sure helped a lot. I'll brief our men on what you told me. I hope you get some good relief," Dean said as he shook his hand.

Dean assigned his men to various places along the line. It was the same defensive warfare they'd experienced on the mountain at Cassino.

A few days later the corporal from Colonel Sweeney's command post came looking for Dean. "Sergeant Brandum, you're to report to Colonel Sweeney right away."

"Now what," Dean thought, puzzled. "Maybe they want to let me know I should have rotated with Sergeant Strong."

STREETS OF HONOR

Chapter 22

In daylight, Dean could have easily found Colonel Sweeney's headquarters in the abandoned farmhouse. Now in the dark, Dean was glad he accepted the offer from the headquarters corporal to take him there. Dean followed the man closely as he confidently made his way through the maze of shell craters and abandoned equipment. The corporal, pointing to a room to his right, "The Colonel's office is in this room."

Dean saluted the Colonel, who was seated at a battered table that served as a desk. In Dean's mind, the scene symbolized the war torn country around them: crumpled maps and a pile of papers perched on one side, large holes here and there in the wall plaster created the background. "At ease, Sergeant. Have a seat. Have you and your men adjusted to night warfare?"

"It's not bitterly cold like Cassino, sir."

"You were briefed on how the Germans like the night patrols?"

"Yes, Sir."

Getting to the point, Colonel Sweeney said, "Sergeant, we have to furnish a detail of men for the hospital project."

Dean looked puzzled.

"You saw all the hospital tents when we landed?"

"Yes, sir. What's happening there?"

"General Truscott wants all the tents dug in the ground for added protection. Even though the tents are marked with a big white patch and Red Cross, artillery or bombs sometimes hit them. Make up a detail and report to the captain of the 36th Engineers."

"Yes, sir. I'll have the men there tonight," Dean said

standing up and saluting.

"You and your men can catch a ride with one of the supply trucks."

Leaving Andy in charge of the platoon, Dean and the ten men he had selected caught a ride with one of the trucks bringing ammunition to the line. Climbing into the cab, Dean told the driver, "My men and I need a lift to the hospital area."

"Okay. It's a mile east of Nettuno and a little out of my way, but I'll drop you off."

"Thanks," Dean said, and lit up a cigarette.

The driver eyed him curiously. "You'll have to be careful with the smokes. The Germans shell any light they see."

"I'm sorry. You're right," Dean said and cupped the cigarette in his hand.

The driver queried Dean, "I see they've been doing some bull dozing around the hospital tents. What's going on?"

Dean explained their mission and the PFC exclaimed, "That's good! Some of my buddies spent considerable time there after they were wounded. They couldn't wait to get out of there. It was safer in a foxhole on the front line than it was in one of those hospital tents."

Dean and his squad were dropped off at the hospital area. Dean told his men to take a break while he went to find the captain from the engineers in charge. Returning Dean's salute the captain said, "Welcome to *Hell's Half Acre*, Sergeant. It's appropriately named by all the doctors and nurses who work here."

"There doesn't seem to be any place that's safe, sir. "

"What we want you and your men to do, Sergeant, is to even out the sides of the hole the 'cats' have made for each tent. The excavated walls need to be reinforced with wire netting and the tents reset again."

"For us, this job will be a nice change, sir."

"Good. The water table is high here, so that the most we can dig is two or three feet. My engineers will fill sandbags and stack them so we'll end up with four-foot walls. The wounded should be safe from anything but a direct hit."

"How long will we be here, sir?"

"We want to finish before there's another bad air raid. I estimate it'll be a week and a half or two at the most. You and your men can bunk in any of those tents."

Dean and the men found the work a welcome relief from the front line. After a few days they were able to detect, by the sound, if the artillery shells were incoming. The chow line was the same for the soldiers working on the tents and the nurses at the tent hospital. Dean became acquainted with a nurse from Iowa. As the nurses were dressed in coveralls, Dean did not realize until later, all were commissioned officers.

"Welcome to the 56th Evacuation Hospital, sergeant," was the cheerful greeting Dean received from Nurse Dorothy, the name sewn on her coverall. A short woman with matching short blond hair, it was her impish smile and twinkling blue eyes that caught Dean's attention.

"So far I'm glad to be here.....as a soldier, that is. My names Dean, Dean Brandum," Dean said and smiled.

"Thanks for digging us in," she replied.

Dean found himself attracted to her. After so many months without talking to a woman, it felt good. He tried to forcibly resist his feelings as images of Carrie and Spencer came to mind. Yet, he looked forward to seeing her at mealtime.

Dorothy told Dean she had nursed the casualties of war in Africa, in Italy at Salerno, Cassino and now at Anzio. "It's much worse here at Anzio because, instead of one wound, the men have several. The good thing is we're close to the front line and can give help right away."

"I've fought in all those places but have been lucky to not visit the hospital," Dean said.

Later in the week, Dorothy confided, "I've seen so much pain and suffering, Dean, I can't comprehend it all. Wounded men get killed here in the hospital by shell or bombs. Six of our nurses were killed when shells hit our tents. My best friend.....I went through nurses training with her.....was killed. I had to go to the psychiatric tent for counseling."

Dean said, "Yah, I've had depression too. My friends have been killed or transferred. Back home, my son recently came down with bronchitis. I want to be there."

Dorothy looked at him steadily and said, "The last two tents at the end of this row are ward tents for the neuropsychiatric center for the beachhead. Tomorrow morning you should visit Colonel Short, the doctor in the last tent. He's been dealing with psychiatric service and trauma here, since the first of March."

"I will, Dorothy. I don't want to crack up and I've seen some men that have." Dean and Dorothy walked up and down the rows of hospital tents, talking, laughing and enjoying each other's company. When he returned to his tent, conflicting thoughts interrupted his sleep.

Dean didn't see the psychologist the next morning. Fate intervened in the form of a German plane pursued by Allied aircraft. The plane had jettisoned its bombs to lighten its load and they landed near the hospital tents that Dean's squad had not yet worked on. Sending up a thunderous roar as they exploded, the bombs made deep craters in the sandy soil and sent steel fragments into the surrounding tents. Dean's detail, working nearby, couldn't see anything through the smoke and dust, but they heard the screaming and moaning. Rushing over to the tents that received the most damage, he was met by Nurse Dorothy.

"Dean, help me get the wounded back on their cots."

Wounded, blood spattered men writhed on the tent floor. Some were trying to get back on cots, others sat with their heads in their hands. In viewing the carnage, Dean felt his head grow hot with anger.

Dean and Dorothy were soon covered with blood.

Several of Dean's squad helped bring order to the chaos.

Afterwards, Dorothy, who was standing by Dean, started to shiver. Dean clasped her small body to his and held her until she stopped shaking. Embarrassed, she stepped out of his embrace and said, "I'm sorry, Sarge. When is this senseless bombing and shelling going to stop?"

Dean looked down at her and he heard himself say, "The blood on your cheeks looks like rouge."

Trying to wipe the blood away, she smeared it worse. "Thank you and your men, Sergeant," Dorothy said as she turned away.

Dean felt the longing and the need in both of them. He looked around at the holes in the tent and at the wounded men. "We better get the tents dug down as fast as we can," he said. Striding quickly from the tent, he added, "Dorothy, I'll see Dr. Short tomorrow."

The next day, he followed through with his vow. Stepping into the tent, he was greeted by a short man with a deep voice. "Hello, Sergeant. What is your name?"

"Sergeant Brandum, sir."

"Oh, yes. Nurse Dorothy said you might stop by. I understand you were a hospital orderly yesterday. Thanks for helping out. What seems to be the trouble?"

"I feel depressed, doctor. My friends are being killed. I haven't seen my family for over two years and I'm feeling edgy. Things seem bleak."

"I see you're with the 34th Red Bull Division. There are three doctors here. A couple of weeks ago, Dr. Nobel was assigned to your Division. He's a psychiatrist."

"I haven't been here long enough to meet him, doctor."

"Captain Nobel has developed the concept of the 'old sergeant syndrome'."

"Well, sir, I'm not that old and I haven't been a sergeant very long. We fought in the Tunisian Campaign. We also did 136 days of combat time in Italy."

"Can you come back tomorrow and talk to Captain Nobel?"

"Yes, sir," Dean said, and left, hoping that Captain Nobel might be able to buoy his spirits.

When he stepped into the psychiatric tent early the next morning, Dean saw that Dr. Nobel was pleased to see him. "The 34th hasn't been at Anzio too long, but we're seeing numerous cases like yours, Sgt. Brandum. You're old in combat days, but not necessarily in years." He continued, "You sergeants started out with social and emotional adjustments of a high degree. You were expected to be highly responsible and extremely motivated. After four or five months on the line, anxiety has set in."

Dean listened closely as the doctor elaborated.

"If you don't come to grips with your thinking, you'll become apathetic, not sick, but indifferent and will no longer be able to tolerate combat distress."

"What should I do?" Dean asked.

"The experience here at the hospital, that is your working with the wounded, the physical work on the tents and the counseling I give you, should help."

"I've lost some of my men in battle and lost some of my self-confidence. I'm worried about my wife and son back home," Dean admitted. "I find myself becoming attracted to nurse, Dorothy."

Dr. Nobel said, "What you're experiencing is natural during war. When we break out of the beachhead and start advancing to Rome, everyone will feel better."

"Thanks, Captain. I appreciate what you've told me. Dean saluted and prepared to leave the tent.

"One more thing, sergeant. We've found severe cases of amnesia develop in men like you who experience a mental trauma. I wanted to caution you about this."

"Thanks for the information," Dean said, departing quickly.

When Dean saw Dorothy at the mess tent that noon he said, "I learned I wasn't the only one who feels helpless. They've made an 'old sergeant' out of me."

"You look young, maybe just a little haggard," she replied.

"With no further interruptions, we should be able to finish our work tonight. The doctor said the work at the hospital was good for me and I have to add that meeting you was the best part of it," Dean said.

Dorothy blushed and said, "The nurses feel that if the men can stand it here we can too."

They both laughed when Dean said, "That's funny. The men say if the nurses can take it, we sure can."

What Dean failed to see in her face was her unexpressed thought, Why are the ones I like the most, married? "By the way, Dean, I'll be working in the nurses' tent late tonight if you want to stop."

Dorothy was the only one there when Dean stepped into the nurses' tent. She gave Dean a hug and said, "I'm glad you came, Dean."

Dean, surprised by her strong emotion, said, "I had to stop and say my good-byes."

"You don't have to rush off. I'm about done and we can visit here."

A surge of emotion went through Dean, conflicted by his feeling for her and the image of Carrie and Spencer that came to mind. Dean gave her an emotional kiss and said, "I'm sorry, Dorothy. I better go. If I get free from the front, I'll come down and see you."

He was surprised by her unexpected reaction. She pushed away from him and exclaimed, "Oh, go ahead! I thought you liked me well enough to stay with me. Just go! I don't care if I ever see you again." She turned away so Dean wouldn't see the tears forming in her eyes.

Dean hated to see their relationship end this way, but he

quickly left the tent.

The next morning, Dean found a truck to take him and the squad back to the front.

"Anything new, Andy?" Dean asked when he and the squad were back at their front line positions.

"No, but look at these leaflets the Nazis have been sending us. They shell us with mortars and artillery. The shells explode, and then we get these propaganda posters."

"The men aren't falling for it are they?"

"No. However, the ones with the naked girls do seem to attract their attention."

Dean added, "We got some on the beachhead too. One was a map of the beachhead with a grinning skull and the words, 'Beachhead - Death's Head' superimposed on it. It said, 'We welcome you with a grin for an appointment with death'."

"By the way, Sarge, I've been saving some mail that came when you were gone."

Dean hadn't heard from his mother in North Dakota for awhile and was happy to have a letter from her. With her minimum education and her closeness to the old country, her grammar and spelling weren't always perfect, but he really enjoyed her letters.

Auburn, North Dakota
March 15, 1944

Dear Dean:

This is Wednesday evening and we sure are having an awful snow storm now. So it sure don't look like spring. I hope its not cold where you are. We thank God we are on soil were we can do things like we do and eat what we do as I guess there are plenty of places where it is not so good.

We are fairly well and up and around doing something. Eric has a boil on his neck. It has been quite painful but it is going away now. He weighed himself on the grain scale today.

He weighs 174 lbs. so he is holding his own.

Peter Jensen was here Saturday and said goodbye to us. He left on Sunday for the Marines and he now is in California. He seemed so happy to go, but it hurt me to see him go. The boys are young and always think of fun and that they will see a lot and that may be true. It is a good thing they feel that way. I suppose I am to serious. I always think of what may happen to them and the hardship they will have to go thru. I guess we just have to wish for the best.

Our new stock is sick. We lost a big cow and one calf and have another sick one. We have vaccinated some of them now. Auction sales will be around again soon. Farmers get disgusted as there help goes to the army, and the old ones get left alone with all the hard work. I have been house cleaning. I am just about thru now.

Carl Walsh is home from Alaska and waiting for a call to go some other place. He was called to an Island but he did not pass as he got a running ear. George and Lloyd have been cleaning grain now and getting ready for field work, if it ever gets nice.

Violet Swenson has moved into her home now. She got all her furniture new so I am sure she will have it nice. Frank Thompson is not feeling so good as his feet swell quite a bit.

Rodney Lindberg, Genevieve's husband left Monday for the army. Genevieve and her little boy are going to stay home with Swen and Lena. Gee, she sure hated to see him go. They had a farewell party on him Saturday nite. You must write a long letter and tell how things are where you are. Hope this will find you well and hope you are feeling good. You are remembered by us every day in our prayers. Love from us all at home. *Skriv snart,*

Love,

Ma

Dean held his mother's letter in his hand, thinking of her

and how real and simple it was back home. He thought about
the young boys that were eager to be in the war. He hoped they
wouldn't experience what he had. He found his writing
material to write to Carrie and Ma.

> *Central Italy*
> *April 2, 1944*

Dear Darling Carrie:

> *It's April and the smell of spring is here mixed with the
smells of war. I wonder if this war is ever going to end.*

> *This last week my squad and I helped at a tent hospital.
I felt a satisfaction I've never had before. After the war, if I
can't get a teaching job, I might go into hospital work or
something like that. Maybe I can help people that way.*

> *We have a psychiatrist assigned to our Division. I had a
chance to talk to him. He said I'm an 'old sergeant' and need
to get my confidence back. He's right. My problems are from
losing so many of my friends and being away from you and
Spencer.*

> *Your letters sure help. I miss you so much and I want to
hold and rock Spencer. Does he still have his blond hair? Do
you think he'll be tall when he grows up? It will be so nice
when we can sit together as a family and talk.*

> *I got a long letter from Ma. I'm going to write her now,
too. She asked for a long letter from me.*

> *If you don't hear from me for awhile, don't worry.*

> *I love you very much and long for the days when I'm
through with war. The distance and time seem to grow too
long. I miss being able to touch you and feel your warmth and
love.*

> *Love,*
> *Dean*

The sector assigned for the Red Bull Division was well
defended by two-man dugouts, bunkers, barbed wire and mine
fields. Truckloads of ammunition were buried ready for the

breakout. When the sun went down, the quiet of the day disappeared. Artillery and mortar shells exploded as they fell on both lines. An occasional flare froze the scene until it burned itself out. Dean was busy organizing the men in his platoon for night patrols and defensive positions.

When dawn started to break over the front on April 6, Paul, one of the squad members who was on the work detail at the tent hospital, hurried over to where Dean was having his breakfast of canned rations and bread. Paul, an inventive man, had built a homemade crystal radio and listened to the German's Axis Sally broadcasts for entertainment. It included the latest popular music from the United States.

Dean, his mouth full of bread said, "I hope the Germans don't shell the bakery. What's up, Paul?"

"Sarge, Axis Sally said the 56th Evacuation Hospital will be leaving the beachhead and she dedicated the program to them. How did she know this?"

Surprised, Dean said, "The Germans must be intercepting our coded messages. Did she say when?"

"Sunday, April 9, Easter Sunday. There's another hospital unit coming to relieve them. Sally didn't say where they're going."

"Thanks, Paul. You and I are both glad they're getting out of here. The nurses and doctors at the hospital have been through a lot."

To ease Paul's concern, he added, "Paul, I've heard when units leave, headquarters protects them extra carefully from German artillery and planes. They should be all right."

After Paul left, Dean thought about Dorothy, her emotional reaction and his words that he would visit her if he could. Now there would be no time for this. His thoughts were mixed. On the one hand he wanted to see her again. But on the other he'd been so lonely, he was vulnerable, and wasn't sure he'd be able to control his emotions.

The night of April 22, 1944, started with a drizzle that

developed into a steady rain. Dean was making the rounds of his platoons positions after midnight with Lt. Marsh. They were slogging through the mud when mortar shells started landing. They scrambled into an artillery shell crater that had begun to fill with water.

Crouched in the hole, Dean thought of Carrie one moment and Dorothy the next. His vigilance distracted, he suddenly heard a noise that startled him. Too late he realized a German patrol had used the rain and the noise of the mortars to infiltrate their lines. A shiver of fear went through him and his stomach muscles knotted. Before they could react, Dean heard a 'thud' and a German 'potato masher' grenade exploded by Lt. Marsh that blew away most of the lieutenant's upper body. The blast from the grenade flung Dean against the crater wall. A sharp burning sensation tore into his left shoulder.

As if in a horrible dream that went on and on, he was trying to claw his way out of the hole. His left shoulder useless, he kept sliding back. "Lt. Marsh, Lt. Marsh," Dean mouthed his name, but no words came.

Dean stared at the mangled body, his mind slowly slipping away from reality. This sensation went on as he drifted in and out of consciousness. He felt as if he were floating above the shell hole. Off to the side, the ghostly forms of Russell, Bill, Nemo and Burt beckoned to him. As if his mind were saying, "No! No!" the curtain dropped.

When dawn came and Dean had not returned to the company area, Andy, Dean's squad leader, went searching for him. Coming upon the lieutenant's body, Andy hurried back to the command center and called Colonel Sweeney. "Colonel, sir, Lieutenant Marsh has been killed and Sgt. Brandum is missing," he said.

STREETS OF HONOR

Chapter 23

A sense of foreboding had haunted Carrie all day. After working all week at the bank, she'd thought that sitting in the rocker on the screened porch of Mrs. B.'s house Friday evening would be relaxing. Spencer played at her feet. A soft, gentle, rain made rhythmical sounds on the roof and the drops from the eaves formed an erratic screen. She enjoyed the smell of the rain-washed, spring air. She noticed a man get out of a car, pull his windbreaker around him and hurry up the walk.

She recognized Mr. Barker from the post office. One of her duties at the bank was to bring the outgoing mail to the post office each day as it needed to be sorted and canceled before the train to Willmar arrived. She always thought he appeared to be a little 'nosey', but perhaps it was because he wanted to be helpful.

Did I forget something? She wondered as she got up from her chair to meet him.

Opening the screen door, Mr. Barker was surprised to see Carrie.

"Oh, I didn't see you there," he said to her. "The post office received a telegram for you."

A wave of fear spread over Carrie as she accepted the telegram. Mr. Barker, curious as ever, made no effort to leave. Ignoring him, she tore it open and scanned the message.

WASHINGTON, D.C.
APRIL 28, 1944

MRS DEAN BRANDUM
APPLEGROVE MINN

THE WAR DEPARTMENT REGRETS TO INFORM YOU
THAT YOUR HUSBAND DEAN BRANDUM IS MISSING
IN ACTION DURING HOSTILITIES AT ANZIO ITALY
APRIL 22, 1944.

J. A. JULIAN THE ADJUTANT GENERAL

Her face turned ashen. "What's wrong?" the postmaster
asked.
"De...Dean is missing in action."
"I'm so sorry, Carrie."
Spencer tugged on her skirt. She picked him up, then
dropped the slightly crumpled telegram. Carrie, preoccupied,
failed to notice the wind's growing onslaught. It surged and
pelted the cold rain against the screen in a loud crescendo.
Carrie, dazed, collapsed into the rocker. Suddenly her
body shook and tears began flowing down her cheeks,
dampening Spencer's clothes. Frightened by the rain and his
mother's crying, he began to cry.
The postmaster hurried into the house and pounded on
Mrs. B.'s apartment door. "Could you help Mrs. Brandum?" he
blurted. "She's on the porch."
Mrs. B. rushed past the postmaster. Noticing the
telegram at Carrie's feet she said, "Oh, no!" and bent over
Carrie, consoling her.
The postmaster, retreating down the steps, said, "I'll
have Dr. Midthune give you a call."
Mrs. B. hugged Carrie and Spencer. "There, there,
Carrie. Is it bad news?"
Sobbing uncontrollably, Carrie managed to say, "Dean's
missing. Someplace in Italy. That's all it said."
"Then we can hope, can't we?" Mrs. B. said
reassuringly. "Dean is such a strong man. It will take a lot to
get him down."
"I...I...I hope you're right. Maybe he's still alive. Oh,

Mrs. B. I'm so scared."

"If you want to drive out to the farm and tell your folks, I'll watch Spencer for you," Mrs. B. offered.

"Thank you, I'll do that. But, would you come with me?"

"Yes, I'll get my jacket. If you get Spencer ready, we can go right away."

Carrie was quiet on the way to the farm. Mrs. B. respected her silence and held Spencer. The gentle motion of the car rocked him to sleep.

Carrie was thinking of all the good times she'd shared with Dean; the trips to the lakes, movies, the games he coached and their last dance. She couldn't visualize her life without Dean. Their plans for the future had suddenly been torn to pieces.

Mrs. B., breaking the silence remarked, "I haven't seen your folks for awhile. I enjoyed working with your mom at church when we lived in the country."

Sophie and Carl were surprised to see the Studebaker drive into the yard this time of the night. Carrie, the telegram in hand, quickly passed on the bad news.

"Oh, Mom and Pa, Dean's missing in action in Italy. I don't know what to do."

Sophie comforted Carrie. Carl took the telegram from Carrie and read it carefully. As she sank into a living room chair, Carl patted her back, not knowing what to say.

Carrie sobbed, "I know you're worried about Joe, but I had to talk to you."

Mrs. B. continued to hold the sleeping Spencer. Now he woke and was surprised to see Gramma and Poppa.

"It's good to see you folks again, but I wish it wasn't under these sad conditions," Mrs. B. said.

"Sit down, Mrs. Bogenreif. Carrie has told us how helpful you've been."

Carl found an old tattered world atlas and searched until

he found Italy. "Here it is!" he exclaimed, pointing to Anzio. "It's on the sea, not too far south of Rome. Maybe he was captured and a prisoner."

"I don't know," Carrie said wearily. Although she did not want to leave the comfort and warmth of the farm home, she knew she must. "The rain has let up," she said. "We better go Mrs. B., before it gets any darker."

Mom gave her daughter a hug. "I could make some lunch, but you probably want to get home."

Carrie said, "Yes, I'd better go. I have to call out to North Dakota and let Dean's mother and his uncle know. This is going to be hard, Mom."

"Yah, but it's good that you'd call. They need to know."

When they got back to the apartment, Carrie thanked Mrs. B. for accompanying her to the farm. She would have stayed, Carrie knew, but she needed to be alone with Spencer. After she'd put Spencer to bed, Carrie called Dean's mother and gave her the sad news. She had just hung up the phone when there was a knock on her apartment door. Carrie opened the door for Dr. Midthune who gave her some personal comfort and left some pills to help her sleep.

Carrie took the pills left by Dr. Midthune and lay there in the darkness waiting for sleep and praying for Dean. With the tear stained pillow clutched to her, she was finally able to relax and drift off.

Both Ma and Eric had similar reactions to Carrie's telephone call. After, they both sought solitude. Pauline took her well-worn Norwegian Bible and went to her bedroom and shut the door.

Eric slipped on his overall jacket and cap. Ignoring the drizzle, he trudged to the blacksmith shop. Here he sat down in his favorite spot, a seat made from an abandoned grain binder.

He sat, looked, and listened in the dark night. Bats, silently weaving in the dark sky, didn't mar the early night's sounds. He listened to the crickets chirping and the sound of the rain running off the roof onto the canvass that covered his wood pile. His hurt was deep.

The old barn cat jumped up in his lap. "Kitty, Dean won't be coming home for awhile," he said. The cat purred contentedly as Eric stroked its fur and continued to talk aloud. "When I came home with the guard from the Great War in '19, I thought we had ended all wars. How many more times, How many more years, How many more deaths will there be? When will man learn their lessons and realize they can't keep killing each other? Dean, Dean, we want you home again," he whispered. The cat meowed.

The first part of June, a smartly dressed soldier strode into the Applegrove Bank. It was mid afternoon and the bank was about to close. Trim and dignified, his dress hat tucked under his arm, he went up to the desk where Carrie was working and said, "Hello, Carrie."

Carrie looked up from her work. Seeing it was a soldier, she became alarmed. Then she recognized Sgt. Bruce Strong. "Oh, Sgt. Strong."

"I promised Dean that I would see you. Could you get time off for coffee at the Applegrove?"

"Have you heard anything about Dean, Sergeant?"

"Nothing more, but I wanted to talk to you."

"Could I meet you around 3:15 after the bank closes?"

Bruce was seated at the counter talking to his older brother when Carrie came into the cafe. When Bruce had left with the National Guard, he turned the operation of the cafe over to his brother. The radio blared the patriotic tune, *"Don't sit under the apple tree with anyone else but me."* Bruce motioned to his brother to turn the radio off. Getting up from his stool, Bruce escorted Carrie to an empty booth. "Would you like a cup of coffee, Carrie?"

"I'd rather have a soda pop."

"You're looking good, Carrie. Are things going all right?" Bruce asked, bringing Carrie her soda.

"Thank you, Bruce." Despite her grief, she'd continued to believe that Dean would return and had been taking care of herself. With the warmth of summer coming, she had decided to wear a colorful skirt and blouse. Her shiny, shoulder length, blond hair was parted on one side. A natural wave dipped on the other side held in place with a small barrette.

"I was sorry to learn about Dean missing. He's a brave soldier and a true leader. Have you heard any more from the Red Cross?"

"No, I check the list of prisoners daily and Dean's name hasn't yet appeared. It's over a month since I heard he was missing."

"I wanted to tell you that when I last saw Dean, he was in fine physical condition. He'd just been promoted to master sergeant. We talked before I left about how he wanted to get back home again and be with you and see his son."

Carrie heaved a big sigh. "There's nothing I can do, Bruce, but wait. The past month has been hard, but it has helped to have Spencer and my job at the bank."

"Listen, I see Colonel Monson quite often. He's in charge of recruiting in a five-state area and headquarters at Ft. Snelling. He's a full Colonel now and before long should be promoted to General. Perhaps he can find out something about Dean."

Carrie brightened, "That would be wonderful."

"Have you been listening to the war news?" he asked.

"Ever since June 6 - 'D' day."

Sgt. Strong, willing to talk about the military, expanded. "That was quite a thing. The army at Anzio, where Dean was, broke out and made it to Rome on June 4. On almost the same day, the Allies started Operation Overlord, landing at Normandy to invade Europe."

"Do you think prisoners will be freed now, Bruce?"

Sgt. Strong answered quickly, "Once the Allied prison camps are liberated, the prisoners should be released. According to the Geneva Convention Code, prisoners are to be treated humanly."

Carrie sighed again, "I just wish I knew where he was." She finished her drink and stood up, holding the tears back. "I have to get back to the bank and mail some letters before the train comes. Thank you, Bruce, for coming to see me and talking about Dean. I feel encouraged after what you told me."

Impulsively, Bruce rose and gave her a hug and said, "Dean would be proud of you. You're a very brave woman."

Carrie hurried out the door before she lost her composure.

Sgt. Strong sat back in the booth for a moment, deep in thought, his coffee growing cold. He was puzzled that Dean's name had not been on any prisoner of war reports. He knew the men in Dean's platoon would have done everything they could to find him.

Picking up his coffee cup, he left the booth to resume his conversation with his brother about the restaurant. Midway he stopped, troubled by the thought that at this time of the year, the rains would wash away bodies and bury them in the mud.

Carrie checked her mailbox each day after work hoping that there would be a letter from Dean. There was no letter from him. However, there was a letter from Dean's mother.

Auburn, North Dakota
June 18, 1944

Dear Carrie:

Will you be home on Sunday, July 2nd? I wrote at Christmas that Eric and I planned to come to Applegrove for Spencer's birthday. After you called me with the news that

244

Dean's missing, we weren't sure about coming. Now I feel I want to see my grandson.

If we don't hear from you we should be there around noon. We wouldn't stay overnight but plan to come home again. It's a lot of driving but Eric says he doesn't want to stay over. He can't get help and he has chores to do when he gets home.

Love,
Grandma Brandum

Carrie decided to have Ma and Eric celebrate Spencer's 2nd birthday at the apartment. They would want to spend time with Spencer and their trip would be too short to visit Carrie's parents on the farm.

On July 2nd, Carrie heard the knock on the apartment door. She hurried to open it and the two women, most significant in Dean's life, clung to each other for a moment and wept. Eric stood awkwardly by, then gave Carrie a hug.

Ma said, "We wanted to come and not let our sadness keep us from celebrating what should be a happy time."

Carrie, drying her tears on her apron, said, "I'm so glad you came, and Dean would be so pleased you are here."

Spencer was confused that this lady also went by the name "Gramma" too. When asked how old he was he proudly held up two fingers and said, "Two." Ma and Eric had brought a small, red, cast iron tractor as a gift. He gripped it tightly in his hands and was soon pushing it around the floor making tractor noises.

Carrie had a good lunch. "That sure was a good meal, Carrie," Eric said. "The apple pie was my favorite."

Spencer rapped his high chair with a spoon when they sang 'Happy Birthday' to him.

"He's getting spoiled," Carrie said. "We're going out to the farm tonight and he will be fussed over some more."

"How are your folks, Carrie?" Ma asked.

"They're fine, but worried about Joe. He's in the army. He'll be through with basic training soon. He wrote that he wants to be a tank operator."

Ma said, "That reminds me, I'll have to tell you about Dean's friend, Charlie."

"Oh", Carrie said, stopping in the middle of cleaning off the table. "What happened to him?"

"Charlie's mom got a telegram the first part of April, right before we heard about Dean. Charlie was wounded fighting on some island, Broganville or Booganville or something like that. Last week his folks heard he's in a hospital in Hawaii and had to have part of his leg amputated."

"No!" Carrie said, a note of distress entering her voice. She told Ma and Eric that Dean and Charlie had a bet as to who would end the war first. "And I remember when we went bowling with Charlie," she added. "We had so much fun."

By mid afternoon, Spencer was ready for his nap. After coffee, Eric announced, "We had better start back, Pauline. Good thing the days are still long; but, we'll be driving into the sun."

Ma gave Carrie a hug and said, "You're doing a good job raising Spencer."

Carrie sat for awhile after Ma and Eric left and Spencer slept. It would have been wonderful to have Dean home for Spencer's birthday. Dean! Dean! What has happened to you? Where are you? Carrie cried to herself.

STREETS OF HONOR

Chapter 24

The uncertainty that Carrie and her family felt would have been lessened if they'd known that Dean was alive. Yet, as they later agreed, it was better that they did not know what had happened to him.

The April rain continued to fall. The cold, the wet, and the pain from his wound brought Dean back to consciousness. He lay for a while, his strength returning. "My shoulder.......my shoulder." With his boots digging into the mud, he crawled out of the crater. Bracing himself with his good arm, he got to his feet. Disoriented, he stumbled along in the dark, toward the German lines.

The German patrol that had made the grenade attack approached the shell crater. The sergeant in charge of the patrol looked down on the grisly scene and told his men, "We're to take prisoners for interrogation if our mortars and grenades don't kill them first. It looks like one of them has climbed out. Keep your eyes open for him, he might be hiding with a weapon."

Dean, weak from loss of blood, stumbled into a thicket of some burned out brush. Drifting in and out of reality, he failed to hear the patrol as they followed their path back through their minefield. One of the German soldiers, looking back, exclaimed, "Look at that! That fellow's following us and is walking through the middle of our mine field."

The surprised sergeant said, "He must be the one from the shell hole. Why is he coming this direction? He must be in shock. It's good that he doesn't have a rifle. If he makes it through the mine field we'll take him prisoner."

The patrol stood back and watched in amazement as

Dean, stumbling and weaving, somehow avoided tripping a mine. Oblivious to the danger he was in, Dean staggered toward the patrol. After mumbling something about needing help, he fell into a nearby soldier's arms. Dean, again, was a prisoner of war.

The young soldier pushed Dean to the ground. "Sergeant," he said. "You said we could have souvenirs from the next prisoner we took."

"Go ahead."

Dean offered no resistance when the German soldier took his billfold. He groaned when another yanked the dog tags from around his neck. Taking out a knife, another soldier tore the sleeve with the Red Bull insignia from his already mangled uniform.

The sergeant said, "He's got a bad shoulder wound. You two. Take him back to the POW (Prisoner of War) collecting point. If headquarters can't interrogate him, they might get a doctor to look at him."

Dean, unaware what was happening, willingly went along with the German soldiers. The German officer that looked him over said, "It's no use to interrogate him. He's in shock. Take him by the first aid tent and then put him in with the British prisoners."

The German doctor examined Dean's shoulder and muttered in English, "Looks like a grenade fragment went through your left shoulder. Medic, see how it missed his shoulder bone and ribs but tore up his shoulder and arm muscles? Sprinkle it with sulfa and bind the arm tight to his body. His wound will have to heal on its own. Turn him over to the prisoner detail."

The British Tommies helped Dean into the prison compound. The British sergeant asked, "Do you know your name and outfit?"

Dazed and not knowing what was going on, Dean slid down the fence with his back to the wire enclosure, his knees drawn tight to his chest. His bowed head rested on his right arm, which lay across his knees.

"Can't tell much about him, other than he's a Yank. Nice looking blond bloke, but he's badly wounded," the sergeant observed.

"Better to be alive than dead like our buddies," one Tommy said bitterly.

The British sergeant said brusquely, "You know most of us were just lucky to get out of that ambush alive."

The Tommy, his lips compressed in a hard line, looked down, shook his head, then walked away.

"What's going to happen to us?" Another Tommy asked the sergeant.

"When the young guard that talks English comes by, we'll ask him."

"Hey!" the British sergeant yelled at the soldier guarding the compound. "What are they going to do with us?"

"Kamerad, you'll get a free train ride to beautiful Germany and you'll see the world from a Stammlager," the guard yelled with a heavy accent.

One of the British soldiers, dismayed, asked the other, "What's he saying?"

"It's what the German's call their prison camps. It's shortened to 'Stalag'. They've got them all over Germany. It depends upon if you're an airman, sailor, officer or foot soldier where you're sent. One of the officers at the beachhead told me about it."

The British sergeant brashly yelled again, "When are we going to get something to eat besides boiled potatoes?"

The guard snapped, "That's all we get," and turned and stalked to the other side of the compound.

The next morning, many prisoners, mostly from the 45th Thunderbird Division, were put in the compound. They had been defending a position well ahead of the Division and were captured when surrounded by German tanks. Dean was slumped against the fence.

"What's with the blond guy?" one of them asked.

The British Tommy spoke up, "We don't know his name, his outfit or how he was wounded. He doesn't seem to remember anything. He doesn't respond to any of our questions."

A sergeant from the 45th tried asking Dean some questions, again with no results. Dean sat quiet, his good arm clutching the tattered shirt of his uniform.

"He looks like a Swede I knew back in Wisconsin," observed the sergeant. Putting his face close to Dean's, the sergeant asked, "Can we call you Swede?"

When Dean didn't react to the question, the sergeant told him, "Well, since you aren't objecting, with that blond hair, that's what we'll call you."

Over the next few days, more prisoners were added, including a large number that had been captured fighting at Cassino and marched to this collection point. The meals now consisted of boiled potato soup with chunks of what appeared to be mutton. Bread, with weevils that some didn't bother to pick out, was added. Dean fed himself with his good right arm.

Under cover of darkness, the motley group of men in varied uniforms, some badly wounded, some not, were marched out of the compound, several miles to a railroad head. Dean struggled along trying to keep up, holding his bandaged arm tightly against his side to ease the pain in his shoulder.

At the rail station, Dean stared at the boxcars. Identical to the 40 and 8 railroad cars in Africa, they looked familiar to him. The prisoners were packed together standing upright and the doors rolled shut and locked just as the sun was coming up. Despite the loud protests about no sanitary facilities and having to stand, the train left the station for Rome.

The train did not stop in Rome, nor Florence, but traveled in daylight up the Italian peninsula, through Austria, into Germany. The beauty of the majestic, snow-capped Alps and the rushing water falls cascading down the mountainside from the melting snow on this first day of May was wasted on the men who had no view to the outside world.

The prisoners were not fed. There was no water. Some tried to knock a hole in the floor to relieve themselves, but ended up living with the sight and smell of their own urine, excrement and vomit.

Dean stood helpless, his body held upright by the closely packed bodies around him. The continuous thumping of the railroad car aggravated the pain in his shoulder. Finally, several of the men cleared a place for him and another wounded soldier so they could lie down.

The men knew night from day only by observing the spears of light that filtered through the cracks of the boxcar. After traveling this way for two days the train slowed, then stopped. The car doors were opened and the vile smell of the interior flowed into the fresh air. The guards, overwhelmed by the stench, motioned for all to get out. Crude boxes had been pushed in place for steps.

One of the English speaking guards shouted, "Welcome to Deutschland. You are now near Munich at Moosberg."

The men were allowed to use the latrine but there was no place for them to clean up. They were each given a small portion of watered, barley soup. Dean drank his down hurriedly.

An officer walked over, looked at Dean's blood stained bandages, then issued an order. He was taken to an infirmary where a doctor removed the wrappings, cleaned the wound and re-bandaged it. After the doctor spoke to an aide, Dean was taken to a building that served as a hospital.

One of the older guards said in English, "You won't be going on the same train as the other men. We send prisoners to the various stalags in Germany. In a few days you'll be leaving."

Dean understood little but when a medic motioned to a

cot, he collapsed upon it and fell fast asleep. The doctor came by a few days later, checked the wound and grasped Dean's arm and shoulder. Dean winced as the doctor tried to convey through motions for him to exercise his arm, so that it might heal properly.

A week later, Dean was put on another train. When some of the prisoners tried to talk to him, he was still very confused. If asked his name, he mumbled, "Swede."

After traveling all day and into the night, the doors were opened and the prisoners were again ordered into formation. One of the German officers barked at them in German. "You're going to Stalag 2-B near Hammerstein. Can you smell the sea? The Baltic is nice this time of the year."

An American prisoner, not wanting to let the Germans know he understood their language, told the men in the formation near him, "Fellows, we're way up in northern Germany near Poland. It looks like this will be home until the war's over.....if we live long enough."

In the darkness, the men were marched onto the road and ordered to double time. A guard with a red scar from a wound ran from his sunken eye to his chin, screamed at them in broken English, "Snell, Kreigies, if you want to sleep at the Stalag!"

In their weakened condition, several of the men could not keep up. Those at the end of the column were prodded along with gun butts or poked with bayonets. Other guards released dogs that bit and herded the prisoners along. The healthier were ordered to help the weaker prisoners. Dean, holding his arm tight to his body, tried to avoid these confrontations by staying in the middle of the formation.

The prison camp, enclosed by a continuous double ten-foot high barbed wire fence, finally appeared out of the darkness. From the guard towers, powerful searchlights illuminated the area and cast eerie shadows into the open spaces. Within the camp were several compounds, each surrounded by double ten-foot high barbed wire.

The prisoners were relieved when an English speaking German officer sent them in small groups to different barracks with the order to, "Find a place to sleep on the floor."

Dean located the latrine, and then stumbled into the barracks where he found an open spot on the floor. Nearing exhaustion, he instantly fell asleep. It seemed like he had barely shut his eyes when a German guard yelled, "Kriege, Appell."

When Dean opened his eyes he noticed a face staring at him from a lower bunk. The prisoner smiled and introduced himself, "I'm Dave." The POW leaned over and offered his hand.

"I'm Swede," Dean said, wincing as he sat up and grasped Dave's hand.

Noticing Dean's confusion he said, "Just follow me. We have to get out for morning roll call or 'Appell' as the Germans call it."

After each of the 4,000 prisoners were counted, the POW's went to the cooks' shack where barley soup was ladled into the men's containers. Dave had brought a tin from a Red Cross package for Dean to use as a container.

"Why" he asked, "are we kept in this fence?" and "Why do they call me 'Kriegie'?"

Dave laughed, "The Germans call all of us 'Kreigies'. It's short for 'Kriegsgefangener' or war prisoner. Are you still hungry? I've got some of my Red Cross package hidden in the barracks."

Back in the barracks, Dave reached down into the bottom of his mattress and retrieved a small parcel. Dean accepted the offer of pork luncheon meat, a biscuit and a piece of chocolate. "You better hide things or the guards will steal it when we're not here during their so-called inspections. Do you understand?"

Dean nodded and said, "I understand."

"Lately we've been getting these packages once a week.

The Red Cross makes sure we get them otherwise the Germans would keep them. If it weren't for the packages, many of us would have starved to death. I've been a prisoner since July '43. What happened to you?"

Dean furrowed his brow, shut his eyes and said, "I don't remember. The doctor said I was wounded with a grenade. I can't remember anything."

Dave said, "I was with the 82nd Airborne paratroopers when the Allies invaded Sicily. We were dropped behind the German lines to pull the Germans off the Straits of Messina beaches. I was captured right away."

Dave, now wise to ways of being a POW, rummaged into his mattress of wood shavings. From his storehouse, he produced a dark green shirt. "Put this on. It was in one of the Red Cross shipments and I've been saving it."

Dean took off his torn, blood stained shirt and donned the fresh one, wincing as he put his bad arm in the left shirt sleeve. "Thank you," he said, and for the first time in many weeks, managed a slight smile.

"We won't be getting any food until this afternoon. We've been getting black bread and hot tea made from barley. It's served from a large barrel. Some of the fellows use it to wash and shave. It might be good to clean your wound," Dave explained.

They were interrupted by the guard ordering them out of the barracks. The English speaking officer told them, "Today you will make room for the new prisoners in your barracks. Lumber has been brought into the compound and the guards will give you what supplies you need to add a third level to your double bunks."

There was considerable activity as the men swarmed in and out of the barracks under the watchful eye of the guards. The men completed the work soon after their bread meal. Dave told Dean, "You take the lower bunk and I'll take the one above you. One of the new POW's will have to take the upper bunk."

Dean nodded, relieved that he would not have to climb.

Dave, sitting on the bunk with Dean said, "They're going to have to build more barracks. One thing we get from the new POW's is how the war is going. When they invade the mainland, there'll be many new ones. I don't know where they'll put them or how they'll feed them."

Dean only nodded, trying to make sense of every thing he was learning. The weeks passed by. Being around the more talkative men, Dean gradually regained his speech. However, his amnesia blocked any memories of his life before his wound. To the men of the camp he was 'Swede,' known for his quiet manner and hard work.

Dean remembered the German doctor's advice to exercise his arm; so he rotated his shoulder as he worked and felt the strength returning. No one knew his rank, so he was assigned the same duties as the other privates and corporals.

Dean and Dave were selected to go outside the camp under the watchful eye of an armed guard and sort and stack lumber needed for the new buildings. Dean was aware Dave did not want to help the German cause by being too cooperative. While Dean was up in the lumber pile, Dave called up, "We're working too hard. I'm going to take a break."

When the guard noticed one of the men was missing, he circled the lumber pile, looking for him.

By now the friendship of the two POW's had been cemented and Dean helped his partner out by using a piece of lumber as a pointer. Dean acted as if he was busy but followed the guard's movements around the pile so Dave was able to avoid him. They kept the charade going until Dave, thinking he shouldn't push his luck any further, climbed up onto the lumber pile. Whistling and pretending that he had been there all the time, Dave nonchalantly stacked lumber. The two friends hid their laughter when the guard's face turned red with anger. But, they couldn't hold back their mirth when the guard began making guttural German noises at them.

Marching them back to the prison compound, the guard had the last laugh when he told the guard from the compound, "These two men are restricted to the barracks and cannot be released for meals until tomorrow."

Dave whispered, "It's a good thing we have the Red Cross."

All this time, Dean tried to remember something about himself. He would sit with his head in his hands trying to recall his past. Every time he tried a different path in his mind, glimpses would flash but disappear. It seemed all he got was a headache.

Toward the end of June, those prisoners captured during the invasion of the French coast at Normandy, began arriving. The D-Day invasion had been a success even though it cost the lives of the soldiers who'd died on the beaches. The news electrified the camp. Would they soon be liberated?

STREETS OF HONOR

Chapter 25

Sgt. Strong stood politely until Colonel Monson looked up. "You wanted to see me, Sir?"

"Yes, at ease, sergeant. Sit down. I want to talk to you about a couple of things. Last June, when you came back from your furlough to Applegrove, you told me Dean Brandum was missing in action and you asked if I could possibly find out what happened to him."

"Yes, Sir. Carrie Brandum has been checking the Red Cross prisoner of war lists ever since she heard he was missing in April. His name hasn't been on them."

"I hope you didn't think I forgot about it," Colonel Monson said, leaning back in his chair. "In July, I contacted my friends in Italy and England. That's three months ago and none of them have seen or heard anything of Sgt. Brandum. But they'll let me know if they learn anything about his whereabouts."

Sgt. Strong drew his lips together in a tight line and shook his head.

Colonel Monson went on to explain, "I plan to send Mrs. Brandum a letter explaining this but I'm hesitant about writing to her. I'm sure she will think it's good news."

"Well, you've tried, sir. And, I know she'd appreciate hearing from you."

The Colonel paused, then continued, "It's too bad about Dean. He was such a nice person and a good soldier. How many young men from Applegrove has our Company M lost in the war since it was called up?"

"I don't know the exact number, but I can check."

"Do you know that's three and a half years ago!"

Colonel Monson exclaimed.

"Yes, Sir. Sometimes it seems like last month and other times like ages ago. There aren't many of the original 135th Infantry National Guard unit left with the Red Bull Division. The Division has replacements from all over the country."

"What I would like to do, sergeant," Colonel Monson sat up straight and leaned forward to emphasize his words, "is have a memorial in Applegrove, one that recognizes all the men who lost their lives fighting for their country."

"That's a wonderful idea! Do you have anything in mind?"

"I'm not sure yet. I'll be going home to Applegrove in December for Christmas and maybe I can think of something. In the meantime, don't mention it to anyone. Now I better write that letter to Carrie Brandum."

"Thank you, Sir." Sgt. Strong stood up, saluted and left the Colonel deep in thought.

Even though it was a Tuesday and a work day for her at the bank, Carrie had planned to have supper at the farm with her folks. Carrie's mother said she would have birthday cake. Colonel Monson would have chosen another day to mail his letter to Carrie if he would have known it would reach her on October 3rd, her twenty-third birthday.

The letter was waiting for Carrie when she came home from work. Her hand shook as she reached for the letter opener. In reading the missive, hope turned to frustration and anger. After she got over these emotions, Carrie hugged Spencer until he wiggled free.

"See Poppa's tractor?"

"Yes, Spencer. We'll go see Poppa's tractor."

Lost in thought about Dean, she drove the familiar road to the farm. A disappointed Carrie told Carl and Sophie, "Colonel Monson wrote in his letter that he wasn't able to find out any more about Dean. He did write he was coming home for Christmas and would let me know if he learned more by then."

Sophie was at a loss for words to comfort her daughter as she put her arms around Carrie.

"What do you hear from Joe, Mom?"

"Last time he called, he said he liked the tank training at Fort Knox; but this time of the year it's too hot for him. Hotter than Fort Riley."

Carrie said, "Did Joe say anything about coming home for Christmas?"

"He should have a furlough around that time," Sophie answered. "He wants to go to Europe and join General Patton's tank Corps. But the army doesn't give them a choice as to where they will be sent."

Spencer climbed down from Carl's lap and pointed at the Blue Star banner in the window. "Daddy's star."

"No, Spencer," Carrie said as she picked him up, "That's Joe's star. Grandma and Grandpa have a star for Joe in their window." As she looked out the window past the blue star at the approaching darkness, she wistfully said, "Wouldn't it be a miracle if Joe went to Europe and somewhere, somehow found Dean."

The subsequent war news was pushed aside by the presidential elections. President Franklin Delano Roosevelt won an unprecedented fourth term. Harry Truman was elected Vice President. Carl told Carrie one Sunday in November, "I'm glad he won. He's been a good leader and his 'New Deal' has done what he could for us farmers."

Carrie had awakened early one morning thinking it was almost Christmas and no word of Dean. She was listening to the singing of *Sentimental Journey* on the radio when the phone rang. It was Carl.

"Carrie, we had a call from Joe last night. He won't be

coming home for Christmas. His tank training group all got orders to leave immediately for Germany."

"How come?"

"The Germans have started a massive attack in the Ardennes Forest. Even some of the instructors are being sent to Germany to fight the bulge. Joe said the rumor is they will be assigned to General Patton's Army, so he's getting his wish."

Carrie hung up the phone. She picked up the sleeping Spencer and laid him beside her in the bed. One thought troubled her, "Will Spencer have a daddy anymore?"

Dean adapted to his life as a prisoner of war in Germany. He found that by listening carefully he could understand what the Germans were saying. Many of the words appeared to be familiar to a language he had heard before. He was careful not to let the guards or fellow prisoners know he understood.

Despite the cracks in the walls stuffed with paper to keep out the summer heat and the approaching winter cold, and despite the wood splinters from the floor, the barracks began to feel like home to Dean. Consequently he was surprised and anxious when the detachment officer spoke to him in English after 'Appell' the last part of September. "You are going to be an 'Arbeitskommando' on a farm. Do you know what that is?"

"No," he replied.

"It's a labor detachment to farms north of Hammerstein. You and others will help families with the harvest and other farm work."

Dean nodded. After breakfast he and several other 'arbeitskommandos' were driven to Koslin near the Baltic Sea. The sandy coastal region shaped by glaciations with the flat farm land, evergreens and woods, looked familiar to Dean.....like this was someplace he had been before.

The truck stopped at a collection of small farm buildings

and the guard motioned for Dean to get out. "Hier ist der Hof Von Twinenockle und Schmidt," the guard said. "You arbiete hier." Dean grasped that it was the farm of two families. Pointing to the six on his watch and then at the ground, the guard indicated he would return. He climbed back on the truck and it continued on the dusty road to the next farm.

An old man came from the largest building, took Dean by the arm, and led him inside. An old woman stood by the stove. The farmer pointed to himself and said, "Rudolf" and then at the older woman, "Mien frau, Elfreide." The middle aged woman seated at the table, he called, "Marlene."

Elfreide handed Dean a cup of barley tea and tried to convey to Dean that old men and women were left to work on the farm and in the fields. Marlene, the younger woman who knew some English, explained he would help harvest the potatoes. Today they would dig potatoes by hand.

The day passed quickly. Dean dug and filled twenty-four baskets of potatoes. After the potatoes were bagged and put in the cellar, he waited contentedly with the family. The truck returned and took Dean and the other prisoners that had already been picked up from the neighboring farms to a large shed that had been converted to a barracks. There they were locked up for he night.

The next day Marlene told Dean, "Our house is in town and we come to the farm each day." Bitterly, she added, "We are prisoners too. All of us must wear these badges with our pictures or the Nazis will beat us."

Sunday, the work group returned to the prison compound. This was the only day Dean saw his friend. Dave, who had been kept off the work detail supposedly for being a poor worker, gave his version. "I don't want to help the German cause, but would rather help our own boys by cleaning the latrines here on the compound. I clean them, pump them out and put in lime," he said proudly.

The next day, before they left to work on the farms,

Dean hid some coffee and chocolate from his Red Cross packages for his farm family. When he presented his hidden stash to them, their eyes grew large with surprise. Their beaming faces, nodding heads and spoken, "Danke, danke," said it all.

The Schmidt farm, which was owned by them, was a small farm of seventy morgens (acres) in northern Pomerania, Germany. Marlene told Dean before the American prisoners came that the farm family received help from Polish slave laborers who assisted in harvesting the barley and wheat. The days stretched into weeks and Dean learned the Schmidt's son had been killed in Italy, and Marlene was the daughter-in-law.

Rudolf often spoke to Marlene vehemently in German. She told Dean, "He tells about my husband, Johann, and how good he was. Hitler no good. He kills many Polish people and Jews. People not in favor of war. Only SS troops and those higher up want war."

Elfreide had turned her back and Dean noticed her shoulder's shaking as she cried at the mention of her son's name. Marlene said, "The mother is sad for her son and I lost my husband. She is afraid of the bombs. She wants a place under the house (unterheims) to go and hide. Don't tell guards how we feel. They will beat us with gun butts."

None of the work group prisoners tried to escape; if caught, they would be punished as a group. The arbeitas were eating better than the prisoners back in the camp and with the Red Cross boxes, ate better than the guards.

Rudolf showed Dean how to harness his oxen and hook them up to the plow. He teased Dean by calling him 'dummkopf' when he hitched them up wrong.

Dean surprised the old man and himself when he answered quickly in German, "Not a blockhead. We have tractors now in the United States." He wondered to himself, How did I know that about the tractors? He felt a headache return when he searched his memory for an answer. His speech had returned but he didn't understand why he knew certain words or their meaning.

The trees were turning various hues of gold and some were scattered with brilliant yellow and orange. The north wind ruffled the trees and brought the smell of the fresh Baltic Sea air. Dean noticed that the early morning sunrises spreading across the farm stirred vague memories.

By November, the Baltic air turned cold and blew across the barren fields. There being no more work for the prisoners, Dean said a fond "auf Wiedersehen' to the Schmidt family and in halting German thanked them and wished them the best.

Marlene translated some words for the Schmidts' and said, "We thank you and hope you will come back in the spring."

Neither the Schmidts nor Dean were aware of the great change that was fast approaching from both east and west. Each time Dean returned to the main camp there were new POW's, as at last the Allied army was now fighting on German soil.

With Christmas approaching, Dave, who'd spent several Christmases as a prisoner of war, told Dean what to expect. "The Germans keep us off work details, but we won't get any more food. We'll pool our Red Cross boxes and eat together. We might occasionally get an extra Red Cross box."

Curious, Dean asked, "Is that only for this holiday?"

"Well they do it for Easter and May 1. May 1st is a special day they celebrate too."

"Why May 1st?" Dean asked.

"It's a spring festival in many countries, not a political event."

Even though the prisoners had occasional church services conducted by a prisoner of war chaplain, Dean had many questions about Christmas. "Where did Christmas come from? Who was Jesus? Tell me about Santa Claus and the children again?" Dave answered his friend's questions even though, to him, many seemed childish.

The prisoners secured evergreen boughs for a makeshift Christmas tree. On Christmas Eve they shared their food and sang the familiar Christmas songs. The guards entered into the festivities by singing along in German to '*Oh, Tannenbaum*' and '*Stille Nacht*' and proudly let the prisoners know they were German songs. The prisoner's lonely Christmas was similar to their fellow G.I.'s of the First Army caught in the Battle of the Bulge defending Malmedy, St. Vith and Bastogne in the winter cold.

The quiet Christmas peace was broken a few weeks later when some of the frightened guards spread the words throughout the camp, "Ruskie Komme, Ruskie Komme."

STREETS OF HONOR

Chapter 26

After the holidays, Colonel Monson's wife, Phyllis, came into the bank. Spotting Carrie as the receptionist, she came over and said, "Hello, Mrs. Brandum. Good to see you."

"Oh, Hi, Mrs. Monson. I wondered if Colonel Monson had been home. When he wrote me, he hadn't learned anything about Dean, but he mentioned he planned to be home for Christmas and might know more then."

Phyllis explained, "He had so many more duties with the Battle of the Bulge that he couldn't come home. I last saw him at Thanksgiving. We talked about some of our past holidays and we remembered when we visited with Dean. He was so nice to talk to when we had dinner at Camp Claiborne. He talked about you and how he appreciated his pretty young wife."

Carrie blushed and with a far away look recalled that particular trip. She said, "It seems like that was such a long time ago."

"Bob called and said he'd be home sometime before Easter. I'm so glad it's early this year. Easter Sunday is April 1st."

Carrie said, "Wouldn't it be wonderful if the war was over by then?"

"A lot of people are praying that will happen. Bob said he had a lot of business to do in Applegrove. He didn't say what."

The fears of the German guards were real. If they were captured by the Russian troops coming from the east, the Russians would retaliate. Feeling the pressure of the Allied Army from the west, they would rather surrender to them.

By January, 1945, Stalag IIB at Hammerstein had now swelled to over 8000 prisoners. Many had been captured during the fierce fighting of the Battle of the Bulge. Dave remarked to Dean, "Things are sure changing around here. The Germans must think the war will soon be over. The guards are treating us like humans. I saw one of the guards click his heels together and salute our camp leader. And he's not even an officer."

The increased air attacks, while devastating the German railroad and road system, also cut the supply of Red Cross parcels and the pitiful German rations. The cold winter weather and meager rations consisting mostly of potatoes, drained the morale of the prisoners. If it had not been for the Red Cross food parcels many more would have died.

The first part of January, word came down from the German High Command that the German camp commanders and guards must take their prisoners and evacuate their camp. The Germans did not want the Prisoners of War to be liberated.

Stalag IIB evacuated their compound on January 29, 1945. The prisoners were divided into three sections so the German guards could more readily control the smaller number of men.

Dave said, "I can't believe they're doing this to us. Where are we going? Where are we going to sleep? And what will be have to eat?"

Dean listened to Dave's ranting. His memory had not returned. By now he had become immune to any changes in his life as a prisoner of war and placidly accepted them.

They walked west in knee-deep snow. Taking as many Red Cross boxes as they could carry and many pulling an improvised sled, they traveled over 30 kilometers a day. The column marched mostly on country roads and occasionally passed through small towns. Out in the winter air all day, they slept at nights in open fields or barns.

The first problem the column encountered was handling the stragglers. Dean, who had benefited from better food while working on the farm and from the Red Cross food parcels, told Dave, "I'm going to walk at the end of the column and help the weak ones."

Dave, surprised, said, "Go ahead, you're stronger than I am."

Occasionally farm wagons were allowed to carry the sickest. Sometimes the Germans could not or would not get horses to pull the 'sick wagon.' Then Dean volunteered to be one of the twelve men on the non-medic teams that alternated pulling the wagon by manpower.

Dean told Dave, "The few chances I've had to drive the wagons with the horses has felt so natural, like I've done it before."

Dave answered, "You must've, sometime in your past."

Dean had compassion for many of the sick and was anxious to help them. Each night when the medics took over a section of the barn for the sick prisoners, Dean assisted in cleaning the barn out, spreading straw and laying out the sick. The prisoners called it the 'hospital'. Those POW's that could, stood for hours in the cold for a drink of boiled water or a few potatoes.

Each day was the same through February, March and into April. The men marched in circles from the Eastern front to the Western front, then doubled back to the Eastern front and back West. Dave, who'd been keeping a tally on a battered card board one day said, "We've been on the march for 70 days."

As a result of drinking unsafe water from ditches, dysentery and diarrhea hit everyone. Dean and his fellow prisoners were forced to relieve themselves out in the public. Half of the men soiled their own clothing and discarded their underwear. Dave, after one bad session, told Dean, "We've left a trail of slime and bloody crap across Germany."

Dean agreed and said, "Yah, and we'll have to wear these clothes all winter."

The men suffered from exposure, dysentery, frost bite, pneumonia, diphtheria, malnutrition or fear. Many had a combination of illnesses. If they passed a Stalag compound that still held prisoners, they were not permitted to stop. Sometimes they were allowed to leave their sickest prisoners.

The column occasionally received a bonus when Allied planes on strafing attacks killed horses nearby. These were quickly cut up, and the meat roasted over a fire. The German guards suffered. There were no extra rations for them. Dave, sitting with his back to the barn wall, mouth full of the fresh meat said, "No steak back home tasted better. We need this. According to my figures we've marched over 1200 miles. It's a good thing the terrain in northern Germany is plains and we don't have to march in the mountains."

Dean eyed Dave's cracked, mud-covered leather boots, his weather-beaten jacket and cap, and simply said, "Yes."

Since German military vehicles intermingled with the prisoners, many days the column had to dodge aerial strafing by friendly aircraft. On the bright, sunny, April 14th morning, the column returned west, crossed the Elbe further south and was strafed by three American Spitfires. Dean looked away from the blood-spattered body of a prisoner. The image of a headless figure beside him in a shell hole came to mind. He slumped to the edge of the road with his head in his hands.

That night Dave whispered to Dean, "We can make a break for the American lines from here, Swede. There's about ten of us ready to go. We've been prisoners too long. Two of the friendly German guards said they'd guide us. They don't want to be captured by the Russians. Will you come?"

Dean stared at his friend in disbelief. Dean felt the spirit of comradeship that often becomes evident in such instances. The loyalty to the whole group, instilled in him the long months living together and working on the farm, and the last few months helping the weaker prisoners, won out. His eyes shut to everything else, Dean embraced his friend, "I will stay here with my fellow prisoners, Dave. Some say we will be liberated and then maybe I can learn about my life before...." His voice trailed off to a whisper.

Dave, ten American prisoners, and the two defecting guards walked westward for nine days. On April 22 they met an American tank battalion at a camp south of Hamburg at Dannenberg. The tank crew welcomed them with backslapping celebrations. A tank driver came over and asked one of the freed prisoners, "Did you have a blond fellow by the name of Dean Brandum in your camp?"

The prisoner looked at the name sewn on the tanker's field jacket and replied, "No, Joe, we had a lot of blond guys but no one I knew by that name."

"My brother-in-law has been missing for a year and I promised my sister I'd look for him."

By the time the intelligence officer strode over, Dave had joined the prisoner and they saluted. The officer said, "Come along with me, we need you for debriefing on conditions to the east."

On the way to the debriefing area, the prisoner that Joe had talked to asked Dave, "What was the name of your blond friend? The tank driver, Joe, was looking for his brother-in-law."

Dave answered, "I never knew his real name, so we called him, 'Swede.' He didn't remember anything about his past. When we get done here I'll describe him to Joe."

The debriefing officer asked the men, "Have you heard that President Roosevelt is dead?"

A shocked murmur of denial ran through the group.

"He died a week and a half ago of a cerebral hemorrhage. Truman is now president. He was sworn in a few hours after Roosevelt died."

Joe had returned to his tank to continue his maintenance routine. The command came to the tank battalion, "Start your engines and into formation." They continued northeast to their rendezvous with the infantry regiment.

After the debriefing, the officer told Dave and the others, "Stay here until the relief column can take you to the rest area."

Anxiously Dave said, "Can I talk to Joe, one of the tank drivers?"

The officer glanced at his watch. He replied, "They've gone. They had orders to leave immediately for the front."

Dave, feeling a pang of remorse and sadness, said to himself, "Probably wasn't his brother-in-law anyway."

Dean was awakened the morning in mid-April after Dave left, by the chirping of birds. The sun was a mere red orb barely creeping over the horizon. The fetid smell of soiled clothes was all around him as he glanced around the barn. He noticed that Dave and a few others from his section were gone.

He couldn't dwell on this sense of loss long, as the guards ordered the men out for their usual breakfast of a small portion of black bread and watery potato soup. Nothing was said about the missing guards. If they noticed that some prisoners were missing - they didn't seem to care. It would mean that many less to feed and guard.

As they marched east again, the men felt the warm spring sun on their faces. With the warm weather came a change for the better, and the guards became more humane. Dean made friends with one guard, Hans, and shared some of his Red Cross package with him. Han's attitude was different from the guards who had gun-butted the stragglers and those guards who had fired shots over the prisoner's heads to hurry them along. These last weeks, the Germans were finally realizing that the end of the war was close.

One morning, Dean heard shots fired at the head of the long column of men. A Russian patrol met the column and immediately shot up the lead guards. The remaining guards threw down their weapons and surrendered. A sense of relief swept through the column.

Not long after, a Russian patrol car with two officers arrived and drove the length of the column waving a bottle and firing an occasional shot in the air. Hans said, "They're drunk on Vodka from celebrating May Day and are dangerous."

Dean said, "Stay close to me and maybe they won't hurt you."

Several Russian soldiers ordered the German guards into formation. Hans shook hands with Dean and hurried to blend with the other guards. They were marched in the direction the Russians had come. Now they were the prisoners of war.

That evening the Russian patrol mingled with the newly released prisoners of war. Calling them 'Komrads,' they offered them C rations, which the troops gladly accepted. One of the American prisoners, after he examined his package, laughed uproariously, "Look at this. The rations we get from the Russians are packed in Palisades Park, New Jersey."

The next morning a Russian officer who spoke English told the men, "You're free from German control. Our patrols will travel west to contact the Americans or British. Now you will go back west, but I suggest you stay together until we locate a patrol."

A few days later, two British sergeants in a reconnaissance car met the column and the cheers erupted from the men. One of the sergeants bellowed in his British accent that everyone understood, "For you the war is over!"

Dean felt relief as well as fear and apprehension. Who am I? How can I find out about my life? What will happen to me now? These were questions he knew he could not answer on his own. The life as a prisoner was all he really knew, and now that too would be gone.

The British sergeant stood up on the seat of the reconnaissance car and told the men in the column, "The war should be over soon. B.B.C. announced that at the end of April the Russian army had circled Berlin, and reports are that Hitler killed himself rather than be captured." This news was greeted with cheering and shouts. "If you march south from here, you'll meet American troops." The additional news that they have been on our right flank brought more cheering and shouts.

A few days later, the column moved slowly out of one of the valleys that the Ice Age had scattered over Germany's northern plains. The sides of the valley blotted out the sun, turning the solitary evergreens into friendly sentinels. A joyous shout went up from the men at the head of the column. One of them yelled, "We've found GI's." They had met an infantry regiment that was bivouacking on the flat plain before the valley. There were cheering, smiles and handshakes as the two groups merged.

Dean heard one of the GI's say as he hugged one of the marchers, "What in hell are you guys doing walking around out here? Don't you know the war is over?" The word spread quickly down the long column of men.

The infantrymen welcomed the marchers as long lost brothers. Their rations and treats that had been sent from home were passed around freely.

The commanding officer of the regiment spoke. "Welcome to Camp Bravo. We're happy to have you as guests. The good news is the war in Europe is over as of today, May seventh. We've been monitoring Armed Forces Radio and Germany surrendered unconditionally at 2:41 this morning in a little red school house in Reims."

A roar went up from the assembled men. The officer continued, "There's a collecting depot at Hamburg for liberated prisoners. It's about seventy miles from here. I can spare trucks to take those of you that need help. I suggest the rest of you walk down the highway. The trucks from the Hamburg Replacement Depot will pick you up. You can stay here with us; but I know you are anxious to start on your way home."

At the mention of 'home', cheers and yells went through the column. Dean stood silently. He felt only sadness as a person with no roots. He had no memories of home.

The staging depot in Hamburg had been hastily put together in an old college area. The bombing had left the buildings primitive, and the men passing through were glad to leave. The major in charge addressed the men, "Planes have been renovated in order to fly some of you to Camp Lucky Strike at Le Havre, France. Unfortunately, there are so many of you that some will have to go by truck convoy. It's a three-day trip by truck. The other bad news is some of you will have to stay here for an additional two weeks, or until transportation is available."

Dean was anxious about the unknown and with no particular urge to hurry, followed those who elected to remain behind, to the former athletic field.

STREETS OF HONOR

Chapter 27

Two weeks later, after traveling across part of Germany, Netherlands, Belgium and into France, Dean's convoy arrived at Camp Lucky Strike. It turned out to be a sprawling city of more than 12,000 tents. It was located northeast up the coast from Le Havre at Cany-Barville. The camp was like a U.S. town with theaters, hospitals, PX (Post Exchange) and gift shop. At times more than 100,000 US soldiers stayed there. Many were, like Dean, liberated American POW's on their way home.

To the men who had passed through the camp from the States, living conditions were poor. To Dean and the former prisoners of war, it was luxury. Not having a close buddy, Dean clung to the group. Many stood in the hot shower until the ones griping behind them moved them out. A clean shave, fresh fatigues and a meal prepared for the liberated prisoners followed.

"Wow, fresh vegetables and real hamburger," one prisoner exclaimed.

"Yah, but they haven't run out of dried milk," another retorted.

The newly released prisoners were ordered to an assembly tent. One of the medical officers stood at the podium. "The Medical Department welcomes you. You're wondering what's going on? Why won't they give you a meal of doughnuts and hot dogs with mustard and sauerkraut? Or why aren't you getting that steak and ice cream you dreamed about? You have to liberate yourself from your appetite and your digestive system. If you obey rules, you can once again eat anything you want and as much as you want, without getting severely ill. Eat only as much as you get in the chow line.

Don't eat candy, peanuts, spicy food and liquor." Some of the men groaned. "Your stomach has shrunk and your linings are sore and delicate. If you have trouble, sick call is from 0800 to 1700 hours."

On the way out of the tent, a lone voice muttered, "They could have left out the part about the liquor."

So far Dean had escaped any problems, and no one had questioned him. The next morning that changed. The airfield continually brought in soldiers to the depot for reassignment to the Far East or orders to be rotated back to the States. As Dean went through the reassignment line to fill out the necessary paperwork, the sergeant processing the men asked Dean, "Where are your dog tags, soldier?"

"I don't have them anymore."

"What's your name?"

"Ah, Swede."

"I mean your full name."

"I...I...I'm not sure," Dean stammered. "I can't remember."

"Hey, corporal. Take this one over to the hospital. He can't remember things."

Dean followed the corporal. They threaded their way on the graveled paths through the rows of tents to a series of much larger tents. Dean was put in a cubicle and was told to wait for the doctor to see him. As he sat alone, he mulled over the questions he'd just been asked. His torment and worries made him break out in a sweat.

"I'm Doctor Watson," a tall graying man said, as he stepped into the cubicle and shook Dean's hand. "The corporal says you can't remember things. I'm going to ask you some questions. Just say, Yes, or No. Do you know your name?"

"No."

"Do you know your serial number?"

"No."

"Do you remember what happened to you?"

"No."

"Do you have any buddies that would know?"

Dean put his hands to his head. "No.....no."

"I'm going to put you in the adjacent hospital tent. We aren't set up here to handle injuries of your type. You're going to have to wait until you get back to the States. Do you understand what I'm saying?"

Dean answered, "Yes."

"We'll try to get orders cut to put you on one of the troop ships leaving Le Havre as soon as we can. Okay?"

Dean blended in with the other cases in the tent ward even though physically he was better than many. The orderlies had him sweep out the tent and take out the wastebaskets. Afterwards, he was content to doze in a chair and enjoy the quietude.

The next morning when the day nurse came on duty, she saw Dean carrying the wastebaskets out the back tent door. She stopped at the orderlies desk, put her hand to her mouth and exclaimed, "I know that man!"

The orderly smiled, "You've met a lot of men on this post, Dorothy."

"No, seriously. His name's Brandum. Dean Brandum. What does it say on his medical report?"

"Nothing. He can't remember anything. He has to go back to the States for treatment."

"Maybe I can help him remember?"

"First, you better check with Dr. Watson, Nurse Dorothy."

"I'll just talk to him like any nurse would."

Dorothy waited until Dean came back and settled into his chair. She had not forgotten how Dean rejected her at Anzio. "How are you feeling, soldier?"

Dean stared into her blue eyes. Briefly he felt a flash of something that quickly disappeared. "I'm better, but confused. That's why I'm here."

"My name's Dorothy."

At the mention of her name, Dean gave a start. A look of recognition appeared but was immediately replaced with a vacant stare. "Are you married, soldier?"

"I don't know."

"Aren't you tired of being cooped up here? I could show you around Rouen. The Hotel Metropole has the best selection of French wines and food."

"I'm content to stay here. I'm not supposed to drink liquor." He glanced at the nameplate on her uniform blouse. "Nurse Dorothy, thank you for asking me, but they said a troop ship might be leaving soon and I better not be gone."

Dorothy, frowning as she felt the color rising in her face, said, "Maybe another time, soldier," and hurried toward the tent door.

She told the orderly, "I'm going to see Dr. Watson."

Entering the doctor's tent area, Dorothy went directly to his cubicle. Seeing she was flustered, he asked, "What can I do for you, lieutenant? I'm getting ready to make my rounds."

"I want to talk to you about the blond soldier that was just admitted to the psychiatric section."

"He can't remember his name, Dorothy. He must be one of the missing in action. His case requires treatment back in the States. The longer psychiatric casualties are untreated and hospitalized; the more fixed their symptoms, the more difficult their treatment and recovery. It'll be some time before his long term memory returns."

"I know his name. It's Dean Brandum. He helped at the hospital in Anzio."

"Are you sure?"

"Positive identification, sir. I tested him and he reacted."

"If you're absolutely sure, I'll give his name to the War Department. They'll verify it and send a telegram to the next of kin. It's unfortunate, but this is a notoriously slow process."

The next morning, Dorothy walked into the psychiatric tent. Not seeing Dean, she asked the orderly, "What happened to the blond soldier?"

"His orders came for him to ship out on a Liberty ship for the States early this morning."

"The February 22, 1945, meeting of the Applegrove Village Council will come to order." Mayor Ken Johnson rapped his gavel to emphasize his words and quiet the men visiting around him.

General Monson sat straight in his chair in front of the Council. Even though these were his friends, and he had faced danger many times in Africa and Italy, he was still uneasy. What would these men think of the proposal he was about to make?

"Nice of you to spend some of your leave time coming to visit us, Bob," the Mayor teased. Having known General Monson all his life he addressed him as his friend.

General Monson looked over the group of middle aged and older men and fired back, "Ken, I was hoping to find some new recruits, but I think I came to the wrong place."

The mayor smiled and said good naturedly, "I had trouble calling you 'Colonel Monson' and now," glancing at the single silver star on his lapel, "you mean I've got to call you General?"

"Yes, last month the government made a five star general rank that included Generals' Marshall, McArthur, Eisenhower and Arnold."

"How come they left you out?" The good natured joshing continued.

"Well, their promotion helped for some of us to move up in rank from Colonel to Brigadier General."

"At ease, gentlemen," interjected Councilman Brown with a grin. "What brings you here, General?"

The banter had relaxed the General. "For some time now I've been thinking of a suitable way to memorialize the men from Applegrove that have died in service. Not only those from our Company 'M' National Guard unit, but those killed in the other branches of service.....Navy, Air Force or Marines."

Now very curious, the mayor leaned forward in his chair, put his large, beefy hands on the oak conference table and inquired, "What are you suggesting?"

"Sgt. Bruce Strong, who is with me at Fort Snelling, has determined there are twenty-eight men from our community that have been killed in service."

Councilman Brown whistled his amazement, "There are that many?"

"That's a lot of young men from our community," Councilman Schmidt said.

Mayor Johnson asked, "What do you propose?"

"I'm suggesting naming the streets and avenues in Applegrove after these men."

Several of the councilmen appeared thoughtful. Schmidt said, "I like that idea."

Councilman Beirmeyer said, "How are we going to put up signs? Our snowplow is worn out. There's no steel for a new snow plow."

"I've thought of that. The cabinet shop can make the signs with the names out of wood. And, the lumber yard has cedar posts. The signs and posts will last until steel is available again."

The mayor said, "I'll bet Al would make the twenty-eight signs for nothing if the city paid for the wood. He's got a son in the Air Force."

"That sounds like a good idea," Councilman Beirmeyer said.

Councilman Brown said, "I'll move the City of Applegrove go ahead with the proposal made by General Monson. I think the community will support this overwhelmingly."

"I'll second the motion," Councilman Beirmeyer said quickly.

The Council unanimously approved the proposal.

Mayor Johnson said, "In the meantime, we can map out the streets and avenues. Bob, you'll have to give the city clerk the names."

"I'll leave the names at the City Hall."

"One more thing, Bob. We'll discuss your proposal further and work out the details. If everything goes all right, we may be able to dedicate this project on Memorial Day. May 30th is on a Wednesday this year. Could you arrange to be here for the dedication? We would like you to be our speaker."

"I would like to do that. It would be an honor for me."

"After next month's council meeting, I'll call you."

"Thanks, Ken, and all of you, for your help."

"That's okay. Proud to be a part of it."

The Applegrove community had a long tradition of honoring the dead of all wars with a Memorial Day service that included a parade of veterans, the service in the band shell at the cemetery with the band, an airplane flyover, recitations by the high school students of Lincoln's *Gettysburg Address* and the poem, *In Flanders Field*, and a speaker. All knew that the morning, May 30, 1945, would take on an extra significance since the dead of all wars would be honored and the community's memorial to the dead of World War II would be formally dedicated.

The acrid smell of gun smoke from the rifle salute by the firing squad drifted over the crowd and the last note of taps died away as General Bob Monson, immaculate in his uniform with his chest full of campaign ribbons, strode to the microphone.

"It is difficult for me to express the feeling of pride and yet humbleness that I feel at this moment. Having watched many of our young men in action fighting and dying to protect our country, I know personally what sacrifice they have made, so we can be free.

"The defeat of the fanatics that led Germany and Italy into war has been accomplished. The threat to expand their boundaries and spread their dangerous beliefs is over. We hope the War in the Pacific will soon end.

"The Applegrove Village Council has approved the project to name the streets and avenues in our village to honor members of the Armed Forces who gave their lives in this war. The names of these honored dead are on the twenty-eight temporary wooden signs displayed here on the panels in front of the stage. The signs will be erected in our community. They will provide an acknowledgement of the sacrifices made by these men on behalf of their community and their country, as their names will always be before us.

"The program that some of you received has a map showing the streets and avenues as they have been named by the Village Council. I have been informed that the Village Council has placed a call for bids for 150 permanent steel street name signs, 90 sign posts and brackets and 1,800 house numbers. When steel again becomes available and the order can be filled, these temporary signs will be replaced.

"Last week I was notified of another young man who has died as a result of wounds received in action in the Pacific Theater on Okinawa. His name and others, if necessary, will be added to the street signs and the village map."

Carrie, startled when the General said he was notified of another young man who had died, relaxed when she realized it wasn't Dean. A feeling of sadness came over her for that soldier's family.

"I hereby dedicate the streets and avenues in the Village of Applegrove and these signs of honored servicemen, as a symbol of our unending respect to the memory of these men, so we may never forget the greatest sacrifice one can make for his country. As these young people reminded us earlier in reciting Lincoln's *Gettysburg Address*, '*that we take increased devotion to that cause for which they gave their last full measure of devotion*."

In a spontaneous response, the audience, with a thunder of applause, rose as a body of one. Many with tears streaming down their cheeks, searched for a handkerchief.

Carrie cringed when the General spoke of the greatest sacrifice made by these men. Now, one of the hundreds who'd gathered at the cemetery with Spencer and her parents, she felt the tears run down her cheeks.

The Master of Ceremonies asked the band to play, *America, the Beautiful,* and asked the audience to sing along. With the phrases - "America! God shed his grace on thee...and...from sea to shining sea," running through their minds, the crowd left the cemetery.

Carl picked up Spencer and carried him to the car. Now three-years-old, Spencer's interest had been kept by the rifle fire and band music. Laying his head on his grandfather's shoulder, he was content to let his eyes go shut.

STREETS OF HONOR

Chapter 28

One day as Carrie was sitting on the porch she became alarmed when she saw Mr. Barker from the post office drive up. A feeling of *deja vue* came over her. Quickly opening the screen door, he saw Carrie rising from her chair. He said, "I have a telegram for you, Carrie." This time Barker didn't wait for her to open it. He shut the screen door and scurried back down the walk.

Trembling and faint she opened it.

WASHINGTON, D.C.
JUNE 22, 1945

THE SECRETARY OF WAR DESIRES ME TO INFORM YOU THAT YOUR HUSBAND, SGT DEAN BRANDUM RETURNED TO MILITARY CONTROL 20 JUNE 45.

J. A. JULIAN THE ADJUTANT GENERAL

Carrie held her breath as she read the telegram again. Her eyes filled with tears as she grabbed Spencer, and swirled around the porch. "I knew it. I knew it. Daddy's alive."

She rushed to knock on Mrs. B's door, calling her name. Mrs. B. opened the door and could tell by the happy glow on Carrie's face that something special had happened. After Carrie read the telegram to her, she said, "I'm not really surprised, Carrie. You never lost faith and prayed for Dean to come home."

"I always believe in miracles, Mrs. B. Oh, I'm so happy! Now I have to call Mom and Pa and Dean's mom with the wonderful news!" Carrie sang over her shoulder.

As the weeks wore on, Carrie became increasingly nervous, as she wanted to hear more from the army. It was a different kind of waiting, a new anxiety, just as powerful. After a month and still no word, she wondered if Dean really was alive. She considered calling General Monson if she didn't hear anything soon.

"Lt. Rosen, you're satisfied that you've done all you can for Brandum?"

Marty Rosen, familiar with his superior's penetrating look, replied, "Yes, sir." The early morning sun bathing the office of Walter Reed Hospital's neuropsychiatric section made the young man squint. "You were with me when we tried the intravenous Pentothal injection. Remember, after he went under, we tried different hypnotic suggestions."

Dr. O'Leary leaned back in his swivel chair. His bushy black eye brows failed to hide the intensity of his stare as he looked at the young, clinical therapist seated across the desk. "Yes," Dr. O'Leary agreed. "What we learned about his life prior to the army didn't make any sense. I recall he couldn't tell us anything about what happened after he left home with his Guard unit."

Lt. Rosen, perplexed by the case that had been assigned to him, ran a hand through his thick black-gray hair and rubbed the back of his neck. "I tried your suggestions, Doctor. I increased the Pentothal percent to 20 cc's, imitated some battle noises and conversed with him as a friend in the present tense. The drug was working and he was definitely under hypnosis, but he wouldn't respond."

"Did you get any other response?" Dr. O'Leary asked.

"Nothing, sir."

Dr. O'Leary leaned on his desk. "I've been here at Walter Reed for two years and we seldom see cases this bad."

He addressed his therapist by his first name, "Marty, we've done all we can here. Make arrangements to send Dean Brandum to San Antonio. Brooke has the trained staff to handle these psychiatric cases."

"Yes, sir."

"I'll have to send a letter to Mrs. Brandum. I'd hoped we could give her better news."

Lt. Rosen stood up. "Let's hope the neurologist at Brooke will be able to help release the mystery in his mind."

The long awaited letter was there when Carrie came home from work. The return address indicated it was from the Walter Reed Hospital in Washington, D. C.. Anxiously she tore it open.

Neuropsychiatry Section
Walter Reed Hospital
Washington, D.C.
June 22, 1945

Dear Mrs. Brandum:

Your husband, Dean Brandum, has been a patient of mine since he returned to the United States on June 6, 1945.

Although progress has been made, he's not responding as rapidly as was anticipated. He has a severe long-term memory block and he will require special treatment. Our hospital is not equipped to handle his case.

The rehabilitation center at Brooke General Hospital at Fort Sam Houston, San Antonio, Texas, has the necessary neurological equipment and training your husband needs. He will be transferred by air on June 25, 1945, to this facility.

The neurologist at Brooke General Hospital will keep you apprised of your husband's progress.

Thank you for your patience in this matter.

Sincerely,
Dr. T. C. O'Leary, Major

Carrie, in hearing this news, felt discouraged. She picked up Spencer and said, "Daddy doesn't feel good, Spencer. He has to stay in the hospital."

"Daddy sick? Daddy sick?"

"Yes, Spencer. But he's going to get well. Then he can come home to us."

She told Mrs. B., "Dean's being flown to Texas for treatment. I looked up San Antonio on the map. It's a long ways away. It's about 150 miles from the Mexican border."

Mrs. B. noticed how crestfallen Carrie was and tried to encourage her, "He must need special help."

"I don't know why they have to send him so far away," she moaned.

"There, there, Carrie. It's unusual for you to be upset."

"I'm sorry. I don't want to take it out on you."

"Maybe they'll allow you to see him."

"One good thing, it's straight south of us."

Major Tom Harper, chief doctor of the electroencephalography section, Brooke Army Hospital in San Antonio, Texas, and Captain Richard Gibbs, his next in rank, sat at a long table. File folders of cases were spread out before them.

"It looks like you've had a busy week, Dick."

"Remember last week when we discussed one of our more critical cases?"

"Oh, yes. That was the Dean Brandum case. What have you learned, Captain?"

Brandum's had so many emotional experiences his mind has blocked them out. However we are making progress."

"Good!" Dr. Harper said emphatically. "Did you try those different electrode positions and combinations we talked about?"

"Yes, the tracings were very good and easy to interpret.

The therapist has uncovered many of the incidents that have been blocking his mind. Soon we should find out the incident that caused his physical and mental wound."

"You've done well, Dick."

The next Monday, Captain Gibbs gave his report to his commanding officer. "Dr. Harper, Sgt. Brandum has improved so that the therapy counselor believes a visit from his wife would assist his recovery."

"Excellent. I will write a letter to his wife right away."

Carrie apprehensively opened the letter from the army hospital in Texas.

Brooke Army Hospital
San Antonio, Texas
July 9, 1945

Dear Mrs. Brandum:

You are undoubtedly anxiously awaiting news of your husband's condition. Sgt. Brandum has progressed to the point where we think your visit here at the hospital would be advisable. This, we hope, may hasten his recovery.

If you could arrange to come here, I can explain his treatment to date. Otherwise, I could write to you.

The hospital is sending a map of San Antonio if you decide to come. The Brooke Army Hospital is located on the east edge of the city.

Please let me know your plans.

Sincerely,
Dr. Tom Harper, Major

Carrie hurried to the telephone. "Mom, I just got a letter from the hospital in Texas. I can go and see Dean. Would you be able to take care of Spencer when I'm gone? I'll have to take the bus. It will be a week and a half of travel at least, maybe more. Mrs. B. might be able to help too."

"Oh, yes, yes," Ma didn't hesitate.

"I'll let you know after I find out from the bank if I can get time off. I need to call the bus depot for the bus schedule, too."

The sun was barely coming up Friday morning when Carl and Carrie drove to the neighboring town, intending to catch the Greyhound bus. Carl had insisted on driving her there. "Good thing we got going early," Carl observed. "Sun's at our back now. It should be high enough so it won't bother on the way home. According to the map you'll be going straight south on Highway 75."

Lost in thought, Carrie was glad Carl rambled on. How will Dean feel? Will he know me? What should I say? Will he think I've gotten old? She continued to be lost in her own thoughts, so she didn't even hear Carl's rambling.

When they got out of the car at the cafe that doubled as the bus depot, Carl pulled forth his wallet and handed Carrie some cash. "Would you do me a favor and buy me one of those felt cowboy hats? I always wanted one and I didn't want to say anything when Ma was around."

"Sure, Pa. I'll be glad to do that," she smiled, wondering to herself how she would keep from getting the hat crushed on the way home.

Carl gave her a hug and said, "Let us know when you're coming home."

STREETS OF HONOR

Chapter 29

To save money, Carrie decided to ride straight through and sleep on the bus for the three-day trip. She was awake through Sioux Falls and Omaha, and slept through Kansas City and Wichita. She was awake again in Oklahoma City and Dallas, Texas. On the long bus ride through Texas she dozed off and on, a thousand thoughts invading her mind. It seemed to her she'd never get to San Antonio.

The hospital administrator had suggested that Carrie stay at the Robert E. Lee Hotel in downtown San Antonio. She was not prepared for the noisy, fast paced traffic or the oppressive Texas heat. The taxi driver, when he learned she was from Minnesota said, "I've got relatives in Iowa. It's hot here, but you get used to it. It's a dry heat. We don't have the humidity like up north." This, however, didn't stop the beads of sweat that formed on her forehead.

Carrie took special care dressing the next morning. Dean once said, "Aqua is your color. It goes with your blue-green eyes." She brushed her hair and applied makeup. She'd kept her hair long, hoping now this would help Dean recognize her. It swirled about her from the Texas breeze as she hurried to the hospital.

The receptionist showed her into the doctor's office. Major Harper was wearing a blue hospital gown. With his short cropped, red hair and bushy moustache he could have passed for a Minnesota country doctor.

"Please sit down, Mrs. Brandum. I'm happy that you could make the trip to Texas. I think it will help your husband's recovery."

"I'm so anxious to see my husband."

"First I want to review his treatment and his current diagnosis with you. Dean's repressed his memory for so long that it's fixed his symptoms and made his treatment and recovery difficult. It's only been recently that we have been able to treat these cases."

Carrie fidgeting in her chair and clasping her hands tightly, said, "Dr. Harper, it's over a year ago since I heard he was missing."

"I understand how hard this wait must have been for you. But, you need to be aware of some things. We've been working to unlock the traumatic experience that led to the amnesia. The doctors at Walter Reed Hospital tried giving pentothal intravenously, so as to induce hypnosis. A therapist acted like a friend in order to help Dean relive the battle experience and restore his memory. Both drugs and conversation were tried but neither relieved his amnesia."

"But you wrote that he's gotten better."

"Yes he has. For awhile it was thought he suffered from 'Blast syndrome' from an exploding shell. But we've ruled that out, as there was no damage to his central nervous system. Here at Brooke we're trained in clinical neurology and electroencephalography. These procedures have helped Dean. The electrode positions and the reading of the resulting graph tracings have been the tools that unlocked Dean's problems."

"Oh, I'm so thankful for that."

"We've figured out that the loss of so many friends and the ugly death of his officer led to his breaking point. He also received a shrapnel wound in his left shoulder. The only noticeable thing is a long scar."

"Does he remember me and his family?"

"Yes, his memory is returning; however, it is a gradual thing and each day he remembers a bit more. He just had a therapy treatment and it would be better if you saw him tomorrow rather than today."

"Oh, I had hoped to see him..." Carrie's voice dropped

off to a whisper.

"I'll tell him you're here. If he responds favorably to this bit of information, we can schedule a visit for tomorrow morning."

Carrie, disappointed, left the hospital. She took a bus back up town, then decided to walk the riverbank to sort out her thoughts. Will he love me? How will he and Spencer get along? I wanted to see him so badly. Why can't I? I've waited all these years, I should be able to wait another day. Round and round Carrie's thoughts went.

Dean sat on a bench. The late morning sun streamed through the window of the hospital arboretum. The cactus and rose bushes filled the space around him. The quiet was disturbed only by the whir of the ceiling fan blades. Major Harper had told Dean, he was well enough to see a woman named Carrie. At the mention of Carrie's name, Dean's face showed puzzlement and then relaxed.

Dean clutched his hospital robe around him.

Carrie followed Dr. Harper into the arboretum. "Dean, this is Carrie."

Dean raised his head, his mouth slightly open.

Carrie dropped to her knees in front of Dean and hugged him, the tears flowing freely.

All of a sudden the familiar scent of the Chanel #5 perfume he had given her years ago triggered the memory the doctors had hoped for. A shiver went through his body. Dean leaned over, stroking her hair and kissing the top of her head, his tears dampening his hands, her hair and head. He tilted her head to look at him. "Carrie, Carrie, my beautiful Carrie."

Dr. Harper, seeing Dean's reaction, left.

Carrie, studying Dean's gaunt face, took in the lines around his eyes. "You're the same, Dean. Just as handsome as ever," she said.

"You were never good at lying, Carrie."

Standing, he pulled her to her feet. They stood swaying

in an embrace. Dean leaned her head back, looked deep into her eyes and kissed her hard on the lips.

The pair dropped back on the bench. "The doctor says I have to stay here awhile."

Carrie squeezed his hand. "That's okay, Dean. We want you to be well. It's all over now. Soon you can come home and we'll begin again."

Over the next few days, Carrie reminisced with Dean or just sat peacefully by him.

Dean refrained from telling Carrie of his prisoners of war experiences, except for one such experience.....working on a German farm. "It was natural for me to be in the field and around the animals. I should have realized then that I grew up on the farm," he said.

Carrie said, "You were sick, Dean."

Carrie told him about General Monson's efforts to have the streets and avenues in Applegrove named for the twenty-nine servicemen that had been killed in the war. She said, "The dedication ceremony on Memorial Day was an honor for those men."

When he asked about Charlie, she said, "Your mother told me that he had been wounded on Bougainville and lost part of his leg." Dean grimaced and shut his eyes. "But the good news is he gets around fine with a wooden one. In fact, so good he married a Silseth girl after he got out of the army."

The corners of Dean's mouth edged up in a slight smile. "I wish I could have been his best man. I remember there were a lot of Silseth girls."

Carrie smiled too. "I can tell you're getting better."

"Charlie owes me five bucks. You remember the bet I told you about."

Carrie smiled again, "Yes, now I know you're okay."

Their parting was hard, knowing he had to stay longer. Carrie, with time before the bus left, went hat shopping. She found a store uptown that sold farm and ranch wear. The salesman noticing her northern speech, asked, "Who are you buying the hat for?"

"My dad," she answered quickly.

"Do you know what size he wears?"

Flustered, Carrie said, "I think his head size is a seven and a half."

"I suggest you get one that's a little larger. He can always put newspapers in the band."

She picked out a tall, cream colored felt with a wide brim.

"I'll put it in a hat box for you."

Carrie bought a cotton scarf for Ma and a pair of cowboy boots for Spencer. The clerk helped her find a perfect pair for a three-year-old.

The bus driver stored her packages in an overhead cabinet. On the bus ride home, Carrie was comforted with Dr. Harper's parting words that Dean could be coming home in a couple weeks.

Carl, Sophie and Spencer were waiting for her at the cafe. Carrie had telephoned when she would be arriving. When she struggled into the cafe with her suitcase and packages, Spencer ran to her.

Sophie asked, "Now what in the world did you bring home?"

"Slide over in the booth and I'll show you." As she handed Carl the hatbox he made a knowing smile. After opening the box, he promptly switched his cap for the cowboy hat. It fit perfectly.

Sophie said, "Carrie, you shouldn't have spent so much."

"Pa sent money along with me."

"Carl, you're the one that shouldn't spend so much. You do look nice though," she admitted. She softened even more when she opened the tissue around the beautiful, cotton scarf.

After Carrie had put Spencer's cowboy boots on, he proudly stomped around the cafe.

On the way home, Carrie chattered about Dean and answered their many questions.

Carrie spent the next week and a half working and preparing for Dean's homecoming. The doctor had sent Dean's travel arrangements.

Carrie and Spencer waited on the platform of the Milwaukee Line in Applegrove August 1, 1945, for the 4:10 passenger train. Five years had passed since National Guard Unit Company M, 3rd Battalion, 135 Infantry Regiment, 34th Infantry Red Bull Division was notified they would be activated.

The iron rails shimmered, creating wavy mirages in the August sun. Spencer had found small rocks the train wheels had kicked up on the platform from the rail bed and was busy throwing them back. Carrie had decided only she and Spencer should meet Dean. Off in the distance, she heard the lonesome, muffled sound of the train whistle as if it was pressed down to earth by the heat.

"Here comes Daddy, Spencer. Remember he has a hurt shoulder."

At those words Spencer moved in next to Carrie. Although she had talked with him about Daddy and showed pictures of him, he didn't know the man he was about to meet.

Dean pulled his small bag off the baggage rack and stood expectantly by the exit at the end of the car. "Going home, Soldier?" the porter asked.

"Yes, sir. Going home!"

When the train stopped he was the only Applegrove passenger. Carrie wasted no time in giving him a welcome home hug that knocked his cap off. Spencer retrieved it and shyly handed it to Dean.

Dean crouched down by him. "Hi, Spencer. Looking into his deep blue eyes that matched his own, he said, "Have you got a hug for Daddy?" Before he could respond, Dean picked Spencer up and tossed him in the air. Spencer squealed delightedly.

"This is my baggage. Let's go."

"We walked, Dean. You can drive the Studebaker another day."

On the way home, Dean glanced up at the sign - Bradford Street and Wagner Avenue. He was overcome with sadness, stifled a sob when the rush of vivid memories of his friends' deaths flooded over him.

"Does your sholjer hurt, Daddy?"

"Yes, Spencer. This soldier hurts."

"Are you okay now, Daddy?"

Taking his small hand in his, Dean said, "Yes, Spence, I'm okay. Let's go home."

Epilogue

The performance of the Red Bull Division at Cassino must rank with the finest feats of arms carried out by any soldiers during the war. When at last they were relieved by the 4th Indian Division, fifty of those who had held on to the last were too numbed with cold and exhaustion to move. They could still man their positions, but they could not move out of them unaided. They were carried out on stretchers, and it was one of the final cruelties of this battle that some of them, having survived so much, were killed on their stretchers by shellfire on the long torturous way down to safety. They had earned the praise which for soldiers is the best to receive - that of other soldiers who have moved in to relieve them and who alone can see at first hand what they have done, what they have endured. It was the British and Indian soldiers of the 4th Indian Division moving in to relieve them, who proclaimed the achievement of the Americans the loudest.

Three years after the end of the war a party of British officers were walking over these same mountains, studying the battle of Cassino as a military exercise, under the direction of officers who had fought there. As they clambered over the rocks, incredulous that anything resembling organized warfare had been waged there, they came at one point upon a grim sight. Crouched against some rocks, in the position in which an infantryman would take guard with his rifle, they found a human skeleton. At its side were the rusted remains of a rifle and steel helmet, both identifiable as American. It seemed a final comment on the endurance of the 34th US Division and the men of the 36th who shared their ordeal in the later stages of the battle...Cassino, so costly in human life and suffering.

1st Lt. Fred Majdalany, British Infantry
The Battle of Cassino

After the breakout at the Anzio beachhead, the 34th Red Bull Division fought up the Italian peninsula to Rome, Pisa and Bologna. When the Italian Campaign ended in May, 1945, the Red Bull Division had 529 days of combat.....more than any American Division in World War II.

The Red Bull Division had 21,000 casualties either killed, wounded or missing. The list of decorations the Division earned contained 9 Medal of Honor winners, 107 Distinguished Service Crosses, 1228 Silver Stars, 2562 Bronze Stars and over 16,000 Purple Hearts.

Family and friends may appreciate a copy of *Streets of Honor* as a gift.

Additional copies may be ordered from:

Appleseed Art Works
12276 Tanglewood Rd.
Audubon, MN 56511

Email: ehkanddakkolke @ loretel.net
Telephone: 218/439-3583

Please Include: Your Name, Address
City, State, Zip Code

Cost: $14.95 each + .97 Tax = $15.92
Add $2.00 for Shipping and Handling

Please remit by:
Check, Money Order or Bank Draft

References

Allen, William L. Anzio: Edge of Disaster. New York, New York: E. P. Dutton, 1978.

Anderson, Robert S., Robert J. Bernucci, and Albert J. Glass. Neuropsychiatry in World War II Volume II Overseas Theaters, Medical Department, United States Army, Office of the Surgeon General, Washington, D. C.: U.S. Gov't. Printing Office, 1973.

Ankrum, Homer R. Dogfaces Who Smiled Through Tears: in World War II. Lake Mills, Iowa: Graphic Publishing Company, 1987.

Bergot, Erwan. The Africa Corps. New York, New York: Grosset and Dunlap, 1971.

Blumenson, Martin. Salerno to Cassino. United States Army in World War II, Center of Military History, United States Army, Washington, D.C. 1993.

Bolstad, Owen C. Dear Folks: A Dog-Faced Infantryman in World War II. United States of America. 1993.

Coggins, Jack. The Campaign for North Africa. Garden City, New York: Doubleday and Company, Inc., 1980.

Commager, Henry Steele, Donald Geddes. The Pocket History of the Second World War. New York, New York: Pocket Books, Inc. 1945.

Cooper, Jerry, Glenn Smith. Citizens as Soldiers: A History of the North Dakota National Guard. Fargo, North Dakota: The North Dakota Institute for Regional Studies, 1986.

302

Daniel, Clifton. Chronicles of the 20th Century. Mount Kisco, New York; Chronicle Publications, Inc. 1987.

Dear, I. C. B., M. R. D. Foot. The Oxford Companion to World War II. Oxford, New York: Oxford University Press, 1995.

D'Este, Carlo. Fatal Decision: Anzio and the Battle For Rome. New York, New York: Harper-Collins, 1991.

Encyclopedia Brittanica, Encyclopedia Brittanica, Inc. University of Chicago, 1975.

Fehrenbach, T. R. The Battle of Anzio. Derby, Connecticut: Monarch Books, Inc. 1945.

Fisher, Ernest F., Jr. Cassino to the Alps. United States Army in World War II, Center of Military History. United States Army. Washington, D. C. 1993.

Garland, Albert N. and Howard McGaw Smyth: Sicily and the Surrender of Italy. United States Army in World War II. Center of Military History, United States Army. Washington, D. C. 1993.

Glass, Albert, Neuropsychiatry in World War II. Volume I, Zone of the Interior, Medical Department, United States Army, Office of the Surgeon General, Washington, D. C. U.S. Gov't. Printing Office, 1973.

Hapgood, David and David Richardson. Monte Cassino. New York, New York: Congdon and Weed, Inc. 1984.

Howe, George F. Northwest Africa: Seizing the

Initiative in the West. United States Army in World War II. Center of Military History, United States Army. Washington, D. C. 1993.

Hull, William H. All Hell Broke Loose. Edina, Minnesota: Stanton Production Services, 1985.

Jennings, Peter, Todd Brewster. The Century. New York: Doubleday Publishing Group, Inc. 1998.

Keegan, John. The Rand McNally Encyclopedia of World War II. Greenwich, Ct: Bison Book Corporation. 1972.

Majdalany, Fred. The Battle of Cassino. New York, New York: Ballantine Books, 1957.

Merriam, Robert E. The Battle of the Bulge. New York, New York: Ballantine Books, 1957.

Remarque, Erich Maria. All Quiet On the Western Front. Boston, Massachusetts: Little, Brown and Company, 1928.

Rosten, Leo. The Joy of Yiddish, New York, New York: McGraw-Hill Book Company, 1968.

Schorer, Avis D. A Half Acre of Hell. Lakeville, Mn: Galde Press, Inc. 2000.

Smith, E.D. The Battles for Cassino. New York, New York: Charles Scribner's Sons, 1975.

Vaughn, Thomas, Wynford. Anzio. New York, New York: Popular Library, 1962.

World Book Encyclopedia, World Book, Inc. 2001.

Wright, Michael, The Readers Digest Illustrated History of World War II. The World at Arms. Reader's Digest Association Limited, London, England: 1989.

Young, Desmond. Rommel, The Desert Fox. New York, New York: Berkley Publishing Corporation, 1958.

Zemke, Hub and Roger A. Freeman. Zemke's Stalag: The Final Days of World War II. Washington, D. C.: Smithsonian Institution Press, 1991.

Reference Excerpts

Bixby, Wallace W. Adjutant, Take the Doctor's Advice. Surgeon's Bulletin, Camp Ramp, ETOUSA. May, 1945.

Caplan, Leslie, Minneapolis, Mn. Death March Medic, Air Force Association, Washington, D. C.

Caplan, Leslie, Testimony - Mistreatment of POW's at Stalag Luft IV. Minnesota Military District, The Armory, Minneapolis, Mn. December 1947.

Goldman, Ben, German Treatment of American Prisoners of War in World War II, Office of TAC History, US Air Force. Wayne University, 1949.

Internal Medicine in World War II, Office of the Surgeon General, Washington, D.C. 1968.

McHale, Tom, The POW Story.

Parquette, Roland G., Three Months of Hell in Stalag 9B.

ABOUT THE AUTHOR

Erling Kolke was born and raised in Moorhead, Minnesota and is a graduate of Concordia College in Moorhead and the University of Minnesota in Minneapolis, Minnesota. He is retired and lives on Big Cormorant Lake, southwest of Detroit Lakes, Minnesota with his wife, DeVaughn. They have six children and twelve grandchildren.

After serving in the army in Korea, he was a teacher, coach, high school principal and school superintendent in Minnesota schools. He was able to combine his experiences in schools and in the army into the story of how one small community honored its war dead. Through interviews with friends, prisoners of war and references on the history of the 34th Infantry Red Bull Division, he takes the reader on the journey to the *Streets of Honor*.

ABOUT THE COVER ARTIST

DeVaughn (Bakke) Kolke is originally from Hitterdal, Minnesota and is a graduate of Art Instruction School in Minneapolis. Her paintings are found in schools, churches, public buildings and homes throughout the United States. One of her paintings was chosen by Courage Center, Golden Valley, MN for a 1997 Courage Card design. This painting is entitled *"Waiting for Winter"*.

DeVaughn conceived the idea of the Minnesota State High School League sponsoring Visual Arts as part of their Fine Arts Program. It was adopted by the League in 2000. She did the cover art for a book, *Bridging The Gap - Tales of the Cormorant Lakes Area*. For the Detroit Lakes City project, 'Sunny in Detroit Lakes', she painted three large fiberglass sunfish statues.